wrong
about
the guy

Also by Claire LaZebnik

Claire LaZebnik

wrong
about
the guy

HARPER TEEN
An Imprint of HarperCollinsPublishers

HarperTeen is an imprint of HarperCollins Publishers.

www.epicreads.com

Library of Congress Control Number: 2014952546
ISBN 978-0-06-225230-2

Typography by Torborg Davern
15 16 17 18 19   CG/RRDH   10 9 8 7 6 5 4 3 2 1
❖
First Edition

I am exceptionally fortunate in the niece and nephew department. I love and admire not only those I'm related to by blood, but those I was lucky enough to acquire through marriage (both mine and theirs).

For Maren, Eric and Cori, Adam and Molly, Emma and Hal, David, Jack, Teddy, Marie, Libby, Ben, Rudy, Dexter, and Freddy

one

It was my idea for Mom and Luke to make a big deal out of their fifth wedding anniversary. And it wasn't just because I was hoping to get a tropical vacation out of it—although, of course, I *was*. It was also because I had been there for their wedding and knew that they deserved a do-over. A ten-minute-long Vegas ceremony didn't seem weighty enough to maintain a lifelong marriage, and I didn't ever want to see them get divorced.

First I needed to get Luke on board—the proposal had to come from him, not me. It was hard to catch him when he was actually home and Mom wasn't within earshot, but I finally found my chance when he was pushing my two-year-old half brother on the swing.

Jacob liked swinging. A lot. You started pushing Jacob in the swing, you were stuck there for a solid half hour because he'd cry if you tried to take him off. After half an hour, he'd *still* cry but your arms would be so tired and you'd be so bored and annoyed that you'd let him.

Anyway, I glanced out my window and spotted the two of them at the swing set and instantly flew down the stairs and out the back door and across the lawn to join them.

"Oh, good," Luke said when he saw me. "You ready to take a turn? He won't let me stop."

"I actually came out to talk to you. I have an idea."

"Of course you do," he said with a smile.

"Your fifth anniversary's coming up in just a couple of weeks. You need to take Mom out to dinner and tell her you love her more than ever. . . ." I stopped and peered up at him. "You do, right?"

"Eh, she'll do," he said. "Since I'm stuck with her and all."

I shoved his arm. Sometimes Luke felt more like an older brother than he did a stepdad. "Be romantic for once. Tell her that this anniversary should be a bigger deal than your wedding was because you love her even more now than you did then and that you want to take her somewhere amazing to celebrate. Somewhere like Hawaii."

"Ah," he said. "Now I see where this is going. And we bring you along, right?"

"If you insist." I grinned. "Come on, Luke! You guys need this so badly. You know you do. You've been so busy lately, and she's been stressed out, and you had such a crappy wedding the first time. . . ."

He stopped pushing long enough to hold his hands up in surrender. "Okay, okay! I'm totally up for this. But only if your mom likes the idea."

"I'll make her like it."

He shook his head and gave the swing an extra-big push. "I can't wait for the day when you figure out how to use your powers of persuasion for something worthwhile."

"This *is* worthwhile!" I said. "I'm saving your marriage. You know what? Don't wait until you go out for dinner. Something always comes up when we try to plan things ahead of time. Go ask her right now. I'll push Jakie."

"You just know I'll agree to anything to get you to take over." He stepped aside and I took his place behind the swing. But he lingered a moment longer. "You don't really think our marriage is in trouble, do you?"

"Do *you*?" I said, a little alarmed by the seriousness of his tone.

"Of course not. I just wish she'd stop worrying so much about—" He gestured toward Jacob's back. "So he's a late talker. Lots of kids are. But she gets herself so worked up about it. She's going to take him to see a speech therapist, you know."

"Yeah," I said. At Jacob's last checkup, the doctor

had given Mom the name of a speech therapist to take him to. But Luke said the pediatrician was being a typical alarmist Westside doctor, and I kind of agreed with him. There was nothing wrong with Jacob—he was just still really little.

"The speech person is just going to say he needs lots of therapy," Luke said. "It's how they make money. And that's not going to help your mother's anxiety."

"And that's why she needs to go to Hawaii!" I said. "So she can relax!"

He laughed. "Right. Hawaii. I'll go talk to her."

"Or Tahiti," I called after him as he moved across the yard. "I've always wanted to go to Tahiti!"

And then I had to push Jacob for about three million more hours. Every time I'd stop, he would arch his back and kick and cry. I eventually had to drag him off the swing. He sobbed and grabbed on to the chains, and I said, "Stop now or I'll never push you again," and he said . . .

Nothing. Jacob never said anything except "Yes," "No," and sometimes the very last word you said. Like if you said, "You want to watch *Pajanimals*?" he would say, "Pah-mulls," or something like that. Sometimes. But that was pretty much it.

He probably didn't even understand my threat, which was fine, since I didn't really mean it.

I carried him back to the house. He calmed down

on the way, burrowing his head into my shoulder and cuddling close, and I couldn't stay mad at him. It helped that he was so cute, with his big brown eyes, narrow chin, and wavy light brown hair.

My face was heart-shaped, too, and my eyes were also large and dark—we both looked a lot like Mom—but I had crazy curly dark hair, thanks to my biological father's genes.

When Jacob was born, I wasn't sure how I felt about sharing Mom with this little squishy stranger. There had already been a lot of adjusting in my life. She and I had been alone together for so many years, and then Luke came along and they were always going out without me. And then she had a baby, and I felt like here was someone needy and cute who was going to take even *more* of her time and attention away from me. But she kept urging me to hold him, and the more I did, the more I loved the way he smelled and his weight in my arms and the little noises he made, and finally one day I said to Mom, only half joking, "He can be mine, too, right?" and she said, "He already is."

two

I was twelve years old and safely at home with my grandma the night Luke Weston met my mom in a Philadelphia alleyway. (It's not as skanky as it sounds, I swear.) At that time, Luke was a singer/songwriter/ guitar player who had so far scored only one moderate and esoteric hit, which played occasionally on a few alternate-rock stations and was loved by a very small handful of music geeks. That song had gotten him some early afternoon small-tent gigs at music festivals and the occasional booking as the opening act for better-known musicians.

That's what he was doing in Philadelphia that summer—opening for a Portland band that had a lot more fans than he did. He had finished his set and was wandering out back into the alley to smoke a cigarette when he spotted a pretty, petite young woman with chin-length black-brown hair squinting down at her phone a few feet away. He assumed she was a fan, since she had chosen to duck out after he had left the stage, so he approached her with a cocky grin.

"Like the set?" he asked.

She stared at him blankly. "The set?" She was simply on a break from her job slicing onions and mushrooms at the hibachi restaurant next door.

A little sheepishly, Luke explained that he'd just been performing at the club, and she said, "Oh, I heard a little through the walls! That was you?" Later, when she told me the story, she admitted she hadn't heard a thing, but she thought he was cute, so she figured it was worth pretending.

Luke found himself trying to prolong his conversation with the tiny, delicate woman with the surprisingly deep laugh and large, lively eyes. And I can't imagine Mom wasn't equally interested in spending the rest of her break with the thin, long-limbed, wavy-haired musician who had appeared out of nowhere. Still, they'd been flirting for only a few minutes when she spun her phone in her hand and casually mentioned that she had been in the middle of texting her twelve-year-old daughter. The defiant dare in her eyes and the lift to her chin both said, *If you have a problem with that, don't waste my time or yours.*

He didn't have a problem with it.

They talked until she had to go back inside, and by

then they'd agreed to meet up after the restaurant closed.

He lingered in Philadelphia as long as he could, days after his gig had ended, meeting Mom for after-work dates and before-work lunches at our apartment, where he entertained us both with silly songs on his guitar. Eventually he had to return to LA, where he lived and performed semiregularly at a few small clubs, but he and Mom continued to talk and text and video-chat every day, and he flew her west a month or so later to come see him headline at his biggest venue so far, a club on the Sunset Strip.

That was the night that a hit-making music producer named Michael Marquand signed Luke to his label.

It was also the night Luke promised to quit smoking forever if Mom would agree to marry him. (Technically it was the next morning when he proposed, but they hadn't gone to sleep, so it counted as that night.)

My grandmother and I flew to the West Coast in time to join Mom and Luke at a ridiculous little chapel tucked in between two huge casinos in downtown Las Vegas.

"Tell me I haven't made a huge mistake," my mother whispered to me as she pulled off the veil Luke had bought her in the gift shop and gulped at the air as if the veil had been made out of lead instead of lace.

"You definitely haven't," I said. Not that I was a reliable adviser: I was as caught up in the excitement of the sudden wedding as she was, and totally in love with the idea of having this handsome rocker with the mildly devilish smile for my dad.

Mom and I moved into Luke's rental house in LA (small as it was, it was still twice as big as the studio apartment we'd been living in, and I had my own room, which was tiny and miraculous), and Grandma went back alone to Philadelphia, where she worked as a nurse. Her last words to Mom were, "He's got to be better than that last one."

She was referring to my father, a wildly romantic and brilliant older man who had said to the teenage Cassandra, "I love you madly and want to be with you forever." His sincerity and enthusiasm rang true, and Mom had no training in identifying a manic episode. By the time he came crashing down, she was pregnant.

I was born shortly after he had gone missing, but Mom used his last name on my birth certificate, so I was named—and remained—Ellie Withers.

She thought he'd come back. He never did. Total disappearing act. No paper trail, no way for even the child support system to track him down.

Luke was definitely better. For one thing, he *stayed*. For another, he worked hard. The first album he made for Michael Marquand generated two decently successful singles. They became good friends during the process, and Michael arranged for Luke to be featured on songs with a couple of major rock stars, which bumped him into a higher level of fame and exponentially increased his gigs.

It was around then that Michael decided to move into television producing. The show he cocreated, *We'll Make You a Star*, combined a singing contest with an image makeover. While Michael planned to appear on the show as a mentor and judge, he didn't want to commit to a full-time television job. He needed someone else to work with the contestants on-screen every week. Someone with real musical talent, who could also bring a little sex appeal to the show. Someone likable, but not TV slick. Someone with a hit or two to prove his music credentials but not so huge he was unaffordable. Someone teenage girls could drool over, but who wouldn't drool back.

And Michael knew just the guy.

Luke agonized for a while over the decision. It meant he'd have a lot less time to write and record music, and that his life would be far more tightly scheduled than he was used to.

On the other hand, he and Mom wanted to have a baby, and Mom was eager for me to go to a private high school. The money would come in handy. Mom was uncertain, but I was totally in favor of his being on TV. (I was thirteen—of course I was.) And what were the odds the show would actually be a hit? Next to nothing, he and Mom assured each other. He'd probably end up working just a few short months for a fair chunk of change. Then life would go back to normal.

So he said yes. And life never went back to normal.

Luke went from mildly respected musician to A-list TV star in less than a year. He started to be recognized everywhere we went, and audiences packed his concerts, which became a lot less frequent—taping *We'll Make You a Star* took up a lot of time, as did the ten million events a week the show's publicist wanted him to make an appearance at.

We'll Make You a Star was a huge hit, and his agent renegotiated his contract for A Lot of Money.

We moved into our current, much bigger, house the year after that.

"I didn't sign on for this," Mom said one night, after she and Luke had gone out for a quiet dinner and emerged from the restaurant to find a mob of screaming teenage girls gathered there, desperate for a glimpse of him. Some of them were sobbing.

"Believe me, I didn't either," he said.

The loss of privacy was hard to adjust to.

We got used to the money and the perks much more easily.

Being rich was a big change for all of us. Mom and Luke had both had tough childhoods. In the neighborhood Mom was from, having a baby at seventeen—like she had done—was virtually a rite of passage. But she was smart and scrappy and wanted something better for *her* daughter, so she had gotten us a tiny apartment in a neighborhood with a good school system, even though it meant she had to share a bed with me every night and had no room of her own.

The only thing Luke ever said about his childhood was that it had been rough, and he didn't like to think or talk about it. Which was pretty typical of Luke—he preferred to keep things cheerful, even if it meant actively avoiding certain thoughts and subjects. His father was in the military and had moved his family around from army base to army base. Music was Luke's salvation: alone with his guitar, he could create his own beauty, his own world.

So while we all now lived in an enormous house behind a tall gate and could hire people to wait on us and had closets full of beautiful clothing, well, both Mom and Luke had paid their dues.

And that's why they deserved a really nice five-year anniversary celebration to make up for that off-the-rack Vegas wedding.

three

Mom said she loved the idea of an anniversary trip, but couldn't even begin to figure out how to plan it.

"Why don't you ask George to do it?" Luke suggested. "He'd probably love the extra hours of work."

George Nussbaum was my mother's assistant. Sort of. He was also my SAT tutor. Sort of. Basically he did whatever our family asked him to at an hourly rate, while he waited for a better job to come along.

George's older brother Jonathan worked for Luke—originally as his personal assistant but now as the head of his new TV production company (the last time Luke's agent negotiated his contract with the show, he scored him a development deal). Jonathan was the oldest of a big family; George was the youngest and, according to Jonathan, the smartest: he was only twenty and had already graduated from Harvard.

At some point over the summer Jonathan had

mentioned to Mom that his brother was looking for temporary work to pay the rent while he wrote a TV spec script and tried to get an agent. Jonathan had already bragged about how his brother had gotten perfect SAT scores and gone to Harvard so Mom jumped at the chance to get all that brain power into my life—part of her *your life is going to be better than mine* plan was for me to go to an Ivy.

Once George started showing up at our house with SAT books, my mom kept discovering other odds and ends he could do for her. I don't know how much she paid him, but I bet it was pretty generous—her own minimum wage days weren't that far behind her and now she had plenty of cash to throw around. Because she had once been a waitress, she left ridiculous tips at restaurants: forty, sometimes fifty percent of the bill.

The Nussbaum brothers looked a lot alike: they were both slightly above-average height and thin, with gray-green eyes and brown hair. George had a lot more of that though; Jonathan's was thinning at the crown, even though he was only in his late twenties. Fortunately for him, he already had a fiancée.

Jonathan was mellow and good-natured, but George was less sunny. He sighed with impatience and rolled his eyes a lot. Of course, it's possible I brought that out in him: I wasn't in the mood to be studying over the summer, and I refused to take any of the tutoring seriously.

It made sense for Luke to put George in charge of the travel and party arrangements, but it had been my idea, so I wanted to keep some control.

"Tahiti?" I suggested hopefully when I found George in the kitchen the next morning researching resort hotels on his laptop.

"Hawaii's looking like the better option."

"Yes, but I've been to Hawaii," I said. "I've never been to Tahiti."

"Oh, right," he said. "This is about *you*, not your parents. I forgot."

"Try not to do it again," I said loftily.

"I'm going to need more coffee." He got up, went over to the pod coffee maker, put a mug under the spout, and hit the switch.

I was proud of that coffee maker: I'd used one like it in a hotel suite last spring and talked Mom into ordering one for us. I also made her get this wooden Christmas tree decked out with different-flavored pods—coffees and teas and cocoas—all tucked into holes on the branches of a spinning wooden frame.

"Can you make me a cup?" I asked with a yawn. I was still in my pajamas: a tank top and PE sweatpants with the words "Coral Tree Prep" (the name of my school) running up the left leg. It was almost eleven thirty, but I'd only just gotten up.

I love summer.

"Make it yourself," George said as he carried his mug over to the refrigerator.

"You suck as a personal assistant."

He got the milk out and poured some into his coffee. "I'm not your personal assistant. And heaven help anyone who is."

"Hey!" I said. "That was gratuitous."

"Good SAT word."

"I know, right? Oh, that reminds me—my friend Heather's going to come study with us today. I think it will help me focus."

"Let's hope," he said.

Heather didn't go to Coral Tree Prep with me; she lived in the Valley and went to public school there. We'd met at a dance class back when we were both thirteen, and I had decided that my true vocation in life was to be a modern dancer, despite the fact I'd never taken a single lesson before.

We'll Make You a Star had been on the air for a few months at that point and people were already recognizing Luke. No one at the dance studio knew I was his stepdaughter, though—my last name was different, and Luke never brought me there. The only thing that made me stand out from the other girls was my total lack of skill and grace.

There was one other girl there who was also new and awkward and alone. She had a round belly under her leotard and I saw a couple of the other (delicately thin) girls eye it and whisper to each other and giggle, so I made a point of catching her eye and smiling. She smiled back gratefully and moved closer and closer to me. When class ended, we walked out together.

While we waited to be picked up, Heather told me that her mother was making her do the class for exercise. I learned later that it was only one in a long series of attempts on Sarah Smith's part to slim down her daughter. Sarah was a tall, skinny brunette with an angular face, but Heather took after her father, who was rounder and had big blue eyes and dimples. Mrs. Smith, I soon discovered, liked to talk loudly and pointedly about how *wonderful* exercise was and how *good* it felt to be in shape and how people who didn't move their bodies turned into shapeless *slugs*. She also liked to drag me into the discussion: "You are so *petite*, Ellie. Isn't she wonderfully *petite*, Heather?" Heather would cheerfully agree that I was wonderfully petite, which pissed me off because (a) I didn't want to be held up as some kind of example and (b) Heather was adorable exactly the way she was, and the only person who didn't see that was her own mother. Oh, and those jerky girls in dance class, who continued to annoy me.

A few classes later, one of them giggled and pointed when Heather stumbled during a routine. I already disliked that girl, who had long blond hair and expensive dance clothing and acted like she was the queen of the class, so I marched over to her and growled, "What's it like to have a sucky personality? How's that working for you?"

"You're the one with the sucky personality," she said, flipping her hair.

"I guess that makes us twins," I said, which seemed to stump her—she couldn't come up with anything to say except a lame "No, it doesn't."

I walked away from her, grabbed Heather by the arm, and said, "Let's go." She willingly let me lead her out of the practice room. The teacher called after us, but we ignored her. A good teacher wouldn't have let her students ridicule each other.

Sarah Smith was already there, sitting on a bench and balancing her checkbook while she waited for class to end. "What's going on?" she asked when we came out.

"We're done with class," I said. "We don't like it." And Heather echoed me.

"You can't quit," her mother told her. "You'll be applying to college in a few years, and they're going to want to see that you've done more with your life than just go to school and eat junk food. Don't you even want to get some healthy exercise? Don't you care about finishing what you started and about getting some good habits into your life? Most girls would kill to have the opportunities you have, and let me tell you, it's not always easy for us to afford them." And so on.

Heather stood silently, her head bowed, letting her mother's words rain down on her. I thought she was genuinely overwhelmed, but it turned out to be a cunning defensive maneuver—with no one arguing against her, Sarah ran out of steam and eventually stopped on her own accord with a resigned, if frustrated, shrug of acceptance.

Before they left, Heather and I exchanged cell phone numbers and agreed that we wanted to stay friends.

At that point, she and her mother still had no idea that Luke Weston was my stepfather. They found out eventually of course, but it didn't change the fact that Heather liked me because I had been a good friend to her and not because I was related to the hot guy from *We'll Make You a Star*.

Four

While I was waiting for Heather to show up at my house that morning, I worked out for about half an hour on the elliptical machine in Luke's exercise room and then snuck into Mom's bathroom to shower—mine was just a regular shower but hers had seven showerheads all spritzing you from different angles. It was crazily great and I didn't even feel guilty about it, since the house had been built green, and our gray water—water we'd only used a little bit, like for showers and stuff—went directly into our yard and watered the plants.

This house was ridiculous in the best possible sense—huge and comfortable and luxurious . . . practically decadent. It sometimes freaked me out to think that this was the only house Jacob would know, that he would grow up thinking this was normal. He'd never know what it was like to share a one-room apartment with Mom or spend a few years in a small house so close to your neighbors that you could hear them calling to each other from one room to another. The funny thing was, I almost felt sorry for him. This house was so big, I often didn't know who was home and who wasn't. I liked having my space, but in a weird way, I was glad I'd had so much togetherness with Mom when I was little.

I heard the gate buzz right after I got out of the shower. I hit the wall panel to let Heather in and used the intercom to tell George to open the front door. I threw on a pair of shorts and a clean tank top and headed downstairs in my bare feet; it was late July and super hot outside, but the house was comfortable with the air-conditioning running.

Jacob was slowly turning in circles in the big open foyer area at the bottom of the stairs. Our housekeeper, Lorena, was standing on the steps talking to him.

Lorena was roughly my mother's age and had an eleven-year-old daughter of her own, who she talked to about ten times a day on her cell phone. Mom had hired her to clean a couple of days a week when we first moved into the big house. After Mom got pregnant with Jacob, Lorena mentioned that she liked taking care of babies and Mom instantly hired her full-time. I think the whole Westside nanny thing kind of freaked Mom out, so she was relieved to have someone around to help without going down that road. Mom told me she expected me to continue to be responsible for making my bed and cleaning my room, but over the course of the last few years, we'd all gotten a little lazy and used to being waited on. If I left my clothes on the floor, they ended up in the hamper or cleaned and folded in my drawers—so why keep picking them up? And Lorena made my bed much smoother than I could.

We were all slightly terrified of her, even though she was totally sweet. It was just that she could be intractable. Like once she thought that a pillow looked better on the smaller armchair in the formal living room, but Mom had bought it for the bigger one. Every time Lorena was in the living room, she'd put it on the smaller one, and then Mom would switch it to the bigger one. This went on for weeks. They never discussed it or acknowledged there was a battle of wills going on. But eventually Mom gave up and just left it on the smaller chair. "She's stronger than I am," Mom told me with a good-natured shrug.

"Let's do something else," Lorena was saying now to Jacob as I came close. "Oh, look, there's Ellie. Don't you want to say hi to Ellie? Look at Ellie and say hi, Jacob. Jacob! Stop going in circles and say hi to your sister."

He kept turning, his arms wide, his head thrown back so he could stare up at the ceiling. It was a classic Jacob thing to do.

I grabbed his arms and stopped him from spinning

long enough to drop a kiss on his head and tell him he was my baby dude, and then I let him go and went on into the kitchen, while he went back to twirling behind me. Lorena may have been stronger than Mom, but Jacob was stronger than Lorena. And therefore everyone else.

Heather was already sitting at the big round table. George was at the counter, sticking another pod into the coffee maker.

Heather was chattering away—something about how glad she was to be done with junior year but how terrified she was of all the college application stuff.

George put the cup of coffee in front of her and said, "Do you want milk or sugar?"

"Milk, please. I can get it, though."

"No problem. I'm up anyway." He went over to the refrigerator.

"You'll wait on her, but not me?" I said.

"Heather asks nicely," George said, setting down the milk carton and taking his seat. "You should try it. You guys ready to do some work?"

"I should warn you that I did terribly on the PSATs," Heather said. "I may be hopeless."

"That's why you're here," I said.

George gave us a bunch of multiple-choice math word problems. It took me a little while on one, and I made a careless error on another, but I basically knew what I was doing, which he acknowledged.

But Heather kept saying, "I just don't get it. I don't get how you can turn this into something *solvable*."

"You make *x* stand in for the unknown answer," George said, for about the fourth time in five minutes. "And then you create a simple equation and solve for *x*. Did you see how Ellie set hers up?"

"My brain doesn't work like Ellie's."

"I've just done more SAT prep than you have," I said. "That's all."

"I've taken an eight-week class and two one-day workshops," she said morosely.

While we worked, my phone kept vibrating with texts from my school friends Riley and Skyler, who wanted to get together with me that afternoon. The fourth time I picked up my phone to read a text, George plucked it out of my hand and said, "You can't have this thing near you. You're an addict."

"Some of us have social lives. You wouldn't know about that."

He squinted at the screen. "Who's Skyler? Boy or girl?"

"Never occurred to me to find out."

"Whoever it is wants to come over."

"Shocker," I said, because everyone always wanted to come over to my house: my house was where Luke

Weston lived. I grabbed my phone back and quickly texted Skyler and Riley—while George tapped his fingers impatiently on the table—to tell them I'd rather meet at the mall and go see a movie. "If I don't answer, they'll just keep bugging me," I said.

"Whatever," he said. "Ready to get back to work?"

"One sec." Now I had to text Mom to let her know my plans and make sure she wasn't counting on me for dinner or anything. Texting was our main method of communication. Mom liked me to keep her informed, but sometimes I had no idea if she was even home or not (like I said, our house was really big) so . . . texting. The next best thing to being there.

"Okay, now," I said, and put the phone down for the rest of our study time—except when I got bored waiting for Heather to catch up and used the time to check my Instagram feed.

Once George said we were done for the day, I invited Heather to come to the mall with me, and she ran to the bathroom to get ready.

George looked up from his keyboard; he was back to researching anniversary celebration venues. He said idly, "So . . . *is* Skyler a girl or a guy?"

"Does it matter?"

"Yeah. I could be walking down the street and someone could yell, 'Skyler's getting away!' and I wouldn't know who to look for."

"Probably a dog," I said. "In that scenario."

"Yes, but a boy or girl dog?"

"You'd have to look between its legs to figure that out."

"Sounds risky." He beckoned to me and lowered his voice. "Listen, Ellie, Heather's really sweet but you might want to study with someone who can keep up with you."

"I like helping her."

"Very noble," he said. "But if she's slowing you down—"

"I'm back," Heather announced from the doorway.

I said, "Let's go. Skyler texted that she's already there."

"Aha!" said George. "She's a girl."

"Shes usually are," I said.

Five

We saw the movie and then ate and shopped. Heather had to leave early; she checked her phone right after the movie to discover that her mother was freaking out because Heather hadn't returned her six calls and five texts. "My phone was off," I heard her explain. "I *told* you I was going to a movie." Then after a long listening silence: "I didn't mean to worry you. Okay, fine, I'm on my way."

Skyler and Riley pretended to be sorry Heather had to go, but they only hung out with her because of me. The two of them were best friends and I guess I was sort of their third Musketeer, since I ate lunch with them every day at school and sometimes saw them on the weekends, but deep down I didn't feel that close to them. They were perfectly fine high school friends, but I doubted we'd stay in touch once we left for college.

Riley was probably going to be our class valedictorian.

She took all honors courses and was the top student in most of them. She wore her long brown hair in a ponytail and studied incredibly hard during the week, and then let her hair down both literally and figuratively on the weekends, when she liked to go to parties where she got so drunk she usually threw up and passed out on the floor. It didn't appeal to me much as a lifestyle, but she seemed committed to it.

Skyler was more mellow about school, partially because she *could* be. She'd already been recruited by Brown for volleyball. She had red hair and green eyes and was over six feet tall. She and Riley had both been going to Coral Tree since kindergarten and had been best friends the whole time.

They were both smart and entertaining and quick to laugh, which made them fine to spend an afternoon with, but I could never shake the feeling that my greatest appeal for them was the fact that Luke Weston was my stepfather. Maybe it was unfair of me—God knows I could be paranoid about that kind of thing—but still . . . there were moments. Like even that afternoon: we passed a poster advertising the upcoming season premiere of *We'll Make You a Star*, and Riley instantly stopped and pointed to it. "It must be so weird for you to see Luke's picture everywhere you go," she said to me a little too loudly, like she wanted people to overhear our conversation. "Doesn't it freak you out? I mean, you *live* with him."

"I'm used to it," I said, and moved away.

Heather flashed me a sympathetic eye roll. I'd confided in her how much I hated how famous Luke had become and the way it made people act. I couldn't complain to him and my mom about it—they couldn't change anything and they would just feel bad—and I couldn't complain to people I didn't trust, so I only complained to Heather, who had loved me for me right from the start, and who kept any secret I asked her to.

So even though Skyler and Riley were my closest friends at school, I didn't feel relaxed around them. They were always inventing reasons to come over to my house, where their eyes would flicker around hopefully at every noise, like they were just waiting for Luke to come through the door and fall in love with one of them. You'd think the fact that he was my mother's husband would make them a little less obvious about their crushes, but apparently his fame made him some kind of acceptable universal object of lust. I just tried to avoid having them over, which is why I usually met them at places like the mall.

When I got home, I found Mom and Luke lying on their bed, Jacob between them, curled up on his side, staring at some animated show on TV. Luke was reading a script (he read a lot of scripts now that he had his own production company), and Mom a glossy magazine. She never cared much about fashion before Luke got famous, but now they were always going to dressy events, and she felt like she had to keep up.

"There you are!" she said, putting her magazine down. "How was the movie?"

"Moderately not-awful," I said. "But only moderately."

"And the SAT tutoring?"

"About as thrilling as you'd expect."

"Just be grateful we didn't make you get a job this summer," she said. "A few hours of studying won't kill you. Is George a good tutor?"

"Yeah, he's fine." I came over and sat down on the edge of their bed. "Speaking of George, I wanted to ask you something. Could we go to Tahiti for your anniversary party?"

"Tahiti? We were leaning toward Hawaii."

"But I've always wanted to go to Tahiti. Plus . . . you know . . . Gauguin."

My mother laughed. With no makeup on and her hair a little rumpled, she looked the way I liked her best: like my mom. When she was all glammed up for going out with lots of eye makeup and curled hair, she looked Hollywood-wife generic. "So it would be educational? Is that what you're telling me?"

"Totally. I'd read up on Gauguin before we went and become a total expert on him, I swear."

"How can I say no to that?"

"Cool." I slid off the bed and stood up. "I'll tell George."

I may have sounded a tiny bit smug when I told George that he should start looking at resorts in Tahiti.

His eyes narrowed. "Just because *you* want to go there?"

"I convinced Mom. I always get my way, you know."

"Yeah," he said. "I see that. Kind of like Veruca Salt."

"Don't be a bad loser."

Except he *didn't* lose. Somehow, once he had done the research and presented all the options to my mother and Luke, and the final decision was made, they went with Hawaii after all.

I complained, but Mom said it just made more sense, because we only had four days, and Hawaii was a lot closer. "Only four days?" I repeated. I'd been picturing a real end-of-summer blowout, days and days of beaches and walks and lazy meals and long naps in hammocks before having to get back to fall semester and college applications and all that stuff. But now Mom said the show was taping and Luke couldn't take more time off than that.

Luke's schedule ruled our household and was the one thing impervious to my coaxing and begging, so there wasn't much I could do about it except whine to George later that we'd be spending more time flying than actually lying on a beach.

"Yeah, it's rough," he said. "You don't get to go on a tropical vacation for as long as you'd hoped. Complain about it to everyone you meet and bask in the sympathy."

He was coming with us—my mother told him they'd pay for his airfare so long as he shared a hotel room with his brother, who was already coming as Luke's guest. She claimed she needed George to deal with the logistics once we were there, which seemed more kind than true. When I pressed her about it, she admitted she just wanted to give him a vacation. "I felt bad that he was spending all this time looking at pictures of Hawaii and not getting to go. He's never been. A trip like that would have meant so much to me at his age."

"You know, Heather's never been to Hawaii either—"

"Forget it," she said. "I have reached the limits of my generosity."

Jonathan's fiancée was coming as his plus one, and Luke was flying my grandmother out, which would be a big help with Jacob. Luke didn't talk to his own family anymore; they'd ignored and ostracized him when he was struggling, and then came running with their hands out when he got rich and famous. He sent them money but never saw them.

We saw my grandmother a ton, though. She came to visit whenever she had time off from work. Mom had tried to convince her to move out to LA to live with us (or at least near us), but she said she didn't want to be dependent on anyone, which was also why she wouldn't let them buy her a nicer apartment in Philadelphia. Mom sent her a lot of gifts and bought her first-class airplane tickets, but other than that, Grandma took care of herself.

Luke had also invited a couple of his closest friends to join us. Carl Miller used to be his business manager and was now CFO of his production company. And of course Michael Marquand was coming—he and Luke were like brothers.

Mom said she didn't need to invite any friends because Grandma and I were her best friends, which was probably true. Most of the people she'd met in Hollywood saw her more as Luke Weston's wife than a person in her own right, and she'd been too busy working and taking care of me to make a lot of friends back in Philadelphia.

Luke got first-class tickets for the family. Jonathan, George, and Jonathan's fiancée, Izzy, were on our flight, but in coach. Luke and Mom sat together on the flight out, and so did Grandma and Jacob, who happily watched movies the entire way—I'm not convinced he even knew we had left the house.

I was across the aisle from Grandma and next to a businessman who never once made eye contact with me and who quickly popped two pills, drank three cocktails, donned headphones and an eye mask, and fell asleep. I guess he didn't want the fancy lunch with the real silverware and all.

I did. I loved first class. We never flew at all when I was a kid; we had nowhere to go and we couldn't have afforded it anyway. The first time I got on a plane was the summer that Mom and Luke got married, and even though it was fun to go up into the sky, I didn't like much else about flying coach. Then Luke got rich and we all started flying first class together, and it was totally different—you could watch your own movies on a personal screen and the food was good and the flight attendants waited on you hand and foot. It felt like vacation.

Like me, Grandma hadn't flown until Luke came into our lives, but she wasn't a convert the way I was. "It's a necessary evil," she said to me, leaning across the aisle at one point. "I do it because I have to, but I don't trust it. There's gravity. Things fall down."

"People fly all the time," I said. "It's pretty reliable."

"I don't want to scare you," she said, "so I won't argue. Even though I could. What was that noise?"

"Nothing. Oh, look." I handed her the menu card. "Wine. You should have some."

"Maybe," she said primly.

She had some. And soon after dozed off in her seat, leaving me to enjoy the rest of the flight in peace.

six

The hotel manager came in a limo to pick us up; she handed out our room key cards during the ride, which is when I found out that I was supposed to share a room with Grandma and Jacob.

I didn't say anything until we had pulled up at the resort, which was spectacularly beautiful: palm trees and fountains everywhere you looked. But I wasn't in the mood to enjoy it. As soon as we'd gotten out of the limo, I grabbed my mother's arm.

"It's not fair!" I hissed. "Grandma gets up at like five in the morning. And she drives me crazy. I want my own room."

"I'm not letting you sleep by yourself in a place where a lot of strangers have passkeys," she said. "And if you think you can talk me into it, you're wrong, so save your breath."

I let go of her and drifted over to George. "I blame

you," I said. "You booked the rooms. You should have gotten me my own."

"First of all," he said, "I was following your mother's instructions. And second of all, I'm sharing a room with Jonathan and Izzy, which is a lot more awkward than sharing a room with your grandmother, so don't complain to *me*."

"You and I could get a room together!" I said. "That would solve both our problems."

"Yeah, I think that might be awkward in a whole different way," he said, and walked away.

Mom and Luke went up to their suite, saying they just wanted to have a quiet dinner alone there. I wanted to eat in one of the hotel restaurants, but Jacob was in a whiny mood, so we ordered room service and turned the TV on to the Sprout Channel to keep him happy.

When the food came, Grandma criticized me for ordering a pizza. She said that everyone knew wheat was bad for you and that it was no wonder I was so short.

I told her to stop blaming my diet for the fact I was short—hadn't she ever heard of genetics? Mom was even shorter than I was, and she wasn't exactly a giant herself.

She said she was sorry she cared about my health, and she guessed she should just mind her own business from now on, go away, and not bother anyone ever again.

I told her to stop being such a drama queen, and then Jacob suddenly let out a wail. I asked him what was wrong, but he wouldn't answer, just sat there, his mouth open in a roar so wide you could see bits of french fries caked around his teeth. Grandma said, "It's because you let him try the pizza," and I said, "No, it's not," and Jacob kept bawling, and the noise was unbearable, and I was losing my temper with them both, so I said I was going down to the lobby and stomped out.

I punched the down button as hard as I could. It didn't bring the elevator any faster but it felt good.

Once I was in the lobby, I wasn't sure what to do. I heard distant music so I followed the sound across a breezy walkway to what looked like the entrance to a dance club. I peered in, but I was wearing sweatpants and a cotton tank top and everyone inside was dressed up. Plus they probably didn't let in anyone under the drinking age. Plus it looked kind of lame—everyone there was middle-aged. Plus I would never go to a dance club by myself.

Still, it was fun to watch for a while. Most of the women were wearing flowery sundresses and the men had on Hawaiian shirts—it was all so tacky it was kind of endearing.

I turned away just as two youngish guys in suits reached for the door.

"Hey there," one of them said, sidestepping right into my path, blocking my way. "Thinking about coming in?"

"Not really." I flashed a tight smile.

"Come on," the other one said. He had slicked-back hair and his suit was a little shiny. "The night's young and you look like you're a dancer. Don't sit this one out."

"We need you in there," the other added. His hair was thinning, triangles of bare skin making wings at his temples. "Never enough cute girls."

"Wrong shoes," I said, pointing down at my flip-flops.

"Kick 'em off," the other guy said.

"Take off whatever you want," his friend agreed, and giggled.

The first one said, "Don't mind him. We're harmless. Would you rather grab a drink at the bar?"

"I'm good, thanks," I said, and turned.

Slicked-back hair grabbed my arm. "Come on," he said. "Don't leave so fast."

I pushed his arm away and said, "Really, no." I was starting to feel uncomfortable, so it was a huge relief to see someone familiar emerge from the restaurant near the lobby. "Oh, there's my friend," I said, then dodged around them while they were still absorbing that and ran toward George, calling him. He turned around.

"Keep going," I said as I caught up to him. "Don't look back at those guys."

He immediately looked over his shoulder. "What guys?"

"I told you not to look!" I glanced back. They had disappeared. "They must have gone into the club. It's fine. I'm just glad I saw you." We headed back into the lobby.

"Why? What happened?"

"Nothing really." We reached the elevator and I hit the up button. "They just wanted me to go dancing with them and were kind of bugging me about it."

The elevator arrived, but George hesitated, holding it open with his hand instead of following me inside. "Should I be doing something heroic like finding them and telling them to leave young girls alone? Maybe slugging them? How big were they?"

"Let's just go up." I tugged him inside the elevator.

"You're on seven, right?" He punched the button. "Why are you wandering around the lobby at night in a camisole anyway?"

I crossed my arms, slightly embarrassed but defiant. "What are you, slut shaming me? Blaming the victim?"

He flushed. "Don't be ridiculous. But you look like you're wearing pajamas."

"Yeah, well, that's because they *are* my pajamas. I was so desperate to get out of my room I didn't bother changing. My grandmother is driving me crazy, just like I predicted." The elevator dinged and the doors opened onto my floor. "Where are Jonathan and Izzy?" I asked as we headed down the hallway.

"They're still at dinner. The restaurant's really beautiful—it looks out over the beach and there are torches everywhere and the sound of the waves and soft music. . . ." He smiled ruefully. "It was incredibly romantic. And there they were, gazing into each other's eyes . . . and there I was . . . totally in the way."

"I know the feeling," I said. "Mom and Luke were so in love when they first met—I ruined a lot of romantic evenings for them."

"They probably didn't mind. They both adore you."

"And I'm sure your brother is very fond of you."

"Yeah, okay, good point."

I glanced over at him as I waved my key card in front of the sensor to unlock the door. He was wearing his usual khakis with a dark blue jacket over a jarringly different shade of blue button-down shirt. "Is there a dress code at the restaurant?"

"Yeah." He looked down at himself. "This is my suit jacket—it's the only one I packed. Does it look stupid with these pants?"

"Not with the pants. With the shirt." I opened the

door to a scene of chaos: Jacob standing naked on the sofa screaming and Grandma scuttling around on the floor below him, picking up food that was scattered everywhere as she scolded him for throwing it. Neither of them noticed us standing there, so I quickly slammed the door shut again before we were spotted. "See?" I said to George. "See what I'm dealing with?"

"Yeah. That's just . . ." He shook his head. "You can't go in there right now. You want to go back down and check out the beach? Wait for things to calm down?"

"I so do."

We took the elevator back down to the lobby. As we were crossing through to the ocean side of the hotel, someone called my name and I turned.

It was Michael Marquand, Luke's best friend and also his music and TV producer—the guy we all owed our lifestyle to. He was dressed in a T-shirt, jeans, and a Red Sox baseball cap, and was holding his six-month-old daughter in his arms. I exclaimed in delight and instantly reached for her. Mia eyed me with suspicion; it had been a couple of weeks since I'd last held her and she was ready to stranger-zone me. But once she was in my arms, I cooed at her and bounced her gently, and she relaxed.

"Where's Crystal?" I asked. Crystal was Michael's wife and Mia's mother.

"She's checking us in." He gestured toward the front desk. "She always has a lot of specific demands, so I let her take charge." He yawned. "I'm exhausted. Long flight. Someone didn't stop screaming the entire trip, and for once it wasn't me." Michael was a tall, thin, wiry guy, who normally looked very handsome and a lot younger than his fifty-five years but tonight looked a little ragged.

"She's being a very good girl now," I said. Mia was the cutest baby in the world—big dark eyes and a fuzzy brown tuft of hair on top of her head.

"She's just too worn-out from crying for six straight hours to cry any more." He turned to George. "Hey, Jonathan! How's it going?"

"Fine?" George said uncertainly.

I came to his aid. "He's not Jonathan."

"I'm his brother," George added. "People get us confused all the time."

"Thank you for pretending I'm not an idiot," Michael said. "Hey, Ellie, I've got some good news."

"Do you?" I said, blowing gently down at the baby, who batted her long eyelashes against the slight breeze. "Does your daddy have good news? Does he? Does he? What'shisgoodnews? What is it?"

"I really don't think she's going to answer you," George said to me. "No matter how many times you ask her."

Michael said a little impatiently, "Aaron's coming to live with me!"

43

I looked up. "You're kidding!"

"Nope. His mother's husband got a job in Vermont, and Aaron said he's not about to move to the middle of nowhere for his last year before college. He thinks LA will be a lot more fun. Crystal and I are thrilled."

"Yay! Does he know which school yet?"

"Fenwick."

I pouted. "I was hoping he'd go to Coral Tree with me."

"Don't worry, you two will still see plenty of each other. Do we have a room?"

This last was to his approaching wife, who joined us and kissed me on the cheek. "The baby looks so happy with you, Ellie. Would you minding holding her for the next fifteen or sixteen years?" She nodded at George. "Hello, Jonathan." She turned back to Michael. "Megan's still in the bathroom."

"Megan?" I said.

"Our nanny."

"What happened to Tiana?"

"She quit," Michael said with a brief dark glance at his wife, who didn't seem to notice. She was wearing skintight yoga pants, high soft leather boots, and a long cardigan over a low-cut top—I guess in theory it was all comfortable traveling clothing, but she looked pretty incredible. She was a beautiful young woman with long, straight dark hair and large black eyes.

Mia reached her arms out toward her mother. Crystal heaved a sigh, handed Michael her purse and the key cards, then took the baby and propped her up on her hip. "Megan doesn't know which room we're in, so someone has to wait for her." Mia waved her arms and made some complaining sounds. Crystal rolled her eyes and thumped her on the back. "And here we go again. You'd think she'd be all cried out after that horrendous performance on the plane. I'll take her on up. Michael, you wait for Megan. You know you want to. She's very beautiful," she explained to George.

"Not as beautiful as you," Michael said wearily. "And she's standing right over there, near the elevators. Let's go to bed. We're all overtired. Good night, Ellie. And good night—" He stopped. "I've forgotten your name," he said to George.

"Are you serious?" Crystal said. "How could you forget Jonathan?"

"Because he's not Jonathan," Michael said. "This is his brother."

"Oh." She studied George. "Identical twins?"

"He's eight years older than me, actually," George said apologetically.

She pressed her lips together, then said, "Huh. Well, good night." They left.

"You know what the easiest thing would be?" I said to George. "For you just to *be* Jonathan for the rest of the weekend. Especially since you don't seem to like correcting people."

"I couldn't correct Michael Marquand," he said. "He discovered Dense Keys."

"Who or what is that?"

"Are you kidding me? Ellie, you're a Philistine. How can you know so little about music when your stepfather is Luke Weston?"

"I don't know. We talk about other stuff, I guess." We headed down the wide, carpeted stairway that led to the pool-level lower floor.

George said, "So who's Aaron and why are we so happy he's coming to LA?"

"He's Michael's son by his first wife."

"So the wife I just met is number two?"

"Three, actually. There was this young actress in between."

"Crystal isn't exactly *old*."

"This one was even younger. I believe the words 'cradle robbing' were used, but I'm not telling you by who, except it was my mom. It didn't last long."

The hallway at the bottom of the stairs ended in glass doors that led out to the back of the resort. George held one open for me and I stepped through. "Wow, it's really beautiful here." I stopped to look around. Torches were lit all around us, outlining the paths to the pool and the beach, and their flickering glow tinged everything burnt orange. Palm tree leaves stirred against the blue-black sky. You could hear the ocean from where we were, but the sound was just a gentle rise and fall behind the uneven clash of voices laughing and talking from the patio restaurant. I breathed in the salty-smoky air and closed my eyes briefly to enjoy it. "Why is anyone inside when they could be out here? Why would anyone be anywhere else in the world right now?"

"Yeah, it's pretty nice."

I glanced over my shoulder and he was watching me, but his gaze quickly shifted away. "I know what you're thinking," I said.

"I doubt it."

"You're gloating because you were right—this is just as good as Tahiti would have been. Maybe even better." I flung my hand around. "I mean, this is perfect. You can't get better than perfect, can you?"

"I didn't deliberately not choose Tahiti because you wanted it, you know. This was the best choice for a lot of reasons."

"Still, you were right and I was wrong. I admit it. Now let us never speak of it again. Want to go down to the beach?"

"Yeah." As we walked along the curving path, he said, "You never finished telling me about Michael's son. Do you know him?"

"He's my future husband."

"Really? What crime did he commit to deserve a sentence like that?"

"Don't be mean. We're like the same exact age and his father and Luke are best friends. And—" I stopped. If I'd been with one of my girlfriends, I might have also said something about how Aaron had grown from a reasonably cute tween when I first met him to one of the best-looking guys in the world. I'd seen him briefly a few months ago when he was visiting his father and he kind of took my breath away. He had gotten tall and broad-shouldered and his hair was this bronze color and wavy, and he had these light blue eyes and this perfect jaw. . . .

"And . . . ?" George prompted.

I shrugged. "And so he's destined to be my husband. I'm just not sure *which* husband. I don't want him to be my first, because obviously that one's not going to last—"

"Obviously."

"And I want my *last* husband to be much younger than I am so he can take care of me when I'm dying. Obviously."

"Obviously."

"Maybe number three?"

"Would that put him in the middle? Or still toward the beginning?"

"I'm hurt," I said. "How many husbands do you

think I'm planning to have? I'm not that kind of girl."

"Obviously," he said.

I nudged his elbow with mine. "Come on. Let's go down to the water."

When we reached the sand, I kicked off my flip-flops and said, "You'd better take your loafers off, too, unless you like gritty shoes."

He removed his shoes and socks, then cuffed his pants. "How stupid do I look?" he asked as he straightened up.

"You don't want to know."

"*'Don't worry, George, you look fine. Not stupid at all.'*"

"My mama didn't raise no liars."

"Just . . . come on." We left our shoes and he led the way down to the edge of the water. We stood there in the semidarkness, hearing the waves better than we could see them. The water looked black at this hour. Black with white frills that caught the moonlight. The few couples I could see were spread out along the beach, as far from one another as they could be, greedy for privacy.

"Why is the ocean so wonderful?" I asked after we'd gazed in contented silence for a while.

"I don't know," George said. "People can't survive without water, so maybe we're biologically programmed to want to be near it."

"You just managed to suck all the poetry right out of this."

"Sorry."

"It's okay. Doesn't this make you want to *do* something?"

"What do you mean?"

"I don't know." I circled my hands in the air, frustrated by my inability to put the feeling into words. "There's something about how beautiful it is—and how the waves look—and the sound, too . . . and it's like we should go out and build castles or fight evil or just run around in circles screaming. Don't you feel that?"

"Yeah," he said. "It's so big and we're so small. It makes you want to be bigger. To matter."

"Right." I turned and we started walking along the shore. "The sand's freezing. My feet are getting numb."

"You want to go back inside?"

"Soon. Not yet." I glanced sideways at him. "So what could we do that would matter? Build hospitals? Slay evil dictators? Write the great American novel?"

"We could write the great American novel about an evil dictator while sitting in a hospital," he said. "But what we'll really do is walk away and forget that feeling within about five minutes and end up like the rest of the world, working any job we can get and leading lives of quiet desperation."

"You're a cynic."

"No—a realist."

I glanced up at the resort and saw a couple strolling toward the ocean, holding hands. "Isn't that Mom and Luke?"

"I think so," George said, and we headed toward them. There were a few other couples trailing them, acting all casual and indifferent but clearly sneaking glimpses at the famous TV star. At least they were all keeping a respectful distance.

"What are you two doing down here?" Mom asked as we came together.

"I had to get out of that room," I said. "Jacob threw a fit—he was screaming and throwing his food. I ran into George in the lobby and we thought we'd see what the beach was like."

"Jacob had a tantrum?" Even in the dim light, I could see Mom's brow furrow. "He's been having so many lately."

"It's just because he was on a plane all day," Luke said with an easy shrug. "After a six-hour flight, I'm ready to throw things, too."

"Yeah, me too," I said. "And most kids scream on airplanes. It's sort of amazing he didn't."

Mom didn't respond to that.

By the time I got back to the room, Jacob was asleep and Grandma was watching TV with the volume down low—some reality show about a bunch of swollen-lipped women who were drinking wine and yelling at one another.

I curled up on the other bed—Jacob was in a rollaway crib—and texted Heather. I wanted to tell her that Aaron Marquand was coming to live in LA.

He's the cute one, right? she texted back. *With the blue eyes?* She hadn't ever met him, but I'd shown her photos.

Yep. AKA my future husband.

Squeal.

seven

The breeze was blowing strands of hair against my sticky-glossy lips. I had to keep reaching up and pulling them away with my free hand. I wished I'd put my hair up. Or not worn lip gloss.

Jacob's hand was sweaty in mine as Luke made a toast to Mom. I glanced down at my little brother, who was wearing a soft dark-green top over white pants. His thick, wavy hair was neatly brushed for once—it was on the long side because he hated having it cut and would scream when anyone tried, but at least it looked cute that way. He also didn't like having it brushed, but I'd won that battle this morning by bribing him: an M&M for each pass of the brush *and* he got to watch TV the whole time.

He was pretty adorable all dressed up. Kid-model cute. He held my hand tightly and stared up at the slowly rotating fake-palm-leaf fan above us.

We were in a room with floor-to-ceiling glass doors facing the ocean, all of them open for the party. We could hear the waves and feel the breeze, but we had a wooden floor under our feet and three walls to keep the event private. For added security, George had also asked the hotel not to use Luke's real name, so the event schedule down in the lobby read "Anniversary of John and Jane Smith." I took a photo and texted it to Heather with a jaunty *Maybe we're related.*

"I am so brilliant," I crowed to Jonathan after the toast was done, and waiters had started passing around drinks and hors d'oeuvres. "Don't you think this was a brilliant idea? Don't Luke and Mom look happy?" Mom's face had lit up when Luke said that the last five years had been the happiest of his life, and their kiss at the end of his toast had looked pretty passionate from where I was standing.

"It's great," Jonathan said, and squeezed my shoulders.

"It's really pretty here," his fiancée added. Izzy had straight dark eyebrows and straight dark hair. She always seemed very serious and intense to me, but it's possible I was reading too much into the eyebrows.

They moved on to talk to Luke's business manager. I helped myself to a glass of champagne and raised it to Luke, who had caught my eye from across the room. He blew me a kiss. I had definitely lucked out in the stepfather department. And not because Luke had become so rich and famous. Because he was Luke.

My grandmother beckoned to me. She'd had her hair blown out by a professional that morning, and it looked sleek and shiny, instead of frizzy and bumpy like it usually did. Between that and the neatly tailored blue silk dress Mom had bought for her, she looked great. "Are you sure you should—" she began, but then she saw something that distracted her. "Is that a piece of cheese? Why would she give that to him? He eats way too much dairy." She ran toward Mom and Jacob.

George came up to me. "Hey," he said.

"Hey. Were you waiting until my grandmother left to come talk to me?"

"She's a lovely woman. I respect her enormously."

"Try waking up with her in your room."

"Words cannot express to what extent I'd rather not."

"You get drunk enough, anything could happen."

"I'm fairly certain not that."

"That's the same suit jacket you were wearing last night," I pointed out, looking him up and down. "It looks better with the matching pants. And a shirt that doesn't clash." The funny thing was, he looked younger in the suit than he did in his usual jeans and oxford shirts, like a teenager borrowing his dad's clothes for a prom. I forgot sometimes that he was only a couple of years older than I was; he felt a lot older because he was done with college already, and because he was so Georgeish.

"There's sand in the pockets from last night," he said. "I can't figure out how it got there."

"Lax immigration laws? You haven't said anything about how *I* look." I spun around so the ballerina skirt on my dusty-pink dress rose up slightly and then settled back down into place. "Nice, right?"

"You know what your problem is?" he said. "Low self-esteem."

"A compliment wouldn't kill you."

"I could never flatter you as well as you flatter yourself."

I folded my arms over my chest with a humph. "I take back all the nice things I said about your suit."

"What nice things? All you said was it didn't look as bad today as it did last night. Not that I remember asking for your opinion."

"Does anyone help you pick out your clothing? Do you have a girlfriend?"

"Not at the moment. I'm sure that shocks you. What about you?"

"I have lots of girlfriends."

"That's not what I meant."

"Oh, you mean like a girlfriend with a penis?" It's

possible the champagne was getting to me. "Nope. Never had one."

"Seriously?" His surprise seemed genuine. "I would have assumed you went through a dozen a year. Aren't you Miss Popularity?"

I wrinkled my nose. "I would never date in high school. It would be way too embarrassing to look back on."

"Don't you think that depends on who you went out with?"

"There isn't a guy in my grade who I haven't seen asleep in class with his mouth open and drooling. Ugh."

"I hate to break it to you, but guys fall asleep in college, too. A lot."

"I'll skip all my morning classes so I won't have to see them."

Before he could respond, Jonathan and Izzy appeared at my elbow. Jonathan said, "Georgie, the manager thought I was you and wanted to know when they should serve dinner. Can you go talk to her?"

"Georgie?" I repeated with delight.

George moaned. "I can't believe you just gave her *more* ammunition to use against me."

"I would never!" I said. "I'm not like that. Georgiekins."

"I'm going to go talk to the manager," he said,

stepping back. "And then I'm throwing myself in the ocean. Tell Mom and Dad I loved them, Jonny."

"*Jonny's* not embarrassing," I called after him as he walked away. "Not like *Georgie*."

"Poor Georgie," Izzy said seriously. "He's so sensitive."

eight

I spent the next two days digging my toes in the sand while I read and dozed in the sun. They went by way too quickly; I blinked and we were packing.

I was hoping the mellow vacation vibe would stick around, but it was business as usual with George when he showed up for tutoring on Wednesday. "You're going to take an entire practice SAT today," he announced briskly as soon as he walked in the door. "We only have a week before school starts and we won't be able to get as much done then. I want to pinpoint whatever you're still struggling with so we can focus on it."

"I'm not struggling with any of it," I said, following him into the kitchen.

"Prove it. Take the test."

"That takes hours!"

"Where else do you have to be?"

"I have a life, you know."

"Want me to text your mother and ask her what she thinks?"

"It is so uncool to constantly be threatening to tell my mother on me. You know that, right?" I dropped into a chair. It had turned really hot, brutally hot, the kind of hot LA only gets in late August and early September. The air-conditioning was blasting throughout the house, but I was wearing my shortest shorts and a tank top because I could *see* how hot it was through the window.

"I'd hate to have you think I'm not cool," he said stonily.

"Yeah, that ship has sailed. . . . Can I at least have Heather come do it with me so it's more fun?"

"If it will cut down on the whining. I can print up two copies."

I texted Heather and told her to come over but didn't tell her why, because I didn't want her to say no and I knew she hated taking tests.

She wrote back: *Okay. My mom says we should pay for my half of the tutoring tho*

Tell her you make me work harder and we should be paying you to come

That's ridiculous

We'll talk about it later

I didn't want her money. George was *my* tutor and she only came as my invited guest, and that's how I wanted it. I liked being the one in control.

Once he had finished printing up the tests, and we were just waiting for Heather to arrive, George started firing vocabulary words at me. "Define *euphemism*."

"Polite word for something that isn't polite. For instance, instead of saying that someone puked, I would say that they 'prayed to the porcelain god' or something like that."

"*Avuncular*."

"Behaving like an uncle to someone. Michael is very avuncular toward me. But when I marry his son, he'll be more *paternal*. Do you want some tea?" I stood up.

"No, thanks. *Fatuous*."

I put a tea pod into the coffee maker and hit the start button. "I'm not sure I can define it, but I'm pretty sure you're an example of it."

"Wrong," he said. "It doesn't mean wildly handsome."

"Oh, well played, Georgie! You win that round."

Soon after that, Heather buzzed in at the gate. "I have good news and bad news," I told her as we walked along the hallway toward the kitchen. "The good news is we're going shopping later."

"And the bad news is that I can't afford to buy anything."

"Yes, you can. I'm treating."

"Then the bad news is that it's so hot, my car will

melt before we leave." She was dressed for the brutal heat in a pair of Daisy Dukes and a gauzy tee.

"Not that either."

"Then what's the bad news?"

We entered the kitchen and I gestured toward George, who was sitting there in his usual jeans and oxford shirt—dressed for a completely different climate. "First we have to take a practice SAT."

"Oh no," she said, backing away. "You didn't tell me we were going to do that. That's not fair."

"Come on." I took her hand and pulled her toward the table. "It'll be fun. We'll do it together."

"No, you won't," George said. "I'm putting you in separate rooms. You need to take this seriously or there's no point."

"You go ahead," Heather said. "I'll wait. I can watch something or talk to George."

"George doesn't want to talk to you," I said.

"I beg your pardon!" he said. "I'd be happy to talk to Heather."

"Thank you," she said to him. "I'd be happy to talk to you, too."

"You have to take this test so George can help you raise your scores." I turned to him. "I've got it all planned out: Heather and I are both going to get in early to Elton College. We'll be done with all the college stuff before the holidays, and then we'll be together for the next four years."

"We *hope* we'll get in," Heather said. "I mean, I'm sure you will, but I'm not so sure about me. Elton College is hard to get into and I haven't been the best student."

"That's why we're going to apply early. They like people who apply early, especially people who are quirky and interesting, and who's more quirky and interesting than us?"

The dimple on Heather's right cheek appeared. "No one."

"Plus George is going to make sure we do well on the SATs. Now get into the dining room and take that test." I took her by the shoulders and steered her across the kitchen and through the archway that separated it from the dining room.

"Why do *I* have to be in here?" she asked over her shoulder.

"Because I need to be in the kitchen. My tea's in there." I came back in and sat down, folded my hands, and looked up at George like an obedient pupil. "We're ready to take your test, Mr. Nussbaum, sir."

He handed me the packet and told me to get to work.

On Friday, I was coming down the stairs in the morning and spotted George heading out the front door

"What are you doing?" I called out.

He turned around and greeted me in his usual measured way—he never seemed particularly excited to see me, but he was always pleasant enough. "Your mom asked me to get her laptop fixed." He showed me the computer sleeve in his hand. "I'm running to the Genius Bar. Hey, can I talk to you for a second?"

"What about?"

"Heather's not here, right?"

I looked to my left and to my right, then patted the pockets of my jean shorts. "Doesn't seem to be. Why?"

"I just wanted to say that maybe you shouldn't be pushing her to apply early to Elton."

I leaned against the banister. "Why not?"

"After scoring that test you guys took, I'm worried she doesn't have much of a shot there."

I shrugged. "Neither of us was taking it very seriously."

"You still managed to do incredibly well." He shifted the computer from one hand to the other. "Elton would be a big reach for her, I think."

"You're not a college counselor," I said. "You don't really know."

"Right," he said. "And you're not one either. So tell her to talk to hers. And be aware that she'll do whatever you say, even if you're totally wrong."

I scowled at him. "First of all, I've researched Elton

a lot, and they like people who are creative, which Heather totally is." She wrote a lot of fan fiction, mostly about characters from her favorite TV shows. That was creative, right? "They're going to want her. And secondly, you're wrong—she doesn't do whatever I say. That's ridiculous."

"I've seen you order her around. She worships you." He raised his eyebrows. "Which seems to be what you like best about the relationship."

"That's so not true! Not to mention rude."

"Uh-huh." He was really starting to annoy me, standing there with his stupid pants and long-sleeved shirt on the hottest day of the year, large almost colorless eyes blinking at me as he accused me of being a bad friend.

I gestured toward the door. "Aren't you going to be late for your genius?"

"Yeah," he said, sounding tired. "I am. Good-bye. We can talk more about this on Sunday."

"I'm canceling Sunday," I said even though I hadn't thought about it before now. "I have other plans."

"Your mother said I should come."

"Well, she's wrong." I turned my back on him and went into the kitchen. Why should I let him tutor me when he had just proven that he didn't know anything about anything?

* * *

I was kind of lying when I said I had plans, except that it turned out I really *did* have plans, I just hadn't known about them. That night, Luke informed the rest of the family that he'd invited the Marquands over for a barbecue on Sunday, which was the day before Labor Day and two days before the start of school. Aaron was flying in on Saturday, so he'd be coming with them.

I spent a long time getting ready for that barbecue. I washed my hair that morning and scrunched it under a diffuser so it was just about as curly as it could get—which was pretty ridiculously curly—and used some gel that made the copper highlights catch the light. Since it was still super hot and we were planning on swimming, I put on my favorite dark-red bikini and covered that with a floaty, transparent printed dress.

As I was leaving my room, I heard Jacob calling out from his and checked on him. He was just waking from a nap. Mom had recently moved him from his crib to a small bed that looked like a race car, but he never got out of it by himself, just sat up and cried until someone rescued him, like he'd always done in the crib.

"Hey, baby dude," I said, and picked him up. His diaper felt heavy through his shorts. He wasn't any-where close to being toilet trained yet—since he didn't talk or seem to understand all that much, it was hard to explain the whole potty concept to him. "Have a nice nap?"

He rubbed his forehead against my bare shoulder and I nuzzled his sweat-damp hair. I liked him best like this, right after a nap, when he was all drowsy and cuddly.

"We're going to have a barbecue," I told him. "Hot dogs. I know you like hot dogs. And Daddy will be home all day. Fun, right?"

He didn't react, just rested against me, breathing lightly.

"We have guests coming over. You remember Michael? And Crystal? And little baby Mia?" I was never sure what he understood and what he didn't. Sometimes it seemed like your words meant nothing to him and then all of a sudden he'd go and grab something you were just talking about and bring it to you. "Let's find you something special to wear." I pulled a shirt out of his drawer.

Instantly he started arching back in my arms—so violently that I almost dropped him—and shaking his head and making a low moaning sound that I knew would turn to screaming in a second if I wasn't careful.

"Sorry," I said, dumping him back on the bed. I quickly crammed the shirt into the dresser. "It had buttons. I know. Forget that. See? All gone now."

Jacob had a button phobia. And of course he couldn't tell us why.

I changed his diaper and helped him into blue board shorts and a soft white T-shirt—clothing he approved of—and carried him downstairs.

Mom was in the kitchen, getting instructions from Carlos, our part-time chef, who had come in early to make a bunch of salads and marinate the meat. "If you dress the lettuce salad too soon, it will get soggy," he was telling her when we walked in. "But you want the dressing to tenderize the kale salad for at least half an hour. In fact, I think I'll put it on right now—it won't hurt and you might forget."

"Yes, do that," Mom said cheerfully. "I'll definitely forget." She was wearing a navy blue maxi sundress and a pair of amazing sparkling sandals. I eyed those sandals covetously and decided I would borrow them soon.

I put Jacob down and he ran over to Mom and hugged her legs.

"Hey, baby," she said, absently patting his head while she glanced around the kitchen. "Where are the hot dog buns?"

"In the bag on the table. Whole wheat." Carlos was bald, but *shaved* bald, and his eyes were younger than his mouth and chin. He was somewhere between forty and sixty, but I had no idea where. He came twice a week and cooked lots of dishes, which he left in the refrigerator so we could heat them up whenever we wanted a meal; he also prepared food for special events like this. "I wanted to get sea bass for the fish but I didn't like the way theirs looked, so I got cod instead. I made a romesco to go with it. All Luke has to do is grill it and then put the sauce on. But tell him not to overdo it. Fish should always be slightly undercooked. Now, let's talk about the corn."

"As fascinating as this is . . ." I said, and left them to it.

nine

deliberately didn't run downstairs when I heard the guests arrive. I took my time, not wanting to seem too eager to see Aaron—I knew that Luke and Michael were into the idea of matching us up and didn't want to encourage them. It was one thing for me to joke about how he was my future husband and another thing for them to try to make it *true*.

I waited about ten minutes, and by the time I came down, they'd all already traipsed through the house and gone out back.

In addition to an enormous lawn, the swing set Jacob loved so much, an Olympic-sized pool, a hot tub that could fit fifteen people, a guesthouse, and a still-under-construction combination exercise and screening room, we had an entire outdoor kitchen and living room in the backyard. I think Luke enjoyed the idea of himself grilling slabs of meat like any American dad, but I kind of doubted that most American fathers had the setup he did: a built-in propane-fed grill, a wood-fired pizza oven, a full-sized outdoor refrigerator, an ice cream freezer/fountain—complete with spouts for hot fudge and caramel—and a farmhouse sink with hot and cold running water.

"Is this a thing?" I said to Mom when the real estate agent first walked us through the house and grounds almost four years ago. "Do people have stuff like this?"

"Not many," she said.

"Come the revolution, we are so guillotined."

"I'll show them photos from the studio you and I shared back in Philadelphia," she said. "They'll let us go."

Luke was busily firing up the grill when I joined everyone outside. Jacob was relaxing in Mom's arms, gently wiggling his fingers in front of his eyes. (He liked to do that. Lorena called it "making pictures in the air.") Michael and Crystal were talking to Mom, and Aaron was watching Megan the nanny give baby Mia a bottle. Apparently the Marquands didn't go anywhere without her.

I said Aaron's name and he looked up and instantly came running toward me. There was no hesitation or awkwardness: he just threw his arms around me and gave me a big hug.

"Can you believe I'm here for the whole year?" he said happily. "How lucky is LA to get me?"

I laughed. "I don't know about LA, but *I* feel lucky. And your father's incredibly excited to have you here—he hasn't stopped talking about it."

"You can't blame me," Michael called from a few feet away. "Here I was, thinking about how my son would be heading off to college soon and probably be too busy to ever visit me again, and suddenly I have him living with me for the next nine months. It's the best gift I've ever gotten."

"He seems to like you," I said to Aaron.

"That's because I haven't been around lately," he said. "I'm most likable when I'm not here."

He was just as good-looking in person as in his Instagram selfies. Better, because his smile was warm and directed right at me. He was wearing blue board shorts (basically the adult version of what Jacob had on) and a dark gray tee with an unbuttoned oxford shirt over it and flip-flops. Simple black Ray-Ban sunglasses blocked what rays were left from the almost-setting sun. Most guys my age didn't know how to dress—they tried too hard or not hard enough. Aaron seemed to have effortlessly found the simple but classy sweet spot.

I wanted to talk to him more—preferably alone—but that wasn't going to happen. Jacob had left Mom's lap and made his way over and now he was reaching his hands up for me to take him. I held him while Michael interrogated me about what kind of cars my friends were driving; he said he needed to buy Aaron one. Then Mom said she thought we should go swimming before we ate because it wasn't a good idea to go swimming after.

I wasn't too concerned about that from a safety standpoint, but it did occur to me that a big salty hot dog would probably make my stomach puff out, and I wanted to look good in my bikini, so I seconded the "let's swim now" idea.

Crystal turned down the invitation to join us, which didn't surprise me, since she was wearing a ton of makeup and her long, thick hair had been blown silky smooth. Mom also passed: she would have killed for a pool to paddle around in during the hot Philadelphia summers, but now that she actually had one in her own backyard, she'd taught herself to loathe it by doing too many laps for exercise.

Megan was taking care of the baby, and Luke was busy grilling, so that left me, Michael, and Aaron up for a swim.

The pool and hot tub were on the other side of the backyard, on a lower level overlooking the canyon and separated from the rest of the house by a rose garden and an iron fence. We walked back there together, then separated at the pool house, which was divided into four small chambers: three changing rooms, each lined with a mirror and a chest of drawers, and a bathroom with a shower. The changing rooms were stocked with towels, sunscreen, pool toys . . . even swimsuits, in case a guest had forgotten to bring one. Lorena checked once in a while to see if anything needed to be replaced.

It took me about three seconds to pull off my cover-up, toss it on top of the chest of drawers, put my hair in a bun, and grab a towel. Back outside, I dropped my towel onto a chaise longue and then sat down at the edge of the pool and waited for Michael and Aaron to emerge.

We kept the pool at eighty-five degrees, which today felt almost too warm. I dangled my feet in it and leaned back on the palms of my hands, keeping an arch in my back and neck—it was the most flattering way to sit wearing a bikini, and I wanted to look good when Aaron appeared. Which he soon did, since all he had to do was take off his shirt and flip-flops.

He dropped down into a sitting position next to me. "How's the water?"

"Nice."

He put his feet in. "Ahh. It's been way too long."

"When was the last time you swam in a pool?"

"About an hour ago. Right before we left to come here."

His father emerged, looking lean and toned in his bathing suit, and dove right in the deep end, then emerged in a crawl, which he continued down the length of the pool.

Aaron stood up. "Are you a jump-right-in kind of person or a slowly-get-acclimated kind of person?"

I clambered up. "Slowly get acclimated. Or not get acclimated at all and stay dry in the sun."

"In that case, let me help you." He caught me around my waist and spun me out toward the pool. "Ready?"

I nodded, so he gave me a gentle shove and I let myself tumble in. He jumped in right after and I scolded him for splashing me inadvertently, and then when he apologized, I splashed him right in the face.

He mock snarled and whipped his head back to get the wet hair out of his eyes and dove under the water. I turned, trying to see where he was going, and felt him touch the back of my leg. I turned again, in that direction, just as he surfaced on the other side and flicked a palmful of water right at me.

We fooled around like that for a while, splashing and laughing and sinking down and springing up until we were out of breath. Then we swam over to the edge of the pool, where we clung on, slowly cycling our legs in the water, while we talked about stuff like movies and restaurants, and Michael steadily did laps behind us—another adult who saw the pool as exercise, not fun.

After about ten more minutes, he swam to the steps, got out, shook himself off, and said, "That's it for me." He disappeared into the changing room and came back out a few minutes later, dressed and dry, and headed back to the group.

The gates clanged again, interrupting my list of the best coffee shops on the west side of LA. I looked over and was surprised to see George Nussbaum walking in, awkwardly carrying Jacob low in his arms. As soon as he saw me, Jacob struggled to get down. George set him squarely on his feet and Jacob ran over to the edge of the pool and held his arms out to me.

"You want to swim?" I said, and he took a step toward the pool like he was going to walk right into it. "Whoa! Stop!" I reached up to hold on to his leg so he couldn't jump in. "Not yet. You need a swim diaper." I looked up at George, who had come closer. "Can you go get him one? They're in the top drawer in the middle changing room."

"Yeah, okay." He was wearing jeans and his usual long-sleeved oxford—although today the sleeves were rolled to just below his elbow. "Hi," he said, his eyes settling on Aaron. "I'm George."

"Aaron."

"What are you doing here?" I asked.

"Tutoring. I thought."

"Tutoring?" Aaron repeated. "School hasn't even started yet."

"SATs," I explained. "Mom found out that George went to Harvard and practically wet herself. She thinks the Ivy League is contagious, so he comes over once in a while and says stuff like, 'What does *epitome* mean?'"

"And do you know?" Aaron asked.

"Of course I do."

"Brilliant *and* modest," he said admiringly. "The perfect woman."

I fluttered my eyelashes at him before looking back up at George. "I thought I told you last week that I had plans today."

"You always say you have plans. And your mom confirmed the appointment when I texted her a couple of days ago."

Jacob knelt down next to the pool and dipped his fingers in the water, then raised his hand so he could watch the drips fall.

"She invited me to join you for dinner," George said as we all watched Jacob watching the drips. "I feel funny about it, but she knows I'm free for the next two hours, so I don't have much of an excuse to leave."

"You should stay." I decided to be generous and forgive him for being mean about Heather. "There's a ton of food. If you want to come swim with us, there are men's suits in the same changing room that has Jacob's swim diapers. Speaking of which—"

"Oh, right. I'll get that now. Want me to put it on him?"

"He won't let you," I said. "Just bring it here."

He nodded and made his way into the changing room.

"How is he your tutor?" Aaron asked, lowering his voice. "He looks like he's our age."

"He's not that much older—just precocious. He went to college when he was like sixteen. According to his brother, he got a perfect score on the SATs."

"The SATs are overrated. Everyone knows the real test of brilliance is being able to balance a Styrofoam noodle on the palm of your hand." He proceeded to demonstrate with admirable dexterity.

I tried to get Jacob to look at Aaron's trick, but he was too fascinated by the water running off his fingers to glance over.

"Here you go." George had returned and was studying the swim diaper in his hand. "How is it different from a regular one?"

"It holds the poop in but lets the pee out."

"'Out' as in . . . into the pool?"

I nodded.

"I really would have preferred not to know that." Aaron eyed the water with sudden suspicion.

"Oh, relax," I said. "The chlorine kills everything. George, you should go swimming before it's completely dark out."

He hesitated, then said, "Yeah." He started to walk toward the changing room, halted, looked like he was going to say something, then just shook his head and disappeared inside.

"So that's the sort of genius that gets into Harvard, huh?" Aaron said.

"Him's got book larning." I got out of the pool and changed Jacob into the swim diaper. "What do you say, baby dude? Ready to take the plunge?" I picked him up and he wrapped his legs around my waist and his arms around my neck. I walked over to the steps and waded back into the pool. I could feel his body tighten as we entered the water. He dug his fingers into me and frowned with concentration—and maybe concern—but he didn't scream or fight me.

Aaron joined us by the steps and watched as I gently dunked Jacob up to his waist. He shivered and then gave a shuddery laugh.

"I wish Mia were older," Aaron said. "She's still too little to be much fun."

"What's it like living with the three of them?"

"It's fine. No one much cares when I come and go, which is a nice change. My mom can be a little smothering. She means well, but . . ." He shrugged. "She hates that I'm here."

"How'd you get her to agree to let you come?"

"Dad and I were both kind of relentless about it. And I think her husband was all in favor of the idea. But she's worried I'll be corrupted here in Hollywood, with no one to keep an eye on me. Plus she's not a fan of Crystal's—thinks she's a total gold digger."

"How about you? Do you think Crystal's a gold digger?" I wondered myself. Michael was rich and famous and middle-aged; Crystal was young and beautiful and had been a struggling, unsuccessful actress when they met. And Michael's track record with women wasn't too impressive.

"Not sure yet," Aaron said. "I'd believe it though."

I heard a door open and looked around. George was coming out of the changing room in a pair of short purple bathing trunks.

I gave a long wolf whistle and George shot me an exasperated look from across the pool.

"This is ridiculous," he said, flicking at the suit.

"The important thing is that you wear it so well."

"Shut up."

"Shorter trunks are totally in fashion," Aaron said.

"Not in that color, they're not," I said.

Aaron flicked water at me. "You're mean."

"It's not my fault if the truth hurts."

"I'm not hurt," George said, sitting on the edge of the pool. "I didn't pick these out." He slid carefully into the water.

He took off toward the deep end with long measured strokes.

"Do you think—" I started to say to Aaron, but I

was interrupted by Luke's call of "Kids! Time to eat!" from up above.

"Dinner," I said. "We should get out."

"No," said Jacob, to my surprise.

"Hot dogs," I told him. "We're going to eat hot dogs."

He lunged so suddenly toward the steps that I almost dropped him.

"Whatever you do, don't mention the kale salad," I stage-whispered to Aaron as we climbed out of the pool. "That could turn this right around."

ten

After dumping Jacob into Mom's arms with an uncer-emonious "He's all yours," I ran into the house to change out of my wet bathing suit and into a striped boatneck top and a pair of oversized sweatpants, which I rolled down at the waist. I released my hair from its elastic and just left it wild on my shoulders. It was still slightly damp, so it was only going to get bigger as the night went on, but I was okay with that; I had long ago made my peace with having hair I couldn't control.

I ran downstairs and into the backyard on bare feet.

The others had already gotten their food and were eating it at the table, so I filled my own plate at the counter, and then George came up from the pool area, dressed, with his hair still dripping in his eyes.

"This is incredible," he said, looking at the spread.

"I believe the word you're looking for is *obscene*."

The adults were gathered at one end of the outdoor

dining room table, with Jacob on Mom's lap and Mia on Megan's. I sat at the far end, next to Aaron. There was an empty place on my other side, and once he'd helped himself to the food, George eyed the table and, after a moment of hesitation, sat there.

"You kids ready to go back to school?" Luke called down the table.

"Shhh," I said, stabbing my fork into a piece of fish. "I'm in denial. The summer can't be over—I had such big plans for it."

"Oh, right," Mom said. "Weren't you going to start a running program? Train for a 5K?"

"It's been too hot."

"And yet we had an unusually cool July," she said.

"Do you play any team sports, Ellie?" Michael asked. "I want Aaron to go out for something. It's a great way to meet people and make friends."

"I played lacrosse," I said. "Freshman year. And I did a season of softball. Oh, and I was on the swim team for a while last year but they expected us to get there at six every morning and— What's so funny?" This was to George, who looked way too amused, given the fact I didn't think I'd said anything particularly witty.

"Nothing." He sawed his knife through his steak in a quick, clean motion.

"I like to try different things," I said, annoyed.

Mia suddenly let out a huge wail, making table-long conversation temporarily impossible.

Aaron stood up abruptly. "I'm going to grab a beer. Anyone else want one?" We both declined. I watched as he went into the kitchen area and got a beer from the outdoor refrigerator. As he was walking by the adults, Crystal looked up and said something to him. He shrugged in response and she touched Michael's arm and pointed to the beer. Michael gave an identical shrug, and Aaron shot Crystal a triumphant look.

Megan had walked away from the table so she could shush and bounce the baby, and Aaron dropped into her seat, joining the adult conversation.

"She hasn't gotten a chance to eat," George said in a low voice.

"Who?"

He was getting to his feet. "Excuse me," he said, and walked over to Megan, then held out his arms in an offer to take Mia from her. Megan shook her head at first, but he said, "Just for a few minutes, so you can have some dinner." She still hesitated for another moment or two, but then passed the baby to him. She watched anxiously while he tried to find a comfortable way to hold Mia—he clearly wasn't any more used to holding babies than toddlers—but he said, "It's okay. I've got this," and she suddenly flashed a brilliant smile.

"Five minutes," she said. "That's enough." She ran over to the food and quickly filled a plate.

George moved onto the grass and started walking the baby in slow, careful circles. She wasn't screaming anymore, just mildly fretting, but she still had tears on her cheeks; they glinted in the little white lights Mom had asked the gardeners to string on the trellis for the summer.

I had no one to talk to now, so I got up and went to them. "I can take her," I said, and held my arms out.

"It's okay. You should keep eating."

"I'm done. Come on, give her to me. I'm amazing with babies."

George shifted Mia into my arms. I tried to cuddle her against me but she whined and moved her head restlessly. "She's just tired," I said. "Jacob always used to get cranky right before he went to sleep. Actually, he still does. Actually, so do I." I started to bounce her rhythmically, shifting from foot to foot with a little dip on each side, and she stopped complaining. "Ah, see? I bet she'll be asleep in two minutes."

"You're good with kids."

"That's because I relate to them—I'm selfish and demanding and I cry when I don't get my way."

"I guess it takes a spoiled child to soothe a spoiled child," he said.

"I wouldn't go that far." I cuddled Mia against me. "We're demanding but we're not spoiled."

"Mm-hmm," he said.

Video chatting with Heather later that night, I said, "I'm not spoiled, right?"

"Of course not," she said. "You're the best person in the world."

For some reason, the hyperbole was less reassuring than a simple *no* would have been. "I do a lot for other people," I said, sitting down with a thump on my desk chair and peering at her on the screen. "I'm going to be running the Holiday-Giving Program at school—did I tell you about that?"

"No," she said. "What is it?"

"We give families who live in shelters Thanksgiving turkeys and Christmas presents and stuff like that. I'm president this year. Well, co-president."

"That's really cool. You do a *lot* of nice things for people. Especially me." She smiled. "Why are you even worrying about this?"

"George called me spoiled."

"Really? That's so mean."

"He was mostly joking."

"Then stop worrying about it! You're being ridiculous." She had braided her thick fair hair while we were talking and now she whisked the tip of her braid over her lips like she was dusting them. "When do I get to meet Aaron? I'm dying to."

"I'll text him and make a plan. I want to know what you think."

"I can't wait! If he's half as cute as he looks in his photos—"

"He's cuter," I said. "And funny. And smart. He's nothing like the boys from school. He's a million times cooler—but not in a fake cool way, you know? Like he's just his own person. And you should see him with his shirt off. Everyone should see him with his shirt off. It should be like the universal Christmas present for good girls everywhere."

"Happy sigh," she said with a happy sigh. "So you're totally in love."

I shook my head. "In love, no. But there is potential there."

"That's the most positive thing you've ever said about any guy."

"Well, you know how I feel about dating in high school. It's always a mistake."

"But if you and Aaron fell in love—"

"That's a big *if*." I tried to picture the two of us kissing. The thought wasn't repulsive. I shrugged. "We'll see. Hold on—I want you to help me pick out what I'm going to wear tomorrow." I got up and walked into my closet, which was the kind of closet you can walk into, and pulled out a pair of skinny jeans and a long-sleeved transparent top. I brought them over to the computer so she could see them. "How about this? I'd wear a tank underneath, of course, and boots."

"It's going to be hot tomorrow," she said.

"So? There'll be air-conditioning."

"You're lucky. My stupid school doesn't have air-conditioning. Or a pool. Or a library. Or anything good."

"I wish you could go to Coral Tree with me."

"Yeah." A couple of years ago, I talked Heather into asking her parents if she could transfer there. They couldn't afford the tuition, but I thought maybe she could get financial aid. But the school rejected her application before money even got discussed. Heather said it was because she hadn't gotten very good scores on the private school entrance exams. "But it's probably just as well," she said now. "Everyone's so smart there. I'd be at the bottom of the class."

"You're a lot smarter than you think you are. And definitely a lot smarter than most of the kids I know there." I studied the outfit. "I don't know . . . should I go more summery? I have this new Alice and Olivia dress. . . ."

Heather wanted to see it, so I got it out and showed her. It was a simple yellow shift dress with a seventies kind of vibe.

"Wow," she said. "You'd look amazing in that."

"You don't think it's too dressy?"

"Wear it," she said firmly. "It's the last first day of high school ever. That's huge."

I got a lot of compliments on my dress at school on Tuesday. Also a lot of compliments on my hair. And on my brilliant comments in class. And on my smile and my shoes and my makeup and my car and my bag and, well, you can pretty much name it, and someone was complimenting me on it.

A new school year. The same old pattern.

I realized years earlier that I could be annoyed by the fact that people were so desperate to be my friend that they'd say anything to make me like them, or I could just shrug it off. I chose to shrug it off. It wasn't malicious and might not even have been entirely conscious; they just couldn't separate me from my connection to Luke Weston.

So I accepted the compliments without believing them and tried to use my social power for good. I wouldn't be friends with anyone who was mean or cliquish and I rallied people to join the Gay-Straight Alliance and Diversity Council and things like that. Teachers called me a "natural leader," which only made me realize that the adults were as likely to fawn over me as the kids were. It didn't go to my head: I knew people weren't following me because I was so wildly charismatic; they were following me because I was Luke Weston's step-daughter and they all wanted to meet him.

I was most proud of having increased student partici-pation in the Holiday-Giving Program by like tenfold or something ridiculous like that. My freshman year, I signed up to help out with the annual Christmas party at the shelter our school supported, and my closest friends all signed up too. Then the next year, I volunteered to head the gift drive, and got Riley to do it with me—of all my school friends, she was the most organized and reliable.

Luke and Mom came with me to that year's Christmas party, which totally freaked people out—everyone who went was giddy with delight at being at the same event as Luke Weston, and everyone who didn't go regretted it. Junior year, I ran the Christmas party and everyone assumed Luke would show up, so literally half the school signed up to bring presents and help out with games for the kids. Luke actually didn't come that year—he was in Chicago, shooting a remote segment for the show—but with all the help and donations, we had an incredible party, and I ended up being asked to co-run the entire program with another rising senior named Ben Simmons, who had run that year's gift drive.

Ben and I had texted a little over the summer and agreed we'd get together after the first day of school, along with Riley and Skyler, who I'd coaxed into co-running this year's Christmas party, and a junior named

Arianna Hawley, who Ben had put in charge of the gift drive, since she'd helped him the year before.

Ben took the meeting seriously, which I appreciated. He was there on time, was focused on making a plan, and had some good ideas.

Riley had briefly had a crush on him in eleventh grade—he was darkly good-looking in a sort of Joaquin Phoenix kind of way—but after she had spent some time with him at a party, she lost interest and said he was boring. He definitely didn't have much of a sense of humor, which would have been a deal breaker for me in a romance but was fine in someone I only needed to work with. We were pretty efficient as we put together a calendar of deadlines and events based on the previous year's schedule and this year's available dates supplied by the vice principal.

It all went smoothly except for one awkward moment, when Arianna suddenly said, "Oh, I was thinking we should get a celebrity parent to come to the party—I hear that one year Luke Weston showed up and people went nuts. If we could promise that he or someone like that would be there, everyone would sign up. How'd we get him?"

There was a slight pause and then Riley said, "Um . . . because of Ellie?"

"Do you know him personally?" Arianna asked me eagerly.

"He's her stepfather," Riley said, and Skyler added, "They *live* together."

"Oh, God." Arianna's hand flew to her mouth and she gave a mortified laugh. "I am *so* sorry, Ellie. I didn't know. You have a different last name. No one told me," she added with a glare at Ben.

"No problem," I said.

"Will he come again this year?"

"I don't know. I'll invite him, but his schedule can be kind of crazy."

As we were leaving the student center after the meeting, Arianna pulled me aside. "I just want to apologize again," she said. "I must have sounded like such an idiot."

"It's fine," I said.

"I'm really excited to be working on this. Everyone says you're like the nicest senior girl at the school."

I smiled and thanked her, but I felt a little tired.

She threw her arms around my neck and hugged me good-bye.

eleven

Heather said, "I hate reading comprehension! You never have enough time to read the whole thing, and the questions try to trick you every way they can." It was Sunday and I had invited her to join me for tutoring again. "And I don't see how you're supposed to study for it," she went on. "They're going to give you completely different passages, so it's not like you can actually prepare."

George said, "It's about having some strategies."

"You always say that," I told him.

"Oh, what's the point." Heather slumped down in her chair. She was wearing a short full skirt and a tight knit top with puffy sleeves. She looked like a little schoolgirl, and the braids she was wearing only added to the impression. "I'm useless."

"That's the spirit!" I said. "Give up before you've tried."

"Shut up," she said. "I'm not smart like you and we both know it."

"I've just studied more than you have." That was a total lie. I hadn't studied at all. I was good at reading comprehension because I read so much as a kid—there wasn't much else to do in our apartment when I was little. I didn't have a laptop and we didn't have cable or satellite TV. But Mom took me to the library every week, so I always had books. We'd curl up together and read for hours. Mom once said that even though she hadn't gone to college, she could keep up in a conversation with almost anyone who had, because of all the reading she did. "You can do this," I told Heather. "Just a few more weeks of hard work and we'll be together for the next four years."

"Or you'll go to *different* good schools," George said.

I shook my head. "We're going to Elton together."

"What other schools are you thinking about?" George asked Heather.

"I don't know. . . . My dad went to Steventon College. He wants me to apply there."

"Oh, please," I said. "You can do better than that."

"It's a good school," George said, an edge to his voice.

"Whatever. Heather and I are going to get into Elton early decision. I've already decided that."

"It's not exactly up to you," he said.

I shrugged. The truth was, I had a secret plan: I was going to ask Luke to call the school once we'd submitted our applications. He was *Luke Weston*; the school would be thrilled to get a call from him and they'd instantly push our applications through—especially if he offered to perform there at some point.

I knew this would work. He had gone with me on the tour of Coral Tree Prep when I was applying there for ninth grade, and everyone in the admissions and head offices came out to meet him and shake his hand after the tour had ended—and then, of course, I got in. It would be like that all over again.

But I wanted Heather to believe she could get in all on her own—she needed the self-confidence boost. So I just said, "You can do this. I know you can. But we both need to study hard. Give us another reading passage, George." Heather and I bent our heads together over the laptop. "Done?" I asked her after a few moments.

"Not yet," she said. Then, after a few more minutes: "It just doesn't make *sense*."

I sat back in my seat, avoiding George's eyes.

A while later, Mom and Luke and Jacob came home from a trip to the park. Luke was wearing a baseball cap, dark sunglasses, and nondescript clothing, and it occurred to me that celebrities and thieves dress a lot alike.

Mom put Jacob on a chair and dropped into another one, flinging out her legs and arms. "Thank God we're home. All he wanted to do was swing. We tried to get him to play with the other kids in the sand, but he kept screaming and kicking until we put him back on the swing."

"At least no one recognized us," Luke said.

"You are so oblivious," she said. "There were two women who wouldn't stop staring at you and whispering."

"They weren't taking photos of Jake, were they?"

"Oh, who cares?" she said, and I glanced up at that because I wasn't used to hearing that bitterness in her voice. What made Mom great—what had made our lives okay even when we lived in a crappy apartment and never had enough money and what had probably made Luke fall in love with her—was that she brought the fun. She laughed easily and saw the bright side of most things and didn't fret about the future. For someone who looked small and delicate and refined, she had a raucous laugh and a raunchy sense of humor. But now her face was taut with worry and it occurred to me that lately it was like that more often than not. "Photos aren't the issue here. The issue is that Jacob doesn't act like the other kids at the park."

"He marches to his own beat." Luke squeezed her shoulder. "That's good. Being different is good. I was the weird kid in all my high schools, and I haven't done so badly, have I?"

"It's not that kind of different," she said, shifting away from his touch. "You wore eyeliner and had an earring. He's *not talking*. It's not a fashion choice—he literally can't talk."

"You're making too big a deal out of this," Luke said, letting his hand drop by his side. "He wanted to swing and he got what he wanted. More power to him."

"It's not that simple," she said. "I'm worried." She appealed to me. "Right, Ellie? You see it, too, don't you?"

"I don't know. Jacob's a little weird, but he's just Jacob, you know?" I hated this conversation. I hated that she and Luke weren't agreeing, and I hated the thought that there could be something wrong with my little brother, and I just wanted her to agree with Luke so I didn't have to sit there hating those two things.

Mom's shoulders sagged like I had disappointed her.

I glanced around and realized that Heather and George had both retreated to the other side of the kitchen and were quietly talking to each other and giving us some space.

"Ellie gets it," Luke said. He moved toward the doorway. "I'm going to go do some work." He had a small recording studio in the back of the house, lined with a bunch of expensive guitars on stands.

"Can you put a video on for Jacob in our room first?" Mom asked. "I'll be right up." He carried Jacob out. Mom turned to me. "You still okay to babysit tonight?" she asked wearily.

"Yeah, no problem." There was a babysitting agency Mom used when I had plans and Lorena wasn't available, but she preferred one of us to watch him. Jacob didn't always like strangers, and even though everyone at this agency knew CPR and had advanced degrees and had been handpicked from some heavenly sphere, sometimes Mom would come home after hiring a new babysitter to find Jacob curled up in a corner sobbing inconsolably.

For a while she just stopped going out at night— "They only really want Luke anyway," she said—but then Luke's publicist said he was getting calls from bloggers trying to confirm the rumor that the Westons were getting a divorce because no one had seen them out together lately, and she felt bad. Plus Luke said he really didn't like going out without her.

So Mom went back to having a social life, but she begged me and Lorena to babysit as much as possible. I didn't mind. Heather was usually willing to come over to keep me company, and we were both happy just to watch movies in the screening room and eat popcorn.

Mom's phone buzzed and she read the text. "Crap. Roger's car isn't starting. He loves that stupid vintage Ford, but it's always breaking down. He's supposed to come tonight." A couple of years ago, Mom saw some bad photos of herself in a tabloid and decided she needed to take her public appearance more seriously, so she started hiring a hair-and-makeup stylist to get her ready before big events. "Oh, wait! George?" she called across the room.

He came back to the table, trailed by Heather.

"Could you pick Roger up for me?" she asked. "He doesn't live that far away. No rush—you can finish up with the girls before you go. I just need him here before six. I'll pay for your time."

"No problem," George said. "And you don't have to pay me."

"Yes, I do. Don't argue with me."

"Can George pick up some food, too?" I asked. "There's nothing decent to eat in the house."

"Good idea," Mom said. "Is that okay, George?" He nodded and she said, "What do you want him to get, Ellie?"

"Maybe some sushi? Oh, and smoothies from Pressed Juicery. And ice cream from Sweet Rose."

She waved her hand. "Just get whatever Ellie wants. Within reason. I'll text you Roger's address." She got up and left the kitchen.

"Um, Heather?" I cocked my head at her. "What was that my mother just said? Something about how George should get me whatever I want?" I smiled sweetly at him. "I think I may have a hankering for a *lot* of different foods from some very far places."

"She said, *Within reason*," he pointed out. "I'll go to three places, max, and they have to be within a two-mile radius of one another."

I pouted. "You make a really bad errand boy."

"I'm okay with that," he said.

Once we'd made the list, George successfully hunted-and-gathered everything—sushi from Sugarfish, drinks from Pressed Juicery, and ice cream from Sweet Rose Creamery. He also picked up Roger, who tore upstairs clutching his hair and makeup toolkits like he was a fireman entering a blazing house. He was a tall, ridiculously thin guy with bleached-blond hair parted on the side and combed flat against his head. He wore eyeliner and had three piercings in his left eyebrow and dressed in tight pants with loose tank tops, and was—according to Mom—a total "genius" with hair and makeup.

George entered at a more normal pace, carting the take-out bags.

"Food!" I jumped up and helped him get it all on the counter.

The intercom beeped and Mom's disembodied voice said, "Ellie, can you ask George if he can stick around and drive Roger home in an hour or so? We'll pay him for his time, of course."

"Of course," I said to George.

"I can stay," he shouted at the intercom as he dumped the bags on the counter.

"It works better if you push the speak button." I pointed at the monitor.

"Right." He went over and touched the screen and repeated his response.

My phone vibrated on the table. Heather was sitting nearby and glanced down at it. "It's from Aaron. He says he can't come tonight and he's sorry." She looked up. "I thought I was going to help you babysit tonight."

"You are. I invited him over so you guys could finally meet. But I guess it's not going to happen."

George headed toward the hallway. "I'm going to Starbucks," he said.

"Why not just make a cup here?"

"I want to get some work done. Tell Roger to text me when he's ready to go, and I'll come back and grab him. If I don't see you when I get back, don't forget to work through the pages I gave you before Wednesday."

"George, George," I chided him gently. "When have I ever once done the homework you wanted me to?"

"Never."

"Then why do you foolishly persist in thinking that I will?"

"I know there's a responsible person in there somewhere. I'm just waiting to meet her." He slipped out the doorway.

"You wouldn't like her," I called after him. "She's boring."

"I like boring," he called back, and kept going.

"Of course you do," I said, but he was already gone.

twelve

Heather's mother called around seven and said, "Don't you have a Spanish quiz tomorrow?" and Heather said she did, but it wasn't a big deal, and her mother said that she would like Heather to come home and study. So she left, apologizing profusely for abandoning me.

But I was fine. I read a book while Jacob watched TV and then I put him to bed. The thing about Jacob was that so long as you didn't change his routine, he was super easy to babysit. I read the five picture books he loved in the exact same order that Mom always read them in, and he curled up after the last one and let me leave without a single complaint.

I crept out of his room, went to my own, and changed into sweatpants and a soft old Dire Straits T-shirt that had been Luke's when he was a teenager, then got into bed with my laptop; I decided I would do some of the homework that George had assigned me. He expected me *not* to do it, and I liked to be unpredictable.

But first I had to check my email. And then my Tumblr, Instagram, and Twitter feeds.

Riley had posted a link to a music video on her Tumblr page, so I watched that, and that reminded me there was another music video I'd been wanting to see, then I clicked on a link to another video . . . and that led me to some others. . . .

It was past ten when the wall monitor beeped: someone was at the front gate. I touched the screen and said, "Who is it?"

"It's Aaron. I was texting you but you didn't answer—I'm right outside."

"Cool! Come on in." I hit the gate button and ran downstairs. I opened the front door just as a minivan came crunching through the gravel in front of the house. We had a pretty long driveway: Mom and Luke had deliberately chosen a house that was set far back behind high gates to keep paparazzi from getting any shots from the street.

"Hi!" I called out as Aaron swung his car door open. I was happy to see him, even if it was late and I had already gotten ready for bed.

He looked much more elegant than I did. He was wearing slim black pants and a V-neck sweater over a collared shirt. "Hello!" He ran up the steps and kissed me on the cheek. "Look at how adorable you are. I didn't know you were a Dire Straits fan."

"I'm a huge fan—of this very soft T-shirt. You're coming in, right? Luke and Mom are still out, so you're stuck with just me."

"Exactly who I wanted to see. Sorry about ditching you earlier."

"No worries. What happened?"

He followed me into the house and down the hallway into the kitchen. "My father was working late and he gave me this whole guilt trip about keeping Crystal and Mia company. As if either of them cares. So . . . awkward evening trying to make conversation with the ice queen." He sighed. "Family duty. It's a bitch."

"Want a cup of tea? Or something to eat?"

He sat down at the table. "Tea sounds good."

I spun the coffee pod Christmas tree so I could see what kinds we had. "Chamomile okay?"

"Whatever. It's all disgusting as far as I'm concerned."

"Then why do you want some?"

"I just like seeing you bustle around the kitchen. You're so cute when you're domestic."

I smiled at him sweetly as I gave him the finger.

"Ah, a feminist," he said jovially.

"Don't you forget it." I put in a chamomile pod for him. "What did you do for dinner?"

"Crystal's never cooked a meal in her life, so she

dragged me out to some fancy Beverly Hills steakhouse, where she paid seventy-five dollars for a plate of food she only pretended to eat." He glanced around. "So why are you home alone? I'd have thought you'd be out doing something spectacular."

"Nah," I said. "I got invited to a birthday party, but—" I shrugged.

"Not interested?"

"I barely know the kid. He only invited me because I'm Luke Weston's stepdaughter. You know what I mean?"

"Are you kidding?" Aaron said. "People wanting to get close to you because your father's famous? That's like my middle name. Like last summer—this older girl in my film program made this ridiculous pass at me. She showed up in my room wearing a coat with nothing on underneath. I'm sure she'd seen it in a movie."

"Or twenty."

"Exactly. Total cliché. Anyway, somehow I got her to sit down and just talk to me—and of course it turns out that she's a budding songwriter who's wondering if she can make it worth my while to pass her CD on to my father."

"Seriously?" I said. "Were you tempted?"

"Nah," he said. "A naked girl in my room does nothing for me."

"Why not?" I picked up the mug of tea and turned to look at him. "Oh, wait—are you gay?" I hadn't gotten the vibe . . . but he *was* awfully good-looking and he dressed well. It kind of made sense.

"No, just a liar," he said cheerfully. "I like naked girls in my room."

"Oh. So did you really send her away?"

"We talked for a while. . . . She left on her own but it was all friendly. My point is, I know what it's like to have people look at you and only see a stepping-stone to your famous father. The trick is to use that to your advantage." He grinned at me. "There are perks."

"Yeah, I know. No one's going to be playing the tragedy violin for either of us." I brought the tea over to him. "What's it like at your school? Are kids all over you?"

"Here they are. In New York, it was less of an issue. People are cooler in New York. So far, I'm not impressed with the kids at Fenwick anyway. I'm only here for the one year, so I'm not looking to make a ton of friends." He tilted his head at me. "I have you, right?"

"Definitely." We were interrupted by the sound of the garage door, followed by the appearance of Mom and Luke.

There's always something a little less polished and put-together about people coming home from a party than when they leave for one. The twist in Mom's hair was maybe just a little less tight and her dress was the slightest bit crumpled and Luke's sweater had a pull or two in it—maybe that's why it was clear that they were at the end of an evening and not at the beginning of one. Or maybe it was the way Mom's face was tinged pink and she was walking too carefully but not quite straight, despite Luke's guiding arm.

"I was wondering whose car that was," Luke said as he steered Mom into the kitchen. He released her so he could shake hands with Aaron. "This is a nice surprise."

"I just dropped by for a quick visit," Aaron said. "Hope it's okay that it's so late."

"Of course!" Luke nudged Mom with an annoyingly meaningful glance at me and Aaron. "Come on, Cassie. They don't need us here."

"Oh, okay." She took a sudden step back, right onto Luke's foot. He steadied her.

"How much did you drink?" I asked her.

"Not that much," she said. Above her head, Luke mimed tossing drink after drink into his mouth.

"A fine example you set," I said with mock superiority.

"It's not my fault. They kept refilling my glass."

"I can't wait to use that as my excuse when I come back from the next after-party."

"I'm putting her to bed," Luke said, tugging her

toward the doorway. "Good night, Aaron. Really great to see you." He ushered Mom into the hallway and I could hear her giggling a little on the stairs. Well, at least she sounded more cheerful than she had earlier.

"I should probably go," Aaron said, standing up. "I only came by to tell you that I wish I could have spent the whole evening with you, like we'd planned. And also that my new home is one weird place."

"Whose home isn't?"

He shook his head. "You have no idea how good you have it. Your mom and Luke—they actually like each other. My dad's never been married to someone he liked. He clearly can't stand being home with Crystal and he was the same way with my mother."

"If they ever really drive you crazy, feel free to come hang here."

"I wish. The problem is they both want me around as much as possible—I'm like their buffer. Which is about as much fun as you'd guess." He stopped and studied me. "Why is it so easy to talk to you? I don't normally tell people private stuff like this."

"I feel the same way," I said. "Maybe it's just that we have such similar situations. Not many people get it. And if I told anyone else something private about my parents, I'd be terrified of seeing it in the tabloids the next day. Let's make a pact to just unload all this stuff on each other."

"It's a deal." He held out his hand and we shook and then he leaned forward and kissed me gently on the cheek. "I am very glad I came back to LA for this year," he said softly.

thirteen

The school activity fair was that Tuesday. Ben and I manned a booth to get people to sign up for the Holiday-Giving Program. Riley and Skyler circulated around the crowded gym with flyers and pointed people in our direction.

Arianna came over and asked if she could help. Ben suggested she reach out to the juniors she knew and encourage them to come talk to us, and she obediently ran off.

Things were quiet at our post, so I was idly watching the crowd when I spotted Arianna targeting two girls from her class and walking them toward us. They were staring at me, and as they got nearer, I heard one of them say, "Luke Weston? Oh my God!"

They signed up to help at the Christmas party, and after they left, I said to Arianna, "Please don't tell people Luke will come to the party. He might not and

I'd rather people signed up because they actually want to be involved."

"Oh, I'm not!" she said with a wave of her hand. "Don't worry! Everyone's just really excited about helping out." And she went running off to collar some more people . . . who all stared at me as she whispered something to them.

And I was pretty sure I could guess what she was whispering.

Heather couldn't join me for tutoring that Wednesday night. She had a drill team practice. I didn't get drill team—it wasn't cheerleading and it wasn't dance and in all honesty, the videos I'd seen of her doing it were pretty lame—but she loved it and I'm guessing it appeased her mother's thirst for extracurriculars to put on her college app.

Anyway, it was just me and George that night. As soon as we sat down in the kitchen, he asked me why I hadn't emailed him any of the work I'd said I would.

"About that . . ." I said. "The dog ate my homework?"

"No dog," he pointed out. "And it was all on the computer."

"If I *had* a dog, I'm pretty sure it would have eaten my homework. Speaking of which, I'd really like to get a pug. Don't you like pugs? They're so cute with their old faces and sad eyes. What's your favorite breed?"

"Nice try," he said. "But since you didn't do the work this week, you'll do it right now, while I'm here." He brought it up on my computer and then stood behind me.

"You're looming over me," I said, glancing up at him. "That can feel very threatening, you know."

"Really? Good. Consider yourself threatened." He pointed at the screen. "Get it done, Ellie. Oh, and I'm taking your phone." He scooped it up and stuck it in his back pocket. "I can't compete with it."

"Damn right you can't," I said, but I let him keep it.

It took me about ten minutes to answer all the questions he'd assigned and another fifteen to write a five-paragraph essay on the subject "Does social media affect our interpersonal relationships for better or worse?" The writing section of the SATs was theoretically optional now, but the counselor at my school had said anyone who wanted to go to a decent college had to take it.

I looked up from the computer to tell George I'd finished and caught him using his phone. "No fair!" I said.

"Why not? You text all the time."

"Yeah, but I'm not getting paid to be here."

"I'm not getting paid *enough*."

"Really? How much are you getting?"

"That's between your mother and me."

"She paid my driving instructor a hundred and fifty dollars an hour."

"Let's look at your work," he said, sitting and pulling the laptop toward him.

"You're not getting anywhere near that much, are you?"

"I'm not letting you drag me into a conversation about this."

"Anything less than a hundred and you're being robbed."

"Just shut up, will you, and let me read?"

"On the other hand, that driving instructor never once told me to shut up."

"He or she must have been a saint. Or deaf."

I watched him reading through my answers, his grayish-greenish eyes darting swiftly across each line. Something buzzed. "You got another text."

He didn't respond.

"It might be important." I peeked at his phone. "Is Carson a girl or a boy?"

"I'm trying to think of how that might be your business and I just can't."

"You kept asking me about Skyler! Exact same thing."

He shrugged and looked up. "You got all of the questions right."

"Of course I did. And I already know that Carson's a girl. First of all, most Carsons are girls, and second of all, she wrote 'Can't wait,' and no boy would ever write that to another boy, even if they were both gay and in love."

"Do you ever stop talking?"

"You took my phone away," I said. "What am I supposed to do? Just sit here and watch you read? As riveting as that might be—"

"Reflect on your flaws," he said. "Resolve to be a better person."

"It's not possible. I'm already perfect."

"Are you though?"

"How about Carson?" I said. "Is *she* a good person? Or a flawed one?" I was only teasing, but my curiosity was genuine. If George was in love, I wanted to know about it. I felt a little proprietary after all the time we'd spent together this summer, like I should get a chance to review and approve anyone he dated. Besides, talking about his personal life was a lot more interesting than studying for the SATs. "Do we like her?"

"She's a goddess among women," he said. "If I give you back your phone, will you stop talking long enough for me to actually read your essay?"

"If you give me back my phone, I'll leave you alone for the rest of the afternoon," I said. "Maybe even the rest of the decade."

"You get ten minutes with it." He pulled it out of his back pocket and handed it to me, then bent over the screen again.

I sent a couple of texts and checked my Instagram feed. Aaron had posted a selfie with Mia. She was tiny and adorable in his well-muscled arms.

"Okay, done," George said, looking up. "Why are you smiling?"

I showed him the photo.

"Right," he said. "Let's talk about your essay." He swung the laptop around and hitched his chair closer to mine so we could both see the screen. "So you got the format right—everything's there, from the introduction to the conclusion. And it's a good length—you got a lot of words down on the page. You even made some decent points. It's just the way you supported them that I'm not sure about. You're a little glib."

"Glib?" I repeated.

"Slick. Easy."

"I know what *glib* means. I'm just hurt you think of me that way."

"Look at this." He pointed to a sentence. "You're essentially making fun of the topic."

"Just trying to keep it entertaining for my reader. I wouldn't want to bore him."

"I want you to take this seriously."

"I did! I mean, for the most part. Come on! It's a perfectly fine essay and you know it."

"It's not bad," he said begrudgingly. "What's this

book you reference here? *The Smith Saga*? I've never heard of it."

"That's because I made it up." I grinned. "Smith is Heather's last name. A little homage to my best friend."

He groaned. "I should have guessed. That quotation is too perfect. You can't do that on the actual test. It's dishonest."

"The teacher who ran the SAT workshop at school said we could. She said that the readers don't have time to check all the references so we should just make some up if we can't think of anything."

"That's a really bad idea," he said. "If she's wrong and someone *does* look it up, you're going to be docked a ton."

"Says you."

He shoved the laptop away. "If you're not even going to listen to anything I say—"

"Relax." I touched his arm. "I'm sorry. You're right. I promise I won't do that on the real test."

"Good." He moved his arm away. "I want to help you do well on this. But you have to actually work with me a little bit."

"I will. I'm going to be a good student for the rest of the evening, okay? We can even do the most miserable math problems and I won't complain."

"Thank you." He held his hand out, palm up. "May

I put your cell phone away again?"

"Only if you'll put yours away, too. I want your undivided attention."

"Deal." He took the two phones and left them on the counter side by side.

It was easier to dodge work and get us off track when Heather was around, which she was for our Sunday session. Heather was always willing to talk about something—anything—other than what we were supposed to be doing, and while George had no problem telling *me* to shut up and get back to work, he wasn't so blunt with her. In fact, he was nicer to her than he was to me in general—gentle when she got frustrated, patient when she was slow, quick to reassure her and build up her confidence. When she got an answer wrong, he always found something encouraging to say about it— like that she was on the right path or had "some good ideas." When *I* got something wrong, he just told me to be more careful and to try harder.

After he snapped at me for not paying attention, I called him on it. "Why are you so much nicer to her than to me?"

"I'm not."

I appealed to Heather. "Isn't he?"

"He's nice to both of us," she said. "Just in different

ways. He knows you're smarter than me so he expects more from you."

"Ellie's not smarter than you," George said. "She's just more confident than you. We need to build up your confidence."

"And tear mine down?" I asked.

"Someone's got to."

"See?" I said. "That was mean."

He ignored that and pointed to the multiple-choice answers on the screen in front of us. "A, B, C, or D, Ellie? And tell me why."

"B."

"Yes, but why?"

"Because it's *right*."

He let out an aggrieved sigh. "Fine. How about the next one? Try to be systematic: eliminate the obviously wrong ones and narrow your choices down before jumping to a—"

"It's C."

"You need to slow down or you're going to get tricked into picking the wrong answer."

"But it *is* C," I said.

"Yeah," he said wearily. "It's C."

"Wait, why isn't it B?" asked Heather.

Fourteen

The Friday before the SATs, Mom ordered me to stay home to study and get a good night's sleep.

I said sweetly, "Exactly how much studying did *you* do for the SATs?"

"I *wish* I'd had your opportunities! It's a luxury to get tutoring for the SATs. It's a luxury to go to college. It's a luxury—"

"To have someone else do your hair and makeup?" I suggested, because she was waiting for Roger to come.

She shrugged. "So we're both a little spoiled these days."

"Where are you guys going tonight anyway?"

"It's an autism fund-raiser."

I had been idly clicking through some Facebook photos of a friend, but now I glanced up at her. "Really? How'd Luke get involved with that?"

"He didn't. I was looking at their website and read

that this thing was coming up and I offered to come with Luke. They were thrilled. As you can imagine."

"Why were you on their site?"

She leaned against the counter and threaded her slim fingers together. "I was looking for some information. I've been wondering about Jacob."

"Seriously?" That made me feel a little sick to my stomach. Jacob couldn't have autism, could he? He was just a late talker. With some weird habits.

"Yeah. A lot of it fits: the late talking, the rigidity, the way he stares off into space. . . . I want to take him to someone to get diagnosed, but Luke already thinks I'm being over-the-top with the speech therapy and I can't face plunging into something this big without his support. So I'm still trying to figure it all out."

"You don't really think he's autistic, do you?" I tried to picture what that meant. Someone silent, rocking in the corner, ignoring the world? That wasn't Jacob. He loved being held and listening to music and watching videos.

"I don't know. I don't want him to be. I want someone to tell me I'm wrong. But he's still barely talking, even with the speech therapy."

I stood up and hugged her. "Don't worry," I said. "Jacob's still really little. He just needs time."

"Maybe," she said. "But something doesn't feel right to me."

"He's a late bloomer. Like the lion in that book you used to read to me when I was little."

"You loved that book. You used to ask for it every night—you *could* ask for it. You were talking so much by Jacob's age."

I stepped back with an exaggerated toss of my head. "Well, I'm extraordinary. You can't judge Jacob by *me*. That's not fair." I was hoping to make her laugh, but her smile was sad.

Roger showed up a couple of hours later—I guess his car had been repaired—and made Mom look fancy; then he left, and Mom and Luke got picked up by a limousine.

Mom had asked Lorena to babysit so I'd be free to study. Lorena made chicken and rice for dinner, and the three of us ate together. I taught Jakie to clink his water glass with mine before we drank. He loved that and wanted to do it over and over again.

The speech therapist he was now seeing a couple times a week said we should get him to say words whenever possible, and had suggested a few she knew he could do. So I made him say "more" before each click. It sounded kind of like "mah" when he said it, but it was close enough. The second he'd say, "Mah," I'd click my glass against his and cry out, "Cheers!" or "Skol!" or a couple of times "Cheese—I mean, cheers!" which totally cracked him up. I started laughing because he was laughing—Jacob's laugh was like bubbles and puppies; you couldn't resist it.

Mom couldn't be right: no way was this happy, adorable kid autistic.

Eventually Lorena whisked him away for his bedtime bath and I settled down to work on some practice SAT questions. But I kept checking my phone for texts. I wasn't expecting any—I just didn't feel like studying.

The doorbell rang, which meant it had to be someone who already knew the gate code. I ran into the foyer and opened the front door.

"If you're checking up on whether or not I'm studying, I am," I told George, who was standing on the front step with a bag in his hand.

"Why do you assume I'm some kind of study cop?" he said. "I actually think you should just relax and go to sleep early."

"Oh. Well, Mom wanted me to pound the books. So why are you here?"

"I brought you some stuff." He handed me the bag. "Nothing big. I just wanted to say good luck and let you know I'm rooting for you. Even if you haven't always been the most cooperative student."

"Let's not start with the postmortem. Mom still wants you to help me with my applications, you know."

"Terrific," he said. "Lots more opportunities to get on each other's nerves!"

"And I'll take advantage of every one of them."

"I'm sure you will." He started to turn and stopped. "Oh, can you do me a favor and text me Heather's address? I have a bag for her, too."

"You know she lives in the Valley, right?"

"That's okay. It's a nice night for a drive."

"I'll come with you," I said eagerly. "I'm going crazy stuck at home and it's hard to find her house." The second half was sort of a lie, but the first half couldn't have been truer.

He hesitated. "Your mother—"

I cut him off. "She's going to be out late. She'll never even know I left. She and Luke went out and left me here alone the night before the SATs. How mean is that?"

"I'm calling social services."

"You should." I clasped my hands. "Please, George? I'll bring my notes in the car. I'll read them out loud and we'll discuss anything I don't understand. That will be better than studying by myself—my attention drifts when I'm alone. You'll help me concentrate. Anyway, you just said I shouldn't study anymore and I should relax!"

He laughed. "How can you make arguments that contradict each other in the same breath?"

"It takes skill. Wait here!" Before he could say no, I ran away from the front door and shoved my feet into flip-flops.

"This is such a good idea," I said when I rejoined George at the door. I grabbed his elbow and pulled him down the steps toward his Prius, which was parked in the half circle of gravel in front of our house. "Heather needs me. She was freaking out last time I talked to her. She's probably chewed off all of her fingernails by now. Plus her fingertips."

He held the passenger door open for me. "She'd be less nervous if you stopped talking about how you both have to get into Elton College."

I slid inside and waited until he was settled in the driver's seat to respond. "She's always nervous—she panics when she takes a *Cosmo* quiz. And I have faith that we'll both get in. So don't sound all doubty when you see her, okay? That won't help."

He raised his eyebrows as he backed up. "Just to be clear, if *doubty* shows up as a vocabulary choice tomorrow, don't pick it. And speaking of vocabulary, where are those notes of yours?"

"I forgot them. It's too dark anyway."

"All right then." He drove onto the street. "Define *effervescent*."

"Bubbly and delightful, like me." It was too dark for me actually to see him rolling his eyes, but I knew he was.

He continued to test my vocabulary the entire way. Couldn't stump me though.

I texted Heather when we were close to her house, and she was waiting out front when we pulled up at the curb. "Please come inside," she begged us as soon as we got out. "Just for a few minutes. My mother's been quizzing me, and I keep getting everything wrong, and we're both freaking out."

"You're going to do fine," George said. "You've got this."

I texted the word *hypocrite* to his cell phone. He glanced down when it buzzed, shot me an annoyed look, then stuck it in his pocket. "Here," he said to Heather, handing her the bag he'd taken out of the car with him. "I made you both care packages."

"That's so sweet!" Heather said.

"I forgot to open mine," I said as we walked up the path to her house.

"You can look at it when you get home," George said. "It's not that exciting."

"What's that?" her mother asked as soon as she spotted the bag in Heather's hand. She'd been standing inside the front doorway, watching us walk up, and greeted me now with a quick kiss on the cheek. "Hello, Ellie. Who's your friend?"

I explained who George was.

"And you're here . . . why exactly?" she asked with a smile that showed her teeth and made me feel sorry for George.

"I made the girls care packages," he explained. "For good luck."

"How nice," she said icily. For some reason, she always seemed to think that every man she met was on the prowl for teenage girls. Especially blond, pretty ones like her precious baby daughter. "Heather, say thank you."

If my mother ever tried to prompt me to say *thank you* . . . We were high school seniors, for God's sake.

But Heather obediently repeated, "Thank you," as she unrolled the top of the bag and peeked inside. "Oh, fun!" she exclaimed.

"What's in it?" I asked.

Heather started pulling stuff out of the bag: a couple of brand-new number two pencils—

"With good erasers," George said. "I tested them myself."

"You need to get a life," I said.

—and several different kinds of protein bars—

"For your snack break," he told Heather.

—and a bunch of other snacks (candy and crackers) and a little stuffed rabbit—

"For good luck," he said.

"Isn't that supposed to be a rabbit's *foot*?" Heather asked.

"With a whole rabbit, you get two feet," George said. "That has to be even luckier, right?"

"Especially for the rabbit," I said. "What else do you have in there?"

"An eye mask," she said, pulling out a soft black cloth one.

"Won't that make it hard to read the questions?" I asked George.

Heather giggled, and he said, "Very funny. It's to help her sleep tonight."

Mrs. Smith said, "I keep telling Heather that she absolutely *has* to get a good night's sleep or she'll regret it for the rest of her life. Speaking of which, I'm sure your mother wants you home early, Ellie. She *does* know you're out with this young man, right?"

"He's my tutor," I reminded her. "This is basically an extended study session."

But we took the hint and said our good-byes. A forlorn-looking Heather watched us from the doorway, her mother's bony arm draped protectively across her shoulders.

"Heather's mother is . . . interesting," George said once we were safely back in his car.

"Yeah, you could say that. Here's all you need to know about her: Once Heather and I went for a long bike ride. By the time we got back, Heather's mom had already alerted the neighborhood security. She thought we must have been kidnapped because we were fifteen minutes late and Heather hadn't answered her texts."

"Oof," he said.

"Right?"

"So what one story describes *your* mother?"

I thought for a second, staring out through the windshield at the headlights coming toward us. "From before or after?"

"Before or after what?"

"Marrying Luke." I circled my hands through the air. "Things changed so much for us once she met him. I mean, here's the story I would have told you about my mom back *before*: There was this kid who was being a jerk to me at school. She told the other kids I smelled bad and that I wore the same shirt over and over again without washing it. That kind of thing. Anyway, I told Mom, and she said to me that we should do some role-playing—she'd be me and I'd be the girl—and she'd help me figure out how to respond. So I would say the meanest thing I could think of to her and she would do something every time that would make me crack up—either say something funny, or speak in a crazy accent, or sniff her armpits— something weird and unexpected. Just fooling around like that with her totally changed the situation for me. It made the girl's insults kind of silly and meaningless. When she'd say something mean, I'd think, 'Oh, I'll have to tell Mom this one and see what she says' and somehow it didn't matter anymore."

"That's pretty cool."

"Best part? That same girl tracked me down after Luke got famous and tried to act like we'd always been friends. It was fun setting her straight."

"I bet. So how would you say your mom's changed since then?"

"Well, for one thing, she's busy all the time—we're never alone together. They have so many important events and trips, and then there's Jacob, of course—that's the biggest change of all. And I love Jacob. I love Luke. I love our lives. I love that we don't have to worry about money anymore—worrying about money sucked. But . . ." I stopped.

He waited, not saying anything, just driving. And listening.

I said, "She was really present back then, you know? I mean, she worked long hours, but when we were together, it was the two of us and the world didn't matter."

"Yeah. It feels like whenever you gain something, you lose something at the same time."

"That sounds like one of your SAT essay prompts."

He laughed. "It does! I even have a literary quote for it. One I didn't make up."

"Let's hear it."

He recited it slowly, pausing a few times like he had to work to remember it all. "'Progress has never been a bargain. You have to pay for it. Sometimes I think there's a man behind a counter who says, "All right, you can have a telephone; but you'll have to give up privacy, the charm of distance. Madam, you may vote; but at a price; you lose the right to retreat behind a powder-puff or a petticoat. Mister, you may conquer the air; but the birds will lose their wonder, and the clouds will smell of gasoline!"'"

"Wow," I said. "What's that from? And how do you remember all that?"

"It's from a play," he said. "*Inherit the Wind*. And I had to memorize it for my high school drama class."

"That's cheating."

"No, it isn't. Making up quotes is cheating. Memorizing them for a class isn't."

"'The clouds will smell of gasoline,'" I repeated. "I love that."

He dropped me back home with another reminder that I should go to bed early and a recommendation that I have a small amount of caffeine right before the test. "Studies show it really does improve your acuity."

"Oooh, good SAT word," I said. "Too bad I don't know what it means."

"You don't?"

"Just joking." I opened my door.

"Good luck," he said as I climbed out of the car. "Let me know how it goes."

I promised I would.

I followed his instructions and went to bed early, but my mother woke me up when she got home by coming into my room. "What's going on?" I asked, raising my head from the pillow, groggily alarmed by the intrusion.

"Oops," she said. "Sorry! Just wanted to make sure you were sleeping."

And then of course I couldn't fall back to sleep for an eternity.

Fifteen

I forgot about George's care package until I was desperately searching for a pencil the next morning and remembered that he had packed some for Heather. I poked through the contents, which were identical to Heather's bag, except apparently I didn't rate a cute stuffed rabbit. I felt a little hurt. If anyone should have gotten an extra gift, it should have been *me*: I was his actual tutee. Heather was just my guest.

Once I'd taken the test and come back home, I texted him to complain.

No *bunny in my bag. Why do you hate me?*

Just thought Heather would appreciate the extra luck. How'd it go?

It went.

And that was all I said to anyone who asked me that question. I had gotten through it, it was done, and I didn't want to think about it anymore until I had to.

Heather's texts to me were less Zen.

I failed

You did not

I didn't know what half the words meant and math was brutal

You always think you do badly on tests

Because I always do badly on tests

No you don't

Yes I do

This is a stupid argument

Can I come over? My parents are making me crazy. They keep bugging me to try to remember the questions and what I answered and it's not fun

Sorry Mom and L are taking me out to celebrate being done

OK

I felt a little bad not inviting her to come with us, but it was rare for both Mom and Luke to have a dinner free and I wanted to have them all to myself.

Except, of course, I wasn't going to have them to myself: Mom had forgotten to ask Lorena ahead of time if she could babysit and she couldn't, so we had to take Jacob with us.

"You sure he'll be able to sit nicely through a fancy dinner?" I asked as I buckled him into his car seat.

"I'm bringing the iPad," Mom said.

"He'll be fine," Luke said cheerfully.

Dinner was a disaster. The food took a long time to come, and the iPad had to be taken away from Jacob, because he kept turning the volume up on it. He screamed when Mom put it in her purse. Luke carried him out of the restaurant, but came back pretty quickly.

"Spotted," he said, sitting down with Jacob on his lap. "People were coming at me with cameras."

"At least Jacob's not screaming anymore," I said.

People had gathered on the sidewalk to peer in at Luke through the restaurant window, and the waiters were a little too attentive—every time we took a sip of water our glasses would instantly be refilled, and seven different people stopped by to ask us if we were enjoying our meal, including the chef. Diners at the tables near us kept glancing over, trying to catch Luke's eyes. One guy actually came over to our table and said it was his fiancée's birthday and could Luke just please come to the table to say hi to her, because she adored him and it would mean a lot to her. Luke did, as quickly as he could, and I guess it was kind of sweet to see how excited and flustered the girl got when he shook her hand and wished her a happy birthday, but I just wanted my family to be able to celebrate me in peace.

Luke asked the hostess to give the valets our car ticket and once our car was in front, we darted outside and piled quickly into it while flashes went off all around us and people called out to Luke, who waved and said a good-natured "Hey, guys" before jumping in the driver's seat and pulling away from the curb.

And that's when Mom told me that she had decided to accompany Luke to London, where they were shooting the show for three weeks in November.

I didn't mind that she and Luke were going, and I didn't mind that she planned to take Jacob: I'd miss seeing his little face, but I'd survive. (And given his behavior at dinner, I was in a particularly good place to accept the thought of his future absence calmly.)

No, the part that made me groan out loud was that she had arranged for Grandma to stay with me while they were gone.

"That's crazy," I said. "*She's* crazy."

Mom turned so she could look at me over her shoulder. "Don't talk about your grandmother that way," she said primly.

"You talk about her that way all the time!"

Luke laughed, and Mom turned her glare on him.

"Don't pretend she doesn't drive you nuts just because you want to inflict her on *me*," I added.

"She's a very good grandmother. And a very good mother, in her way—"

"Her crazy way."

"She comes through when we need her, which is the best thing you can say about family."

"Okay, fine, but I *don't* need her this time. I don't

need anyone to stay with me. I'm almost eighteen."

"Bad things happen when teenagers are left alone."

"Not with me!" I said. "When have I ever done anything wrong? I'm the best-behaved teen in the entire world."

"You can be a little mouthy," Mom pointed out.

"Everyone needs a hobby. Seriously. You know I wouldn't do anything dangerous."

"It's not you I'm worried about," Luke said, his eyes briefly meeting mine in the rearview mirror. "It's the crazies who stalk me. It's not that hard to find out where I live and I don't like to think of you all alone at night."

"We have the best security system in the world," I said. "And what could Grandma do if someone attacked us? Lecture them to death about the dangers of gluten?"

"We'll just both feel better knowing she's there with you," he said.

I gave up. If they were in agreement, I wouldn't win this one.

My birthday was a couple of weeks later. I turned down my mother's offer to throw me a party in favor of a visit to a day spa in Malibu with Heather. We asked for a "couples massage" so we could be in the same room, and we giggled a lot whenever we glanced over at each other.

On our drive home, we stopped to get coffee at a

Starbucks right off the Pacific Coast Highway. I glanced around the room as we got in line. "Oh my God! There's Aaron!"

"I want to meet him!" Heather said, squinting in the direction I was pointing. "Is that him in the red shirt? Who's he with?"

"His stepmother. Hold on—don't lose our place in line. I'll bring him over."

Aaron and Crystal were sitting at a small table near a window. I called out to them and Aaron jumped to his feet and came running to meet me. He threw his arms around me.

"What are you doing here?" he asked. "Are you following me?"

"Of course I am."

"Next time, show up sooner." He lowered his voice. "The she-wolf dragged me out on the pretense of needing caffeine. Turned out what she really wanted was to ream me out for being too messy to live with."

"Are you?"

He shrugged. "I'm not *un*messy. But it's not like she cleans—we have people who do that for her. She just likes to yell at me."

I squeezed his arm consolingly. "I want you to meet my friend," I said, but Crystal beckoned to me so I went to greet her first. We exchanged an air kiss and I asked after Mia. She said, "She's fine," then abruptly stood up. "It's getting late, Aaron. I have yoga in an hour. We have to leave *now*." She headed toward the door. Aaron rolled his eyes at me behind her back and followed her to the exit.

I rejoined Heather in the line.

"Why didn't you bring him over?" she asked plaintively.

"I was going to, but his stepmother said they had to leave. I promise you'll meet him soon."

"He looked really cute."

"He's even better up close."

That week, the speech therapist told Mom that Jacob's language delay and some of his behaviors "could potentially be consistent with a diagnosis of an autism spectrum disorder." Mom had taken notes at the appointment, and she carefully read that last bit out loud for me and Luke that night, so she could get the wording right.

Luke said, "'Consistent with'? What does that even mean?"

"It means he's autistic," Mom said.

"She didn't say that!" He sounded annoyed so I quickly jumped in.

"I think it means he *could* be autistic. But not that he definitely is."

"Right," Luke said. "This woman who sees him for

less than two hours a week said there's a *possibility* that he has a disorder that would just happen to significantly increase the number of hours we pay her each week—"

"She's not like that," Mom said. "And she admitted she's not a diagnostician."

"Which means she really doesn't know what she's talking about." Luke shook his head. "All I see is a kid who's just like his dad—I was shy and hated talking to strangers when I was little. That's all that's going on here." He got to his feet. "You take a toddler who marches to his own drummer, and people go and slap a label on him. It's ridiculous."

"We can't just ignore this," Mom said. "A developmental pediatrician could give us a definite diagnosis."

Luke shrugged irritably. "You really want to start hauling a two-year-old around to unnecessary doctor appointments?"

"He's almost three."

"Jacob's *fine*," he said. "Why can't a kid just be a little bit different anymore? Jesus!" He took a deep breath. "I need to get some work done. I'll be in my studio." He left the room.

I stared after him. Luke didn't get mad often. He once told me he'd had a bad temper as a kid, but playing music always calmed him down. The only time I could remember him getting really angry at me was when I was thirteen and called my mother a . . . well, best to forget that one. He told me I had hurt her and disappointed him and even though he never once raised his voice, I burst into tears. He was the guy who always smiled at me, and his frown was like the sun going away.

But he was clearly pissed off right now. I turned to my mother, who was still staring at the doorway, even though Luke was gone. There was a line etched between her eyebrows I'd never noticed before. I put my hand on hers. "Don't worry," I said. "I bet Luke's right and the therapist doesn't know what she's talking about."

She pulled her hand away. "So you don't support me either?"

"Of course I support you. I just agree with Luke that doctors like to scare people. Seriously, Mom, you should see how many kids in my class supposedly have ADHD and get tons of extra time on tests. It's insane. Heather told me her mom was convinced she had dyslexia because it took her like a month longer than the other kids to learn to read back in kindergarten. And at least five kids in my grade claim to have Asperger's but they're totally normal. People are out of control these days."

"I know. But still . . ." She shook her head. "Something feels wrong to me."

"He just needs to start talking more. Then you'll feel better. It's good you're doing the speech therapy. That's enough for now."

She nodded wearily.

I texted Luke on the way to my room.

Please don't be mad at Mom.

He replied quickly. *Don't worry. I'm not. I just needed a little time to myself.*

Write a song for me. I always said that to him when he was in the studio composing.

And he wrote back the same answer he always did: *Every song I write's for you, little girl.*

He was a good stepfather.

A week or so after that, I got my SAT scores and there was general rejoicing throughout the household.

Mom came into my room that night and said, "I really am so proud of you, Ellie." She sat down on the edge of my bed, where I'd been reading, and I drew my knees up to make room for her.

"I'm just relieved I don't have to take them again."

She glanced sideways at me. "I did a little research. With these scores, you'd have a good shot at getting into an Ivy."

"I don't want to go to an Ivy. I want to go to Elton College. Remember when I toured it last year and came back and said it was exactly what I wanted? Remember that?"

"I know, but . . ." She leaned back on her hands. "When I was a kid, I heard about Yale and Princeton and Harvard and thought people who went to those places were like a different species. And now I have this daughter who could probably get in. And we can actually afford it—"

"But it's *your* dream," I said. "Not mine."

"I can't help wanting big things for you. You're so brilliant, Ellie. I don't think I appreciated how easily things came to you until all of this happened with Jacob and I see him struggling just to . . ." Her voice sank to a whisper. "Just to talk."

"Jakie's going to be okay," I said. "Me, I'm not so sure about."

"My kids," she said, like those two words were a sentence all by themselves.

sixteen

I didn't hear from Heather that night, which seemed like a bad sign. Since my scores were good, I couldn't text her to ask how hers were—there are rules about these things. I knew I'd hear from her sooner or later, anyway.

And I did. The next day.

Hi said the first text.

Hi! I texted back.

I'm so depressed

My heart sank.

George came by that evening.

"Wondering about my scores?" I said when I opened the door to him. "You could have just texted me."

"This may come as a shock, but not everything's about you," he said calmly. "I'm here to help your mom organize her office."

"So you're not even curious about what I got?"

"She already told me."

"Damn it!" I said. "She ruins everything. I was going to tell you I did horribly just to make you feel guilty."

"Why would that make me feel guilty?"

"Because you were my tutor. My doing badly totally reflects on *you*."

"You didn't do badly," he pointed out.

"But if I had, it would have been your fault."

"So I get to take credit for your doing well?"

"No. That was because I'm smart."

He rolled his eyes. "This may be the stupidest conversation I've ever had with you, and that's saying a lot. Where's your mother?"

I wasn't sure, so I led him into the kitchen, where I hit the intercom on the wall monitor and blasted a message through the entire house that he had arrived.

"Thanks," he said when I had done that and Mom had called down a "Be right there!" He leaned against the counter. "I'm a little scared even to ask, but how did Heather do? Do you know?"

"Yeah."

He studied my expression. "Uh-oh."

"Not as well as I'd hoped," I admitted.

"So—"

I cut him off. "She'll take it again and do better. And even if she doesn't, I've already looked online and there are plenty of people who got into Elton College with similar scores. Well, not plenty. But *some*."

"A lot of people are extraordinary in ways that have nothing to do with test taking," George said. "But I'm not sure—"

"Don't." I put my hand up to stop him from finishing his sentence. "You don't know Heather the way I do. People love her. She'll probably have the best teacher recommendations in the world. And she's really well-rounded." *And Luke will call and make them take her.* "The scores are only one small part of this whole thing. I promise you, she and I will end up at our first-choice college together."

"Make sure you're not assuming it's her first choice just because it's yours."

"I'm not," I said, and he just shook his head and went back out into the hallway.

I got a text a little while later from Aaron asking if I wanted to run out for boba. I said sure, and he offered to pick me up.

I buzzed him through the gate about twenty minutes later. When I opened the front door, he pulled up in a Porsche convertible, which he parked behind George's Toyota. He got out and bounded up to the front door with his usual show of energy and enthusiasm. "Hello!" he cried out, and hugged me tightly. "It's been way too long. Why have you been denying me the inspirational sight of your beauty?"

"I'm pretty sure you're the one who's been too busy to get together." We'd tried making plans a few times, but they kept falling through.

"I blame you. And those rat bastard SATs."

"At least they're over."

"And at least you did well."

"You too, right?" I didn't know the exact numbers, but he'd said he wouldn't have to retake them.

Mom called down from upstairs, "Who's that, Ellie?"

Aaron and I moved deeper into the foyer and tilted our heads back so we could see her; she was leaning over the banister, George a few feet behind her, in the shadows.

"Aaron's here," I said. "We're going out to grab some boba."

"Boba?" Mom repeated. "Okay." She was wearing yoga pants and a zippered hoodie and had her hair in a ponytail, so either she'd been exercising before George came or was planning to after he left. "You sure you don't want to stay here? We could order something in."

"I want to get out of the house."

"You're not going to be drinking, are you?"

"We just said we're going out for tea," I said. "We either have to drink it or shoot it into our veins."

"You know what I mean."

"Do your parents do this to you when you're leaving?" I asked Aaron.

"Only if I flunk the urine test."

We said good-bye to her and headed out the door and toward his car. "Since when have you had a Porsche?" I asked.

"Three—almost four—hours."

"Seriously?"

"Dad made a deal with me that if I got over a certain number on my SATs, I could get one."

"We only got our scores yesterday. You move fast."

"Yeah, I was desperate—I've been driving their minivan. Do you know how hard it is to look cool behind the wheel of a minivan?"

"If anyone could manage it, it would be you."

"True enough." We got into the car and he said, "So . . . that place on Sawtelle? Whose name I can never remember? Or the one in Westwood?"

We settled on the Sawtelle place, and I sat back in my seat as he peeled out through the gate and onto the street. "You know what's weird?" I said. "I smell new-car smell but I also smell perfume."

He sniffed. "Oh yeah. Eau de Evil Stepmother. Crystal made me drive her to the market before I came over here—she was almost out of the blood of virgins to bathe in. Which reminds me: What are you going to be for Halloween? You're coming to our party, right?"

"Yes! We're all going." Michael threw a big annual Halloween party that my family always went to.

Aaron proposed coordinating our costumes, so we spent the rest of the evening discussing what we'd go as, finally settling on the two kids from *Moonrise Kingdom*.

He dropped me off at home around ten. I gave him a quick peck on the cheek and then jumped out of the car. I didn't want a long good-bye—these things can get weird, and Aaron and I were definitely in uncertain territory. We were old family friends—theoretically, at least, since we'd never spent all that much time together—so it made sense that we'd want to get together to complain about our families and just hang out.

But . . . this evening wasn't exactly *not* a date either. I mean, he texted me, picked me up, and took me out to a quiet place where we sat and talked alone for a couple of hours. He even paid for my tea. (It cost a whopping three bucks—and his father was richer than the entire universe—but still. He paid.)

We got along incredibly well. We were practically the same person: we both had to deal with having ridiculously famous fathers, and we'd also both spent a lot of our lives alone with our unfamous mothers. We both considered ourselves Californians, but had lived in other states. We both had these much-younger half siblings who were equally adorable and annoying.

Our personalities were similar, too. We were both outgoing and quick and impatient and greedy. We got each other.

So in a lot of ways you could say we were soul mates. Which maybe meant we were destined to be a couple.

But I wasn't feeling it. Friends, yes. But nothing more. Yet.

seventeen

flung open the front door. "Heather's coming," I told George, who had appeared, at my mother's request, to help me with my college essay. "Only not for another hour, so you can focus on me first. But then you have to focus on her."

"Okay. Where do you want to work?"

"Where do we always work?" I led him to the kitchen and he sat down and took his laptop out of his bag.

"Your mother said you'd send me your essay ahead of time but I never got it."

"I forgot." Which wasn't entirely true—I had remembered a couple of times (mostly because Mom kept reminding me) but never when I felt like running to the computer and actually doing anything about it. "Hold on." I located the document: a rough draft that I had written during a summer essay workshop at school. It was about a trip I took to Haiti a year or so ago—the show had arranged for Luke and Michael to do a PSA calling attention to the need for adequate housing there and I'd gone with them because Luke and Mom had felt it would be educational for me.

My college counselor had said the essay was "good but needed work." I hadn't looked at it since then.

"It's possible it sucks," I said as I opened the document on my laptop and swiveled it around for George to see.

"I'll leave myself open to the possibility," he said, and then read silently. I watched his face for signs of approval or disapproval, but he kept it studiously blank.

"Well?" I said when he finally looked up.

"It's a little too long. You need to cut it by about thirty percent."

"I know. But is it good?"

He leaned back and regarded me. "Here's the thing. It's fine. It's well-written and takes you on the right sort of journey. There's nothing wrong with it exactly—"

"Wow," I said. "Stop all the gushing. It's going right to my head."

He ignored that. "If you want to use this, you certainly can."

"But—?"

"It's just . . . It feels a little generic. Tons of students write essays about being exposed to poverty and having some kind of an epiphany because of it—as if third world countries only exist to expand our rich American minds."

I flushed, embarrassed because he was right and annoyed at him for the same reason.

"Also," he said, "how much did that experience really change your life?"

"What do you mean?"

"Do you actually volunteer more now? Watch the news and stay on top of global events? Donate to groups like Doctors Without Borders? What did you take home with you other than a, um . . ." He glanced down at the screen and read, "'A sense that we draw boundaries and turn our backs to keep ourselves from feeling the pain of people whose only separation from us is geographic'?"

I squirmed at hearing my own stupid words. "Okay, that may have been over-the-top."

"Maybe," he said. "I would definitely rewrite it. But that's not my point. My point is, how did that trip really affect you?"

"I think about it a lot."

"Uh-huh."

"Shut up."

"I didn't say anything."

I glared at him. "Okay, fine, so what do you want me to do? Add in something about how now I give all my allowance money to good causes or something like that? You don't think that will sound smug?"

"I think it *will* sound smug," he said. "Not to mention that it would be totally dishonest, since I'm guessing you don't actually do that."

"So what then?"

"You have a couple of choices. You can sharpen and edit this, and it will be fine. Totally acceptable. Or you could do something completely different."

"Write a whole new essay, you mean?" I made a face. "Ugh."

"You don't have to. It's your call. But—" He leaned forward. "Ellie, you're one of the funniest, smartest, most interesting people I know. You don't think like everyone else and that's mostly a good thing—"

"Mostly?" I repeated. But I felt a little bit better; George never complimented me if he could help it, and he'd just complimented me a lot.

"*Sometimes* a good thing," he said. "And I'm trying to make a point here, so don't get all full of yourself. This essay could have been written by anyone—well, by anyone rich and privileged enough to travel safely to a third world country with her parents, which is a large percentage of the people applying to liberal arts colleges."

"So what *should* I write about?"

"Something only you could write about."

"Which would be . . . ?"

"I don't know," he said a little impatiently. "If I

154

knew, it wouldn't be something only you could write about, would it? Think for a second: What makes you unusual? What do you think about that most people don't?"

"How annoying George Nussbaum can be. No, wait—I bet a ton of people think about that."

"Funny," he said.

I slumped down in my chair. "I honestly don't know what to write about other than that trip. The college counselor said it should be meaningful and that's the only thing I can think of."

He waited a moment, then said, "So I was reading everything I could find about college essays last night—"

"Of course you were."

"And I came across this one article by someone who consults about college applications for a living—she gets like thirty thousand dollars per client—and she said the best essay she ever read was about *napping*. The kid who wrote it just really liked taking naps and he was able to say why in a funny, charming way."

"I don't like to take naps. I never know what time it is when I wake up and I feel all groggy and stomachachey."

He shot me a look. "You may be missing the point here."

I waved my hand. "I get it. I should come up with something offbeat."

He nodded, watching me expectantly.

We sat there for a minute and then I shook my head. "I can't think of anything interesting. My life is boring. I'm boring."

"That's it?" he said. "You're giving up?"

"What was yours about?" I said, almost accusingly.

"About having a lot of older brothers. And about how no matter what I did, I felt like I could never measure up. And a little bit about how I had crushes on all their girlfriends."

All right, so his *was* cooler than mine. No wonder he got into Harvard. "Can I see it?"

He shook his head. "Nah, too embarrassing for me to look at it now."

"Did you have a crush on Izzy? Do you still?"

"If I did, you'd be the first person I'd tell," he said. "Okay, let's go over this essay."

It was painful to read through it with him. I hated every word now that we'd had that conversation. George was right: it was self-satisfied and dishonest. I was trying to make myself look virtuous and caring, when I wasn't really either.

But the college counselor had approved it and it was safe and I didn't have any other ideas.

"You're unusually quiet," George observed after he'd pointed out some minor edits.

"I'm listening," I said.

"You sure you're not getting sick?"

"I am capable of listening quietly, you know."

He raised his eyebrows but didn't say anything. The doorbell rang, and I jumped to my feet. "Heather's turn. Thank God."

Once she had her own essay displayed on her laptop, I asked if I could read it over George's shoulder, and she said, "If you want to, but I don't know why you would. It's not very good."

"Stop that," I said. "You're always putting yourself down."

"But it's not."

"I bet it's better than mine. George hated mine."

"I didn't say that," George protested.

"You strongly implied it." I stood behind George's chair so we could read Heather's essay at the same time, George glancing up at me to make sure I was ready each time he scrolled down. Fortunately we read at the same pace.

The essay was about how Heather had found a stray dog when she was ten and helped to rescue it, and that got her interested in animal rights, so now she worked at an animal shelter once a week. She said we all had to speak for the animals because they couldn't speak for themselves and too many were euthanized or mistreated. The essay finished with "I hope to do something to change this sad situation someday."

"Well?" she said when we had finished.

"It's good." I circled around the table and sat down. "It could maybe be a little less . . ." I stopped. "I don't know. What do you think, George? You're the expert."

"I'm not really an expert," he said. Then: "You did a good job laying out the issues with stray animals and I can tell you're passionate about the subject. It's just . . ." He halted.

"You guys keep stopping!" she said. "It's okay. I know it's bad. The counselor at my school said it was fine, though. And my dad likes it."

"It's not bad," George said. "It just needs more of you in it. Why did that stray dog speak to you?"

"It just started barking."

"No, I mean, what made you want to take it under your wing?"

She giggled. "It's funny to talk about wings when you're discussing animals. I just loved her at first sight— she had this silly scruffy hair on top of her head that was *so* cute."

"Well, see, that's a nice detail," he said. "Details make an essay come alive. You want this to be less about rescuing the dogs of the world and more about who you are."

"Okay," she said, and proved over the next half hour or so to be a far more obedient and tractable student than I was, eagerly suggesting new ideas and word choices whenever he asked her for them.

I stayed at the table with them, aimlessly surfing the net on my own computer. George had told me to edit my essay while he worked with Heather, but I just couldn't bring myself to look at it again right away.

After they'd been working for about half an hour, the wall monitor beeped that someone was at the front gate and as soon as I hit the intercom, a voice said, "It's Aaron, let me in!"

I had the front door open by the time his Porsche had scrunched to a stop in front of our house. "This is a surprise!" I said as he got out.

He came bounding up the steps. "I know, right? I was in the neighborhood. Well, not really, but I was in the car and bored, so I drove to the neighborhood to see you."

"You are brilliant," I said, and we hugged, and then I pulled him inside. "You have to meet my friend Heather. She's the best."

We entered the kitchen and I introduced him to Heather and reminded him who George was. "Right," Aaron said, nodding at him. "You're the guy who's always here doing something."

"That's pretty much my job description," George said.

Aaron turned to Heather. "Word on the street is that you're the best. Is this true?"

She shook her head, smiling. "No. Not even close."

"Don't listen to her," I said. "She is."

"I believe you." Aaron glanced at the table. "Wow. Three laptops. You guys must be doing something important. Should I leave?"

"God, no," I said. "Those two are working together right now, but I wasn't doing anything other than thinking about how hungry I am. Want to go on a food run with me?"

"Are you kidding? I fantasize about going on food runs with you."

"What does everyone want to eat?" I asked.

"Something sweet," Heather said. "Like cookies."

"I'm good." George checked his watch. "How long will you be gone? Will we have time to work more? Early applications are due in two weeks, Ellie."

"Yeah, I wasn't aware of that," I said. "We'll be back in less than half an hour. Shouldn't affect my application process all that much." I whisked Aaron out of the kitchen.

We picked up cupcakes at my favorite place and brought them back to the house. "You should have seen the cashier's face," I told George and Heather when we walked back in. "I'd forgotten to bring my wallet—"

"Oldest girl trick in the book," Aaron put in. He fluttered his hand to his chest. "*Oh, my goodness gracious me! I seem to have forgotten mah li'l ol' purse! I guess you'll just have to pay, you sweet, gullible young man, you!"*

I rolled my eyes. "Yeah, I sounded just like that. Anyway, Aaron pulled out his credit card and the girl at the counter looks at it and goes, 'Wait, are you related to Michael Marquand?' And he says, 'Yeah, he's my dad and he really loves your cupcakes.' And she gets incredibly excited and says, 'We have some new flavors you have to take for him to try' and starts loading them into the bag. So now we have all of these!" I held up the bag. "There's like twenty cupcakes in here. And she wouldn't let us pay for them."

"In retrospect, I probably should have tipped her," Aaron said.

"Are you kidding?" I said. "You made her day. She'll be talking for years about how Michael Marquand's son bought her cupcakes."

"And flirted with her," Aaron said. "Don't forget that I flirted with her. I'd say at least four of the freebies are flirtation cupcakes. The rest are celebrity perk cupcakes." He pulled some out of the bag and lined them up on the counter.

"That is so cool," Heather said. "Did you get any red velvet?"

"Sorry," Aaron said. "That's not a new flavor. We

have one called a caramel crunch wizard, though."

"Blizzard," I corrected him.

"How does that make sense?"

"It's white on top. How does *wizard* make sense?"

"Wizards usually have white hair," Heather pointed out.

"There you go!" Aaron crowed. "Nice save! You *are* the best."

She curtsied and giggled.

I glanced over at George. "Now you're the one being quiet."

"I'm tired. It's been a long afternoon. But a productive one," he added with a quick smile in Heather's direction.

"Have a cupcake," I said as I tossed one toward him.

He wasn't ready and the cupcake just splooshed frosting against his fingers and landed on the floor. "Jesus, Ellie! Next time, give me a warning."

"Next time, catch it." I went over to the paper towel dispenser on the counter.

"*You* try to catch something covered in frosting."

"Like this?" Aaron said, picking up three cupcakes and neatly juggling them. Somehow he managed to keep grabbing them by the bottoms, not the frosted tops.

"Whoa!" Heather said. "That's so good. I tried to teach myself to juggle but I didn't get very far."

"Your mistake was not ignoring everything else in

your life in order to master the skill," Aaron said, focusing intently on the cupcakes circling in front of his face. "I didn't do anything for three months except this. I failed two courses and got kicked off the swim team. But I could juggle three sharp knives and only get cut a little bit. Look, I can even do this . . ." He took a step forward and then back without missing a beat. "And this . . ." He tossed one behind his back. It sailed over his head, but then he bobbled it on the descent, lost his rhythm, and all three cupcakes came tumbling down at his feet. He gazed forlornly at the mess. "And thus endeth the juggling. I hope no one was interested in the peanut butter one." He poked gently at one of the cupcakes with the tip of his shoe. "Or the coconut one. Or whatever that orangey one is."

I picked up the cupcakes, threw them away, and knelt down to wipe the floor with another paper towel. "You know, you could help," I said, looking up at him.

"Some people make the mess; some clean it. And never the twain shall meet."

"Hey," I said to George as I stood back up. "How's this for a new essay? I could write about how Americans waste too much food and we should all grow consciences about that." I tossed the paper towel in the trash.

"And once again your sincerity would shine through." George closed his laptop. "I've got to go. Tell your mom I'm going to pick up those bins she needs, will you? I'll be back tomorrow to see if they work."

"See?" Aaron said to me in a stage whisper. "He's always here."

George said, "I know. I need a real job. Trust me, I'm trying." Then he said good-bye and headed out.

I felt a little bad, although I wasn't sure exactly why, so I ran after him. "Thanks for the essay help," I said, holding the front door open for him. "Heather and I both needed it."

"You're welcome," he said and left.

eighteen

Riley and I were finishing up lunch at one of the courtyard tables at school the next week, when I felt a tap on my shoulder. I swiveled. Arianna was standing over me, clutching a plastic container and a can of coconut water. She gave a little wave with her free hand. "Hey!" she said. "Mind if I join you?"

"Of course not!" I tried to sound more enthusiastic than I felt. "There's always room at the inn."

She sat next to me on the bench, and took the lid off her container, which turned out to be a salad. She then started to carefully remove bits of onion one by one with a single tine of her fork and deposit them on her napkin. "I was going to sit with my usuals, when I saw you guys and thought it would be a good chance to talk about the gift drive, and also just hang out! People totally get stuck in same-friend ruts, you know? I think we should all reach out more. I talked to Mr. Bergeron about doing a 'new friends' day where everyone would have to sit with someone new—like randomly assigned or something—and he loved the idea and is talking to Dr. Gardiner about it. So anyway, about the gift drive? I've been thinking about the posters. I was just going to do a stencil letter kind of thing—but, like, in bright colors and really artistic—only then I had this brilliant thought. At least, I think it's brilliant. You have to tell me if I'm right."

Riley stood up. "Sorry, guys, but before we get too deep into this, I need to go read over my notes for my AP History test next period. Wish me luck."

We did, and she left.

"Ugh, that's zucchini!" Arianna exclaimed, glaring down at her salad. "I thought it was cucumber. Who puts raw zucchini in a salad?" She got busy picking the zucchini out and piling it on top of the onion.

"So what's your idea?" I asked.

"Okay, you know those Uncle Sam posters? The ones where he points and says, *I want YOU?*" She switched her fork to her left hand so she could demonstrate the pose.

"Yeah."

"We do that. Except we say, *I want YOU . . . to give to the gift drive.*"

"Uh-huh," I said. "It's a little military-ish, though, isn't it? Wasn't that for the draft?"

"No, it's okay because we won't actually use Uncle Sam." She switched her fork back to her right hand. "That's the whole point—we use your stepdad! Can you imagine how cool it would be for kids to walk down the hallway and see Luke Weston pointing at them from a bunch of posters? I bet they'd all notice it."

"Yeah, no," I said. "Let's not do that. The stencils sound fine."

"Oh." She raised her chin a little. "It was just an idea."

"I know."

"I just thought he might want to help. Since it's for a good cause."

"Yeah. It's just that I try not to drag him into school stuff."

"But couldn't you ask him? Maybe he'd *want* to do it."

"I'll think about it."

"Do you want *me* to ask him? Since it makes you uncomfortable to do it? I could come over sometime and just put it out there." Big smile. Lots of teeth. "I'm willing to be pushy for a good cause."

I believed her. "Let me think about it," I said again.

She shook her finger at me playfully. "Don't forget the goal is to get a lot of people involved in this! And there's nothing wrong with using connections—if *I* had a celebrity in my family, I'd make him the mascot of the whole program." She picked up her fork again and stabbed some lettuce, then stopped as she was raising it to her mouth to pluck off another microscopic piece of something before finally eating it. She crunched on the lettuce and said, "I mean, most people *like* to do charitable work."

"Luke does tons for charity," I said, stung by the implication that he didn't. "I just don't want to drag him into a school thing. For both our sakes."

"I bet he'd be happy to do it. I don't see how it would hurt to ask."

"Right," I said, just wanting to end the conversation. I stood up. "I've got to grab some books before my next class. I'll see you later."

"Okay," she said. "You sure you don't want me to come by and ask him myself?"

"I'm sure," I said, and walked away.

Mom asked me what I thought we should all be for the Marquands' Halloween party. She wanted it to be something Jacob would like since he'd be going, too.

I told her I'd already made a costume plan with Aaron, but that I'd double-check. I sent him a text.

Still on for Halloween? Me Suzy, you Shakusky?

Shit—totally forgot. Sorry. Crystal got us all themed costumes, even Mia. Must do what the generalissima says. You shd still be Suzy tho—you'd be so cute.

But I couldn't be Suzy without Shakusky. She was part of a set.

I found Mom and told her I was in on whatever she decided. We talked about it for a while and decided we should do *Peter Pan*, since that was Jacob's current favorite Disney movie.

Halloween was the next Friday night. Riley and Skyler asked me if I wanted to do something with them. "We could hand out candy at your house," Riley suggested hopefully.

"No one comes to our house," I said, which was true, because we had a gate and a long driveway, and all the houses in our neighborhood were too far apart to make trick-or-treating worthwhile. "I'm going to a party, anyway."

"Whose?" Riley asked, with the stricken expression of someone who thinks she's been socially marginalized. I quickly explained that it was a family thing.

We gathered in the kitchen before we left for the party so we could take a few family photos. I felt a little stupid in my green tights and tunic but I really loved the over-the-knee slouchy brown boots Mom had let me buy. I'd been coveting them for months, but she kept saying they were too expensive until the day before, when I'd argued that they'd work for Halloween and she gave in. She was funny about money, spending lavishly one second and suddenly frugal the next—her current lifestyle clashing with old habits.

We'd assumed Jacob would want to be Peter Pan, but when we showed him a picture of the costume and said, "For Jakie," he'd shaken his head and pointed to a picture of Michael, the little boy with the teddy bear, and then pointed to himself and said, "Jake." Which for him was practically a sentence. So I became Peter by default. As Mom put it, "It's either you or Luke, and Luke already said it won't be him. He's very excited about Captain Hook's mustache."

"Why not you?" I asked. "Isn't Peter Pan usually played by a middle-aged woman?"

"That sentence alone is enough to send me into therapy for five years," she said. "Green tights would push me over the edge."

She had been torn for a while between Tinker Bell and Wendy, but decided that since she'd probably be holding Jacob/Michael for most of the party, Wendy made more sense. "Plus I'll be wearing a nightgown, so I can go right to sleep afterward," she said. "It's my ideal party outfit."

Lorena took the photos for us. Mom held Jacob, Jacob held his teddy bear, and I stood next to them with my hands on my hips while Luke glowered appropriately from behind us.

Jacob loved taking photos: the second he spotted a

camera or phone pointed at him, he froze, smiled, and said "Eee!" which was his version of saying cheese. He did that now, and Lorena took a bunch of photos on my phone and then she gave him a big kiss on the cheek and said good-bye.

Normally we wouldn't bring Jacob to a big party, since they overwhelmed him, but Michael always hired a cast of young actors to dress in costumes and man booths in the backyard stocked with candy and toys, so kids could trick-or-treat without leaving the house, and Jacob was old enough this year to join in.

Aaron came over to say hi as soon as we walked into their house.

"Aladdin!" Jacob said, pointing at him with delight.

"Smart kid," he said. "The trick-or-treating has started, if you guys want to bring him out back." Mom and Luke thanked him and carried Jacob toward the yard, but Aaron grabbed my arm and said, "Stay with me. I need to know what you think of my vest." He was wearing a small purple one over his naked chest. His body was as taut and muscled as I'd remembered from when we swam, but either he'd been tanning a lot lately or he'd sprayed some bronzer all over himself before the party, because he was a different shade than I remembered.

I said, "It's in a tie with the fez for my favorite part of your costume." I flicked the tassel on his little cap.

"Ah, we're playing that game, are we?" he said, and flicked the feather on mine.

We walked into the living room. There was soft sitar music playing from hidden speakers, the lights were slightly dimmed, and the walls and ceiling were draped with silk—it all felt very exotic and fantastical.

"The palace at Agrabah?" I asked, gazing around in delight, and he nodded.

"Crystal's Jasmine and Mia's wearing a little tiger costume."

"This totally leaves last year's pirate theme in the dust. Why isn't your dad Aladdin?"

"He said he was too old. He wanted to be Jafar."

"But Jafar's evil."

"He preferred age-appropriate to heroic."

I halted suddenly and glanced back. "Was that Lady Gaga we just passed a man?"

"Yep. He's a studio musician, and he already told me he remembers when I was three and visited the recording studio and ate four cookies and threw up. It's going to be one of those nights—one of those 'Oh, you're Michael Marquand's little boy!' nights. And don't get me started on the yold women here."

"Yold?"

"Young/old. You know. They all have those smooth, unmoving foreheads and long hair and big breasts and tiny waists and dead eyes and bony necks."

"Oh my God," I said. "I know exactly what you mean."

"There are a lot of them here tonight and a couple of them are wearing very low-cut costumes and I can't stop shuddering. And speaking of shuddering . . . look at Crystal." He pulled on my sleeve to turn me in the right direction. "You understand why my father and I— and the house—all had to dress the way we did, right? It was all so she could look like *that*."

She was magnificent. There was no other word for it. Her perfectly chiseled abdomen and narrow waist were shown off by a tight aqua-colored bandeau and matching hip-hugging harem pants. Her shining black hair was pulled into a sleek ponytail that was decorated with aqua ribbons, which matched her aqua headband. Her eyes were outlined in black and her lips were bright red. "She does look pretty amazing," I said, staring in open admiration. "You have to admit."

"Do I?" He considered her for a moment. She looked up while he was studying her and I saw their eyes meet. She pressed her lips together and quickly looked away. "Sorry," he said, turning back to me and shaking his head. "I can't. I just can't. I mean, yes, I'm sure objectively she's attractive. I just can't get past the absolute Crystal-ness of her to appreciate it."

"Well, I think she's beautiful."

"*You* are beautiful. She's scary. Let's see what's on that tray. I'm hungry."

The server holding the hors d'oeuvres was talking to someone in a plaid shirt whose back was to us but seemed weirdly familiar for a back.

We circled around.

"George?" I said, totally surprised. "What are *you* doing here?"

"Pretty much the same as you," he said. "Hey, Aaron."

"Welcome," said Aaron before turning to the caterer. "What've you got there?"

"Stuffed mushrooms." She held out the tray so he could take one. "Finish what you were saying," she said to George as Aaron considered his options.

"Nah, it's okay," George said.

"I wanted to hear the rest."

"The rest of what?" I said. "And who are you supposed to be?"

"I'm staff," she said.

"Not you. Him."

"Me?" George said. "I'm a farmer." He was wearing jeans and that plaid shirt.

"That's the laziest costume—you didn't even get a hat!"

"I'm not into dressing up."

"I didn't know you'd be here," I said. He was so out of context, it was weird. The girl was still gazing at him expectantly like she was waiting to hear what he had been saying when we interrupted.

"Jonathan brought me. He said it would be an amazing party. It *is* an amazing party," he told Aaron, who shrugged.

"I can't take any credit for it." He pointed at the mushrooms. "What are they stuffed with?"

The server said, "Crab."

"Weird," Aaron said.

"They're good. Try one." She offered him the tray again, and Aaron selected a mushroom.

"I'm dubious," he said, eyeing it.

"They're delicious," George said. "I ate like three, and I don't like either mushrooms or crab."

The server beamed at him. She was pretty. If you liked blonds with lots of makeup.

Aaron bit into the mushroom. "Ugh," he said, and she held out the pile of napkins in her hand. He took one, wrapped the uneaten part in it, and carefully put the whole package on a side table. He turned to me. "Where to next, Ellie, my love?"

Before I could answer . . .

"Aaron!"

We all turned toward the new voice. Crystal approached us, her hands on her hips. "I was looking for you both. Ellie, your mother could use some help with Jacob."

"Is something wrong?" I asked.

"No, but don't you think you should give her a break so she can enjoy the party?" She seemed a little disgusted with me for not having thought of that on my own. "I saw them out back."

"Okay."

Both guys started to follow me toward the French doors that led to the yard, but Crystal put her hand out to stop Aaron. "Hold on. I want you to talk to some of our *other* guests."

"There's only one person here I want to spend time with," he said, which made me glance back. He caught my eye and winked at me.

I couldn't hear Crystal's response because she leaned in close to him and lowered her voice, but I could guess the tone of it from the scowl on her face. He dropped his eyes to the floor; it was probably impossible for Aaron to look sincerely contrite, but he did look a little less self-assured.

"Families," I said to George as we walked away from them. "Am I right?"

"Yes," he said. "You're right. I have no idea what your point is, but I know you can't be wrong."

"It's theoretically possible," I said. "It's just never happened."

nineteen

We crept around the crowd, keeping to the edges of the room. I brushed my fingertips against the folds of silk lining the walls. I couldn't even begin to imagine how long it must have taken to remove all of their paintings—they had a ton of art because Michael had once dated a very persuasive art curator—and cover the walls with all of this jewel-toned silk. Not to mention how much it must have cost.

"Oh, wait." I halted. "Hold on a sec." I crouched down and snaked my hand into my right boot.

"What are you doing?"

I stood up, now clutching my phone. "This is why slouchy boots were invented," I said. "To hold cell phones." I sent Mom a text asking if she needed my help with Jakie—and, if so, where I could find them—then glanced back up at George. "So were you enjoying your conversation with the server girl? You both seemed very into it. Sorry if we were interrupting something. Were we? Interrupting something?"

"Just a conversation," he said. "Nothing important."

"She was cute. You should totally get her number. Want me to get it for you? I could be very subtle about it."

"Thank you, but I'm capable of managing my own social life."

"Are you, though?" My phone buzzed and I glanced down at it. *We're fine. Enjoy yourself.* "All's well with Mom," I said. I dropped the phone back into my boot. "Oh, look, there's your brother and Izzy."

"I found where the trays come out," Jonathan crowed as we came up to them. Like George, he and Izzy had pretty minimal costumes. Theirs matched: cowboy hats, leather vests over white shirts, bandannas, jeans, and boots. "This is the best place to stand—the food's hot and we get to try everything."

"This is why I'm going to marry him," Izzy told me. "He always figures this stuff out. I never go hungry at a party. Although I do go *thirsty*, because once he's staked out a spot, he won't let us leave it."

"I'll make a bar run," George said. "What does everyone want?"

I asked for a Diet Coke, Izzy wanted wine, and Jonathan said he'd take a beer. I was happy to hang out with them, but Luke spotted me from across the room and beckoned, so he could introduce me to some guy in thick black glasses and a buzz cut—no costume— whose name I didn't catch, but who asked me so many questions about school and my hopes for college that I felt like I was being given an oral exam.

The worst part was that someone else pulled Luke away, so I was stuck talking to the guy one-on-one, which made it hard to extricate myself. Fortunately Aaron suddenly appeared at my side.

"There you are!" he said. "I've been looking for you." He slid his arm under mine. "You can't monopolize her all night long, Samson," he said, and my examiner held his hands up and said, "Wouldn't dream of it—she's all yours," with an annoyingly insinuating smile.

"Samson?" I hissed as Aaron led me away. "Was that Samson Cardoza?"

"You didn't know that?"

"He's like my favorite movie director ever. Rats." I glanced back regretfully. "I would have enjoyed that conversation so much more if I'd known who I was talking to!"

"You do realize that's a ridiculous thing to say, right? You want to go back?"

"Nah, he was still pretty boring. Where are we going?"

He'd steered me out of the living room and back into the foyer, but now he stopped. "I don't know. I just wanted to make sure I had you all to myself again. Sorry about abandoning you before, by the way."

"It's fine. Was something wrong?"

"Crystal just likes to be pissed off at me. Makes her feel all maternal. Apparently I wasn't being a good host because I was spending so much time with you."

"Well, now I feel guilty."

"You should," he said. "It's all your fault. Fluttering those big brown eyes at me, making me forget that I'm supposed to be talking to old people who can't keep their food in their mouths and spew it all over everyone who stands near them—"

"There's no one like that here!" I said, laughing. "And I know this is a weird segue from that, but I'm hungry."

"The dining room's wall-to-wall food. Come on."

The statement might not have been literally true, but it was pretty close, since their banquet-hall-sized table took up most of the room and was covered with platters of roasted meats, small biscuits, salads, and pasta. There were surprisingly few people in there—I didn't know whether it was because most of the guests hadn't discovered it or because no one in Hollywood eats real food.

Aaron found us a quiet spot in a little area off the dining room that was lined with glass-fronted cabinets filled with china. He dragged two chairs in and we sat together and ate, our plates on our laps, wiping our faces with the backs of our hands because we'd forgotten to get napkins.

We talked about the food for a while, but then Aaron fell silent. I looked up after a moment. He was studying my face seriously.

"What?" I said.

He put his plate on the counter and leaned toward me. "Ellie," he said, and glanced around like he wanted to make sure we were alone. "I've been wanting to talk to you. There's so much that I—" He stopped. Then he said, "I just want to get everything out in the open." He stopped again and rubbed his head, like he was a little unsure of what to say next. Or whether he should talk at all.

Suddenly the last bite I'd taken felt all bunched up in my throat and I had to swallow hard to get it to go down. I already knew what Aaron was going to say. It was obvious. He was going to tell me that he liked me. And not just as a friend.

All of the attention he'd been paying me—even against Crystal's orders—and the way he kept tucking my hand against his side and keeping me near him . . .

Aaron liked me. A lot.

And I liked him a lot.

But did I like him as much as he liked me? Or the *way* that he liked me?

My stomach lurched.

I just wasn't ready for things to change between us. Not yet. I needed more time to figure out my own feelings. I had thought all of our flirting was friendship flirting. Like the jokes I made about our future marriage—I had always assumed he knew I was just being silly when I said stuff like that. But maybe he didn't. Maybe he thought I felt the way he did.

And maybe I *did* but just didn't know it. Could that happen? I didn't feel shaky and excited when he was around, just happy to enjoy his company. Shouldn't I be *less* comfortable with him? More starry-eyed? Or was that just in movies and books? I'd never felt that way about anyone. But maybe I wasn't the kind of person who got that way—I never had crushes and most of my friends had them all the time.

My mind raced, while the smile on my face froze.

I didn't want to be mean, but I desperately didn't want Aaron to say something that would change things between us. Not yet. I needed to hold him off for a while, buy myself some time, and figure out how I felt.

I said, "What's up?" as lightly as I could.

"We've gotten so close," he said. "We basically think the same way about everything—"

"Well, not everything." I cut him off with a forced laugh. "There's that whole putting-fruit-on-frozen-yogurt thing that I still haven't accepted about you."

"Right," he said. "I put fruit on mine and you put gummy worms on yours, and *I'm* the crazy one. Anyway—"

"Gummy worms are so much better. Just ask any eight-year-old you see. Well, any eight-year-old girl. Do little boys like sugar as much as little girls do? This is where not having a brother affects my knowledge. I mean, I *do* have a brother—duh—but he's way too little. He doesn't count. Plus he's really weird about food. And doesn't really talk." I was chattering as fast as I could to keep him from saying more. His face kind of fell while I was talking; it was probably pretty obvious that I was trying to avoid having a serious conversation. "I'm really thirsty," I said abruptly, and rose to my feet. "I told George to get me a Coke and then totally forgot about it. I'd better go back to the living room and make sure he's not looking for me."

"Okay," Aaron said, and got up, too.

We abandoned our plates and moved back through the dining room. I threaded my arm in his, glancing up at him uncertainly. I couldn't really acknowledge what had just happened because I hadn't let him get far enough for us to talk about it openly. But I hoped the pressure of my arm told him that I understood what he had been trying to say, and that I did care about him—I just wasn't ready for that kind of a talk yet.

It was a lot to try to squeeze into, well, a *squeeze*, but

he smiled down at me without any noticeable resentment. Maybe he was relieved, too.

The Nussbaum brothers and Izzy were right where we had left them, but they had been joined by a tall, muscular guy dressed like Khal Drogo from *Game of Thrones*. He had the body for it, I'd give him that. Huge biceps.

"Hey!" I said to George. "You never brought me my drink!"

"I *did* bring you your drink," he said irritably. "But you disappeared."

"I'm still thirsty. Hint, hint."

"Yeah, no," he said.

"I'll get it." Aaron disentangled our arms and gave my hand a good-bye squeeze. I saw Jonathan and Izzy exchange a look and knew they were misreading the situation. "Diet Coke, right?"

"You might want to tie her down first," George said. "She disappears."

"I always want to tie her down," Aaron said with a gallant leer, and left.

"That wasn't what I meant," George said to no one in particular.

"I'm Ricky," said the artist formerly known as Khal Drogo, holding his hand out to me.

"Ellie." I shook it.

"How do you know the Marquands?"

"My stepfather's friends with them."

"And who is your stepfather?"

It was a perfectly reasonable question; he had no way of knowing that it made my whole body tighten. "Luke Weston," I said, and his eyes got suddenly wide, so I quickly said, "How do *you* know the Marquands?"

"I'm Crystal's trainer."

"You must be good. Her abs are incredible."

"I *am* good. So . . ." Ultra-casual tone. "Any chance you could introduce me to your stepdad? I have an idea for a show that would combine getting in shape with a singing contest. I wouldn't bother him—just two minutes is all I need, and I know he'd love it."

"Actually," Jonathan intervened smoothly, "I'm the president of Luke's production company. Why don't you talk to *me* about it?" He glanced at George with a little head jerk that seemed to send a message, because George instantly said, "Come on, Ellie. We can't be here when Aaron comes back with your drink, or you'll make it too easy for him."

I was happy to say good-bye and slip away with him.

"That was annoying," George said as we found an empty spot across the room from them.

"Yeah. I hate stuff like that."

"You deal with it well."

"Jonathan dealt with it, not me."

"I mean in general. The whole fame and Luke thing.

It doesn't seem to affect you too much one way or another."

"Thanks." I leaned against the wall, and felt the hanging silk fabric bunch up behind my back. "But it does, in a way. Like . . . I'm tired of people at school trying to be friends with me just so they can meet Luke."

"Does that happen a lot?"

"All the time. There's this one girl right now who— Oh, there's my drink!" Aaron had spotted us and was coming over with a cup in his hand. "You see?" I said to George. "*He* had no problem finding me."

"Clearly I lack his skill and perseverance," George said. "Excuse me." He walked away as Aaron approached.

"Was it something I said?" Aaron asked, nodding in his direction.

"I made him feel bad that you brought me my drink and he didn't."

"You're a harsh mistress." He handed me my soda. "And speaking of harsh mistresses, my soulless, bloodsucking stepmother just said I have to keep mingling. You know I wouldn't leave your side if I didn't have to, right?"

"Fly," I said. "Be free."

"I will come back to you," he said, clutching his heart. "I will find you and come back to you." He held out his hand and I held out mine and we did a whole melodramatic thing where we pretended to be reaching for each other as he backed away, then he suddenly rushed back. "It hurts to say good-bye," he said, and grabbed me around the waist, bent me backward, and planted a pseudo-passionate kiss right on my startled lips. "I couldn't just leave," he said as he released me.

I tottered for a moment, regaining my balance. A quick, embarrassed glance around the room confirmed that Crystal was watching with her hands on her hips; Jonathan, George, and Izzy were all staring; and Mom and Luke were gaping from just a few feet away. Only Jakie, curled against Luke's chest, seemed unaware of what had just taken place, his eyes gazing blankly in a completely different direction.

"My goodness," Mom said as the three of them came close. "That was quite a kiss."

"It was ironic," I said quickly.

"Of course it was," Mom said with a little smile.

I felt my face get hot, mostly because I wasn't a hundred percent sure it *was* ironic. I mean, the whole back-bending part was clearly over-the-top and ridiculous. But was the kiss itself? I hadn't really ever been kissed before—I wasn't convinced I could distinguish a sort-of-real kiss from a totally mock one.

Fortunately Mom was changing the subject. "We've trick-or-treated," she said, holding up a very full plastic pumpkin. "Jacob wasn't crazy about the part where you were supposed to go up to people but he liked the part where you get candy. And he *really* liked the part where you eat candy."

"He's wiped out now," Luke said, and Jacob's smushed face against his shoulder seemed to confirm that. "You ready to go, Ellie? Or do you want to stay and I'll come back to get you later?"

"I am very good to go," I said. I had a lot to think about.

At home, I considered FaceTiming with Heather and telling her about the whole Aaron thing, but decided instead to take a long bath. Heather would probably ask me stuff like "Do you like him? What are you worried about?" and I didn't want to start answering someone else's questions until I could get my own thoughts straight.

So I tried to get my own thoughts straight as I lay in a bath that was more bubbles than water.

Aaron likes me. And he's handsome and funny and charming and I like him.

So . . . why didn't I let him take things to the next level?

Because I'm not ready for that yet. Because I don't want to risk losing him as a friend. Because I don't want to date anyone now. Because . . . I don't know and it's weird because he's very good-looking and I like him so much and it would make our parents so happy.

Because *it would make our parents happy?*

Because *it's too easy, too comfortable, too right, and I'm contrary?*

Because . . . *because . . .*

I got nowhere in the bath. Other than wet and wrinkly.

twenty

On Sunday, Mom, Jacob, and Luke left for London. They'd be staying in some super-grand hotel—VIP treatment all the way—but Luke would either be shooting segments or doing publicity most of the time, so Mom wasn't all that pumped about it.

"I'll miss you lots," she said as we hugged good-bye. "Please be nice to your grandmother." Grandma was coming that afternoon; Mom had arranged for a car to pick her up at the airport.

"I'll be as nice to her as she is sane to me."

"Be nicer," she said. "And get your college application in on time." She turned to George, who had arrived a few minutes earlier to help me work on my essay. "I'm relying on you to make it happen, since I won't be here."

"We'll be talking every day," I said. "You can remind me yourself."

"I don't trust you when I can't see you," she said.

"You'll probably ignore everything I'm saying and text your friends while I'm talking."

I put my hand to my chest. "I would *never.*"

"She would," Mom told George, who nodded in agreement. "Oh, and don't you think Ellie should consider applying early to an Ivy League instead of Elton? I feel like her scores are good enough for her to aim a little higher. I'd hate for her to sell herself short."

George opened and closed his mouth, looking a little panicked. "I'm not sure I'm the right person to—"

He was both interrupted and rescued by Luke, who appeared in the doorway.

"Car's loaded," he said. "And Jacob's in his car seat. He knows something's up—that kid's no dummy. You'd better get out there."

Mom's mouth turned down. "I hope he likes the hotel babysitters, or it's going to be a very long couple of weeks." That little line appeared in her forehead. "I'm worried this is a mistake—taking him out of therapy, uprooting him . . ."

"A few weeks without speech therapy isn't going to change his life, and I want you both with me." Luke put his hands on her shoulders and steered her toward the hallway. "You worry too much. Come on." He shoved her gently in the right direction, then came back to me for a quick hug. "Take care of yourself, Ellie. Sorry we're abandoning you, but we'll be back before you know it."

"Right," I said. "Have fun."

"Fun? I'll be working eighteen-hour days. Fun isn't on the agenda."

"No one feels sorry for you, you know."

He flashed the gently roguish grin that made hearts beat faster all over America, told me he'd miss me lots, and left.

I went back to the kitchen, where George was typing on his laptop. He looked up when I entered. "They gone?"

"Yeah." I threw myself into the chair across from him. "So . . . kegger tonight? You bring the coke."

"As in cocaine?"

I rolled my eyes. "A-doy."

"Just checking. Last time you asked me for Coke, it was a whole different thing."

"Yeah. And you never gave it to me."

"Are we really going to rehash this? Or are we going to work on your essay?"

"My essay sucks. It's boring. And clichéd. I don't like it."

"So what are you going to do about it?"

"Complain a lot and whine."

"You're doing great!"

My phone dinged with a text. I glanced at it.

"Aaron?" he asked.

"Heather. She wants to know if you're here and if she should come over to work."

"Fine with me."

I texted Heather to come and then looked up again. "Did you go back and get that cute catering girl's phone number?"

"Did I? I can't remember."

"Don't be a jerk. What's her name?"

"Ethel? Maybe Gertrude. No—Brunhilde."

"You're no fun." My phone dinged again. "Aaron?" he asked.

"Riley."

"Don't you have any friends with gender-normative names?"

I texted her back that I was busy and couldn't hang out, then looked up. George was watching me. "You want to work?" I asked.

"Only if you're not too busy," he said with exaggerated politeness.

"Never too busy for you," I said genially. My phone dinged again.

"Aaron?" he said.

"Yep."

"Ha! Guessed right."

"It's not a good guess if you've made it three times and were wrong the first two." I read the text then said,

"Hey, what time do you think we'll be done?"

"The usual. Two hours from when we start. Assuming we ever actually start."

"Hold on." I sent a text to Aaron, who had asked if I wanted to go see a movie later: *Yah. You okay if Heather comes?*

The cute blonde? Why wouldn't I be?

I smiled at my phone, relieved. I had been wondering whether we'd be able to go back to normal after the other night's weirdness, but he sounded like himself. And also like he didn't care whether or not we were alone together, which meant he was in no rush to start pushing things forward again.

"I really hate to interrupt the love affair you're having with your phone," George said. "Any chance I can get you to put it aside for . . . I don't know, ten seconds? To start?"

I tossed the phone onto the counter. "Look how I obey you," I said. "Use your power over me wisely."

"I'll try to," he said, with a sort of odd seriousness that made me feel anxious—was I about to get in trouble? And why did George always make me feel like I was about to get in trouble? But all he said was, "Let's read through the essay again. Did you make those changes we talked about last time?"

"Um . . . about that . . ."

He sighed and we bent over my laptop together. We

went back through all his notes and I made the changes right there and then, with him at my elbow, pointing at the screen. But even though he kept me on task, he wouldn't actually cut anything or dictate any phrases; he had said earlier that every word of it had to be mine and apparently he meant it.

I worked hard for twenty minutes, which, as I explained to George, was as long as my attention span ever lasted. He said, "I guess that is true," so I got up and made us tea and found some cookies in the freezer in a big bakery box that someone must have brought my mom as a hostess gift.

We sat and ate our microwave-warm cookies and drank our tea and talked about some of the short essays on the application and what I could say about extracurricular activities since I didn't really have much other than the Holiday-Giving Program—I showed up to meetings for the Gay-Straight Alliance and Diversity Council, but I didn't run anything other than the H-G.

Then Heather arrived, looking extremely adorable in a pink-and-gold sundress, and George asked her if *she'd* made the changes he wanted, and she dimpled up and said that of course she had, she'd made every one of them and all of his comments had been so helpful and made it so much better, and he glanced at me like he wanted to make sure I'd heard that, and I shrugged because Heather was the kind of girl who did what you told her to and I . . . wasn't.

While they went over her changes, I worked on the common app, adding the information we'd just discussed. A while later the intercom let us know that someone was at the gate. I jumped up and buzzed in Aaron's car.

"We did good work here today," I announced to the kitchen in a "Let's wrap this up now" kind of way. It had been almost two hours . . . if you considered an hour and a quarter almost two hours.

"Oh no," Heather said, looking up. "Do we have to be done? Can you look at this one more time, George?"

"Call him Georgie," I said. "He likes that."

"I can stay as long as you need me," he told her. "I'm doing some organizing for Ellie's mom, so I was going to stick around to work on that anyway."

"Do you really like to be called Georgie?" she asked.

"No," he said. "I hate it."

"I figured. Ellie likes to be mean sometimes."

"I do not!" I said, but before I could defend myself more, there was a knock at the front door. I ran out into the hallway and swung it open. "Yay, you're here!" I said to Aaron. Then, a little less enthusiastically, "And you brought my grandmother."

"'Brought' isn't entirely accurate," Aaron said. "But we got here at the same time."

"Am I supposed to tip him?" Grandma asked me in

a loud whisper. "He looks like he expects a tip." For a second I thought she meant Aaron, but then I spotted the cabdriver coming up behind them with her suitcase.

"It's taken care of," I said.

"Are you sure? I think maybe I should tip him." There was no way he hadn't heard her stage whisper.

"It's good. We're good. Thank you," I said more loudly to the driver, who handed the suitcase to Aaron, wished us all a good day, and stepped away.

She looked back over her shoulder. "I just don't like having someone out there who thinks I'm ungenerous. Bad energy always comes back to you."

"He doesn't think you're ungenerous." I led her into the foyer, and Aaron followed us. "Mom already paid the tip online. You know she would never expect you to use your own money for this. You're doing us a favor."

"I *am* using up all of my vacation days on you," she said. "Not that I mind." She pressed me tight against her ample chest. "We're going to have so much fun together." She released me. "Aren't you going to introduce me to your friend?"

I explained that Aaron was Michael Marquand's son and then reminded her that she had met Michael and his wife at the anniversary party.

"She's very beautiful," Grandma said to him. "Your mother, I mean."

"Crystal's not my mother!" Aaron looked horrified

at the thought. "She's, like, twenty-five."

"I see. Well, I hope you get along with her. The step-mother/stepchild relationship can be a very meaningful one, if people are willing to be open to it. Have you let her into your heart?"

"Uh, yeah, sure," he said, but he looked like he wanted to both laugh and vomit.

"Come into the kitchen," I said quickly. "More people to meet there."

Both Heather and George had already spent time with my grandmother, so no introductions were needed. Heather hugged her warmly, loving her because she was my grandmother and Heather was the kind of person who loved other people's grandmothers. George was going to shake her hand, but she threw her arms around him, which seemed to surprise him but not in an unpleasant way. He nodded over her shoulder at Aaron with a curt, unenthusiastic "Hey."

Aaron was more focused on Heather, anyway, dropping the suitcase on the floor so he could go in for his own hug after Grandma got hers. Leaving his arm slung possessively over Heather's shoulder, he said, "I want you to know that I only came over because Ellie said you were here. You're my favorite."

"Favorite what?" she asked.

"Human being."

"What about Ellie?"

"Her? Ugh." He made a disgusted face, then pretended to realize I was watching and flashed me a big fake smile and a double thumbs-up. "I mean, she's great!" I rolled my eyes at him, and Heather laughed. "So, what are we all up to here?" he asked.

"Just finishing up some college application work," I said. "Heather had a few more questions for George, then we can go. What movie should we see?"

"I've narrowed it down to four possibilities," Aaron said, and removed his arm from Heather's shoulder so he could tick them off on his fingers. "A superhero movie, a movie about a gang of superheroes, a dark thriller featuring a superhero, and a romantic comedy starring someone who usually plays superheroes. But I should warn you that I only threw in that last one to make you girls think I'm sensitive. I don't really want to see it."

"That's okay—neither do I," I said.

"I do," Heather said.

"Me too," said Grandma. "I vote for that one."

There was an awkward moment of silence after that. Aaron coughed. I couldn't tell if it was real or fake.

"Don't feel you have to chaperone us or anything," I said to Grandma. "You've got to be pretty tired after getting up early and flying."

"I feel fine. I just need to visit the restroom and I'm good to go. So what movie shall we see?" She gazed around happily.

Aaron caught my eye and opened both of his wide for a moment in telegraphed panic before collapsing into a chair like his legs couldn't support him any longer.

"You can come if you want to," I said, "but it might be weird for you."

"Why would watching a movie be weird?" Grandma asked, her smile fading a little.

"The movie wouldn't be, I guess—not that much—but we were going to walk around the mall and just sort of hang out for a while afterward. I don't think it would be that much fun for you."

"You mean," she said, "that it wouldn't be that much fun for *you* if I came." She blinked a few times, patted her hair as if she were making sure it was still there, and said, "That's fine. Really. I understand. Who wants a grandmother cramping their style?"

"It's not that," I said. "It's just . . . we all made this plan a long time ago, and you and I will be spending a lot of time together over the next couple of weeks, so . . ." I trailed off.

"More than you probably want."

"No, no." I'm not sure how convincing I sounded. "It's great. We'll have a lot of fun. I was just . . ." *What?* "Just expecting you to show up later, so I made these other plans for today. But if you really want to go . . ." I stopped because Aaron was slowly shaking his head at me, telling me not to finish that sentence.

"I'm sorry," Grandma said into the silence. "I didn't mean to get in the way of your fun." She picked up her suitcase with a slight grimace of effort. "I'll just take this up to my room. I assume I'm staying in the same one as usual?"

"Wherever you want is fine," I said. "Seriously. Take your pick. You could sleep in the master or Jacob's room or either of the guest rooms—even my room if you prefer that." Guilt was making me chatter idiotically.

"I wouldn't want to get in your way," she said. "My usual room is fine."

"Let me carry that." George took the suitcase from her.

"I was just about to offer," Aaron said, leaping to his feet.

"I've got it." George gestured to Grandma to go ahead and followed her out of the kitchen, listing to one side to balance the weight of the suitcase.

twenty-one

"Phew," Aaron said before they were even out of earshot.

Heather shushed him and whispered to me, "She could come with us, you know. I don't mind."

"But *I* do," I said. "You don't know how annoying she can be."

"Really?" Aaron said. "Because I only just met her and I get it."

"Yeah, it's better this way. We couldn't have relaxed with her around. And I'm sure she's fine with it." I was trying to reassure myself as much as Heather. I felt bad: Grandma had traveled a long way to be with me, and now I was blowing her off. But she really would ruin our fun. Not deliberately. Just by being there and by being herself. Anyway, she and I would have plenty of time together—she was staying for a small eternity.

"She was probably relieved not to have to go," Aaron

said. "Why would she want to hang with a bunch of teenagers?"

"I agree. You guys mind if I run upstairs and get changed?" I plucked at my sweat shorts. "Not exactly dressed for the movies."

"We'll figure out what to see while you're gone," Aaron said.

I reached the stairs just as George appeared at the top. "Hey," I said as we were passing at the landing. "I'm just going up to get changed."

"Hold on," he said. He put his hand on my arm to make me stop, so I did—reluctantly. I wasn't in the mood to be yelled at and he looked like he wanted to yell at me.

But then, George always looked like he wanted to yell at me.

He didn't exactly yell; his voice was quiet as he said, "That wasn't very nice."

"What are you talking about?" I said, even though I knew.

He just waited, his dark eyes flickering across my face with a strange mixture of hope and concern.

I waved my hand dismissively. "You mean Grandma and the movie thing? She was fine with it."

"You hurt her feelings."

"Did she say that?"

"She didn't have to. I could tell."

"You're projecting. She was fine. I know her better than you and I could tell she didn't really care about going." I wanted to believe that more than I actually believed it. I hated feeling guilty.

George shook his head. "I know it's weird having your grandmother tag along," he said, his voice even lower. "And she drives you a little crazy. But put yourself in her shoes for a second. She left her home and flew out here just so you wouldn't be alone. After dealing with all the stress of packing and getting to the airport and flying and taking a cab, she gets here and you make her feel like you wish she hadn't come."

"I didn't." I looked down and rubbed at an imaginary stain on my shirt, so I didn't have to meet his eyes. "I mean, she knows I'm glad she's here."

"Does she?"

"Of course she does."

There was another pause and then he said, "Did you ever think about how strange this must all be for her? That you and your mom live like this?" He gestured around the house. "She told me she used to babysit you all the time back in Philadelphia. She still comes running the second you or your mother calls her even though she knows you have these incredible lives that she's not part of. Would it kill you to try to make her feel a little more welcome when she comes?"

I felt sick. Because he was right: Mom and I used to

depend on my grandmother and now we barely saw her. There was a time when I actually thought that Grandma brought the fun, when her arrival at our apartment door meant I got to watch TV and do messy art projects and bake cookies. (She wasn't into health food back then—that came later.) And now . . . my heart sank when Grandma appeared, and I didn't even bother to hide it. Yes, she was maddening, but George was right—she would do anything for me and Mom and Jacob. And I was an ungrateful pig.

But I didn't want George to think so. It was one thing to have him tease me about being spoiled and self-ish, and a very different—far more painful—thing to feel like he actually thought I was. I struggled to think of something to say to defend myself, but it was hard. "I welcome her," I finally said.

He waited another moment and then sighed. "Okay." He lifted his hand off my arm. "I know it's none of my business. I just . . ." He stopped. Then he said, "I just wanted to speak for her, I guess."

I nodded. I still couldn't look him in the eyes. I felt ashamed and desperately wanted the conversation to end, so I said, "It's okay. But I should go. The others are waiting."

"Right," he said, and walked down the rest of the stairs.

In my room, I sat on the edge of my bed and curled

my knees up, hugging them to my chest.

I was such a jerk.

When did Grandma's presence stop being fun and start being annoying to me? I couldn't pinpoint the shift; it was too gradual. Part of it was moving to LA, where people were suave and sophisticated and savvy. And part of it was Luke's getting rich and famous— she was so clearly from our past, from a time when I was bored and lonely. Now I had cool places to go and every amusement at my fingertips. I had stopped craving adult attention, so Grandma's company had become just a drag.

What did she even have in her life these days? She worked long, hard hours at the hospital, then watched a ton of TV and read articles about stuff like karma and meditation because they gave her boring daily tasks meaning. Her life had narrowed while ours had expanded, which made her refusal to live off Luke sort of noble. She never complained. She deserved a lot more respect and sympathy than I ever gave her.

I got up off the bed and changed out of my sweat shorts and tank top and into jeans and a sweater. I stuffed my feet into low boots, and then I marched out of my room and down the hallway, where I knocked on the guest room door before opening it. I said, "Please come with us to the movies."

"I don't want to be an imposition," Grandma said, looking up from the suitcase she was unpacking.

"You're not. If you don't want to go, that's fine—I'll stay home with you. I'd rather be with you than see a movie."

"In that case"—she flung her skirt back in the suitcase—"I'll be ready to go in two minutes!"

I found Heather and Aaron sitting close together at the kitchen table, watching a movie trailer on her laptop.

"Where's George?" I asked. I wanted him to know that Grandma was coming with us.

Aaron hit pause and looked up. "He took off. Said he had to get something but he'd be back to work on your mother's office later. Does he have a key to your house?"

"Everyone has a key to our house," I said. "Which makes all of the security cameras and stuff kind of pointless. You guys settle on a movie?"

"I let Heather decide," Aaron said. "I'm a gentleman that way."

"He is," she said. "And because he was nice to me, I was nice to him and picked the movie he wanted."

"He played you like a fiddle," I said.

"I'm devious." Aaron stood up. "I'm going to run to your bathroom before we go."

While he was out of the room, Heather closed her laptop and arched her back in a long stretch, then said, "I feel really good about my essay now, Ellie." She nodded toward the hallway. "He's so smart. And sweet."

"I've always thought so."

"Can I ask you something weird?" I nodded and she lowered her voice. "If you are, it's totally cool . . . but . . . you're not interested in him romantically, are you?"

It was funny to hear the question I'd been agonizing over simply asked out loud. And a relief. Because having someone else question how I felt about Aaron brought an immediate answer to my lips that seemed right as soon as the words were out.

"No," I said. "He's just a friend."

"Really? Are you sure?"

"Totally." I was. I was totally sure. I loved him, but deep down I knew there wasn't even a shred of sexual attraction or romance in that love. And here was Heather, *asking* about him. I felt a smile creep over my face. "Why? Do you like him?"

She ducked her head, blushing, and barely whispered, "I think, maybe, yeah. He's really nice."

"He is." I considered her for a moment, and it was like light dawning. I clasped my hands. "Heather, this is brilliant. You two are perfect for each other."

"You really think so?"

"I can't believe I didn't realize it sooner."

"You don't think he's too . . ." She groped for the right word. "Too sophisticated for me?"

"Why do you always sell yourself short? You're plenty sophisticated. You're also the sweetest, best girl in the world. He'd be lucky to get to be with you."

"You're just saying that because you're my friend."

"It's true."

"So what do I do now?"

"I could say something to him—"

"Oh God, no! That's so middle school! I want to seem older, not younger."

"Okay. But you should reach out to him somehow—let him know you're interested."

"Right," she said. "I'll try. I'm just not—shhhh." Aaron was coming back into the room. I grinned at her and she blushed.

"What'd I interrupt?" he asked, looking back and forth between us.

"Secrets," I said.

"Girl talk? Can I join in?"

"No," Heather and I said at the same time, just as my grandmother entered. She had made herself fancy: a bit of her hair was pinned against her temple with a big fake flower and she'd traded her black elastic-waist pants for a long black elastic-waist skirt.

"I'm ready," she sang out.

Aaron gaped at me.

"Grandma's coming with us," I said, and hooked my arm through hers, avoiding Aaron's accusing glare. "Let's go."

twenty-two

I did my best to encourage things between Heather and Aaron that night. The more I thought about it, the more I was convinced they would be a perfect couple, the one so domineering, the other so compliant. I made sure they sat next to each other at the movies and shared their own bag of popcorn. I shared with Grandma, popcorn being one of the few junk foods she approved of. (*It's high in fiber, you know, Ellie. So long as you don't put that fake butter on it, it's really not bad for you.*)

Now that I knew Heather liked Aaron, I could see the signs of it—nothing major, but they were there. Like the way she talked to me more than to him—of course Heather would be all shy and self-conscious around a guy she liked! And she didn't scarf down popcorn the way she normally did; she only nibbled a few pieces at a time. A classic case of shrunken love stomach.

I wasn't sure Aaron was getting the message, though: it was all pretty subtle. She was smiley and responsive to anything he said directly to her, but in pretty much the same way she was smiley and responsive to anything *I* said to her. I worried that Heather just didn't know how to send out vibes that were more flirtatious than friendly.

I wished I hadn't promised not to say anything to him. I felt like just a few careful words might have made him see her in a whole new light. Plus it might make things clearer between him and *me*. A simple *Hey, maybe you and my friend should go out* seemed like an effective way to get across the message that I wasn't interested in him for myself but had nothing against him.

Alone that night in my room, my grandmother's snores audible through the wall, I searched my ego very carefully, poking and pricking to see if there was any soreness there, any discomfort at the thought of Aaron and Heather's falling in love. But there wasn't. Picturing the two of them together only made me feel happy. And a little relieved.

I knew that Heather would be a much better girlfriend for him than I ever could. She was sweet and easygoing and generous. I was too used to getting my own way and dominating everyone around me—just like Aaron. As a couple, we would have clashed constantly. But he and

Heather would complement each other perfectly, and I would do everything I could to make them happen.

I squidged down into bed and waited to fall into the deep sleep of the virtuous and celibate.

Except I couldn't.

Now that I felt settled about the Heather/Aaron situation, a far less serene memory bubbled up to the surface: my conversation with George about my grandmother. I never liked when people called me out on something I already felt guilty about, and I couldn't get his last disappointed look out of my mind.

I wished he knew that he'd convinced me to include her. But sending a text that said, "Enjoyed the movie— my grandmother did, too," seemed too embarrassingly transparent. Anyway, I kind of wanted to tell him face-to-face. I wanted to see him smile and nod, the way he did when he felt I'd done something right for once. Those moments were rare enough.

I flipped around in my bed. The house was too quiet. Usually I could hear someone moving around after I went to bed: Mom getting up and wandering along the hallway (she had insomnia issues); Jacob crying after a bad dream; Luke coming home late from work. . . . But tonight it was just Grandma and me, and the faint sounds of her rhythmic breaths made me feel even more alone: she was so deeply asleep and I was so awake. I wasn't exactly scared—we really did have a ridiculously impressive security system and I had double-checked that it was set before going to bed—but I didn't like the quiet. It made me glad Grandma had come after all. If I felt this isolated *with* her, the loneliness would have been unbearable without her.

I couldn't fall asleep. I sat up and reached for my laptop. When I opened it, the screen was still filled with the Word document for my college essay. I skimmed it again and hated it even more. It was so boring. So . . . just okay. So upright and good citizen–y. So uninspired. So not really me in any way at all.

I opened up a blank page and started to write a response to the essay. Just to have something to do, something to take my mind off how empty the house felt.

I didn't try to sound formal and smart. I just wrote down the sentences that came into my head.

I want to be exceptional. But my expectations of who I should be always run ahead of the reality of who I am. I see myself as a writer, a philanthropist, an athlete, a dancer. . . .

But I'm not any of those things. Not really. I've tried my hand at so many different

*activities, been enthusiastic and optimistic
about each one until it turned challenging or
repetitive, and then . . . stopped. I never make
it to the next level, where I might actually get
good. I'm strong with beginnings; it's sticking to
something that's hard for me.*

*I used to dream about being really good at
something and I've managed to convince myself
that the reason it hasn't happened yet is because
I just haven't found the right "thing." So I keep
trying new things, just waiting for the magic to
happen.*

*But maybe you aren't born with a talent
that's like a key that fits into a lock. Maybe it's
the sticking-to-something part that makes you
outstanding—and that's what I don't have.*

*So now my dream has changed. Now instead
of dreaming of being brilliant, I dream of being
consistent. I dream of being dedicated. I dream
of finding something I love so much that even
someone like me—a mercurial, inconstant,
lifelong dilettante—could honestly say, "This
time, I'll make myself proud."*

I sat back and looked at what I had written. It was
way too short. It was probably too negative. It wasn't

particularly clever or well-written.

But it was honest.

I went back to bed and this time I fell asleep.

When I got home from school the next day, I worked on the essay some more, expanding it, making it funnier and adding in some examples. I talked about our trip to Haiti and how I had vowed to find a way to help—the stuff the other essay had been about—but this time I told the truth about how little I had followed through on my resolution.

When I finished rewriting it, I stayed in my seat for a while, staring absently at the keyboard and thinking.

I wasn't actually sure I should use it as my college essay. In fact, I was pretty sure I shouldn't. It made me sound like someone who couldn't get her act together, which wasn't exactly what colleges looked for in their students.

But if I didn't think I could use it, why was I putting all this time into it?

Could I use it?

I needed George to help me figure it out, I decided.

So that night, after I had fiddled with the new essay some more and felt like maybe it was in decent shape, I sent it as an email attachment to him. In the subject line, I wrote, *Possible new essay?* And in the body of the email I wrote, *I want to be a good person. I just get in the way sometimes.* ☺

I deleted the smiley face and put it back in several times, finally leaving it in.

And then I hit send. And waited.

An hour later, I got an email back from him.

Re: Possible new essay?
Yes. Will discuss on Wednesday.

I spent the next hour staring at music videos and obsessing over those five words. The *Yes* seemed positive. Maybe that meant he liked it? Although . . . it could also have just meant he agreed that I got in my own way. And the *Will discuss on Wednesday* wasn't exactly helpful feedback.

I had wanted more from George. I felt like I'd cut myself open and exposed some hidden nerve-ridden and embarrassing part of my anatomy with that essay. I'd spent years trying to convince myself that I was someone who did what she set out to do, so it wasn't easy to admit that I wasn't really like that.

I wanted something back for my honesty—some sense that George appreciated it and valued the courage it took. I also wanted him to see that the essay was my way of saying I screwed up with Grandma and that I was glad he called me out on it, because I really *did* want to be a decent person, even if I didn't always act like it.

But as good as I was at talking other people into things, I couldn't succeed at convincing myself that George was saying he understood all that in those five short words.

twenty-three

Ben and I needed to write an official email about the Holiday-Giving Program's annual Thanksgiving Food drive, which would have to be approved by the head of the school before we could forward it to all the parents. We had the previous year's letter as a template, but we had to change the dates and some other minor details.

He offered to drop by my house on Tuesday evening, which was fine—with Luke and Mom out of town, I was happy to host. When he showed up, I was surprised to see he'd brought Arianna with him. I'd thought it was just going to be the two of us.

It didn't really matter—actually, I figured an extra set of hands and eyes could come in handy—but she kind of annoyed me right at the start by saying, "Oh my God, your house is amazing!" as they walked in the door. Not that there was anything wrong with the compliment. There was just something about how her eyes were darting around, greedily sucking in every detail, that made the words grate on me.

"Thanks," I said. "We like it."

"It's so big. I can't believe how big it is. How many of you live here?"

"Just my family. And the house may be big, but we always end up doing everything in the kitchen. Which is where we're going now." I led them that way. "You guys want something to drink?"

"Water's fine," said Ben.

"Can I see what you have?" Arianna asked, and opened the refrigerator before I could even respond. She seemed a little disappointed by the slim choices there. "I guess I'll take a Snapple," she said, and grabbed a bottle. She turned around. "So is there, like, a big music studio in the house?"

"There's a small one out back," I said.

"Can we see it?"

"No," I said, a little more curtly than I probably should have. I softened it: "It's kind of Luke's private place. I don't go in without him."

"Are you musical, too?" she asked. "He must have taught you how to play the guitar and stuff, right?"

"He tried once, but it didn't take." I was totally tone-deaf, and even though I learned to strum a few chords, I never practiced and got fidgety when Luke sat down with me, so we both lost interest in the attempt. For Luke's sake, I hoped Jacob would be more into the music thing; he certainly liked to sing along to Disney songs—always in his own language, but he nailed the tunes.

While Ben and I were working on the letter, Arianna leapt up to explore the kitchen. She kept opening cabinets and drawers, checking inside, and then closing them again.

"What are you looking for?" I asked.

"A snack, I guess. I haven't eaten dinner yet. But don't mind me."

I got up, went to the pantry, and pulled out a bag of crackers. "Will this do?" I dropped it on the table and sat back down.

But a few minutes later, she was back on the prowl, glancing into everything she could open.

"Do you need something else?" I asked, trying to keep the annoyance out of my voice.

"Uh . . . silverware?"

"Why?" We were eating the crackers with our hands. I mean, obviously.

She just shrugged and came back to the table, where she looked over our shoulders and agreed with everything either of us said, but then she must have drifted away again without my even noticing because the next time I looked up, she was over at the opposite side of the room flipping through our mail, which was stacked up on the counter for Mom and Luke to sort when they came home.

"Hey!" I said.

"What?" She turned around, after quickly dropping whatever she was holding back onto the pile.

"Are you looking through our mail?"

"Not really." She gave a little laugh. "Honestly, I don't even know what I'm doing. I'm just sort of wandering around. . . . Short attention span, I guess. Do you mind if I use your bathroom?"

I minded that a lot less than her pawing through our private correspondence. "It's down the hallway, take a left, and then another left."

"Thanks." She disappeared.

"That was weird," I said to Ben in a low voice.

"What?" He looked up from his laptop.

"She was going through our mail."

"Arianna? Why would she do that?"

"I have no idea."

"I'm sure she wasn't." He pointed to the screen. "Shouldn't this be a period instead of a comma?"

I let it drop and just focused on finishing the work as quickly as possible so I could get Arianna out of my house.

Later that night, after they'd gone, Grandma and I were watching TV together when she said, "Which friend of yours is that blond girl?"

"Blond girl? You mean Heather?"

"No, I know Heather. I mean the one who was wandering around upstairs earlier tonight—I heard a noise in your mother's room and there she was. She said she was working on a school project with you and you'd sent her up to find something?"

"Oh. That's Arianna. We *were* working on a project, but I didn't send her upstairs."

"Hmm," Grandma said. "She had her phone out. I think she may have been taking some photos."

I swore and pulled my phone out of my pocket. I didn't follow Arianna, but I was able to find her Instagram account pretty quickly. And see her most recent photos.

Luke Weston's driveway! Luke Weston's living room! Luke Weston's closet—and shoes!! Luke Weston's drawer full of T-shirts! Luke Weston's bed (squee!)!!!!!!!!

There was even a photo of me working on my laptop at the kitchen table, completely oblivious to the fact that my picture was being taken. She had posted it with the caption "Luv ya, gorgeous gurl!"

"Oh, for God's sake!" I said.

"What?"

I showed Grandma the photos.

"The curse of fame," she said cheerfully. She'd already had a cocktail or two. "But no harm done."

"I guess not." I felt violated though.

I complained to Heather a little while later, when we were video chatting. I made her check out the photos on her phone.

"Ugh," she said. "People are jerks."

"Right?" That was more the response I was going for. Grandma's "live and let live" attitude was a little too easygoing for my current feelings about Arianna.

Heather said, "Did you see how Riley commented on every photo? About how much she loved your house, too, and how you're both so gorgeous? It's a little much."

I checked to see and she was right: Riley was almost as annoying as Arianna. To be fair, she'd been over a bunch of times and never taken any photos—or snuck upstairs without telling me—so she wasn't in Arianna's league or anything, but the fact that she wanted everyone on this stupid Instagram feed to know that she'd *also* been to Luke Weston's house was a little nauseating.

"Do you see why I need you to come to Elton College with me?" I said. "What if everyone there is like them? What if there aren't any Heathers?"

"There are Heathers everywhere," she said. "There's nothing special about me."

"Stop it," I said. "You're special to me. You're the only friend I trust. Well, you and Aaron."

"It's good he moved here," she said.

"Yeah, I know *you* think so," I said with a grin.

She shrugged with an embarrassed smile and swiftly changed the subject. "Applications are due tomorrow at midnight East Coast time, right? I was thinking it would be fun to click submit together. Is George coming that night?"

"Yeah. I just need to go over my essay with him one last time. Why don't you come at eight? That'll give us an hour to check everything before hitting send."

"Can I? I'd love that—if I stay home, my parents will be standing over me, worrying about every sentence. If I tell them your tutor will read it over for me, they'll back off."

"For a good girl, you can be very devious."

"You taught me everything I know."

twenty-four

Before George came on Wednesday, I reread my two essays and decided I hated them both. One was too insincere, the other too negative.

I felt anxious and unsettled, so when Grandma came down to make a cup of tea, I snapped at her that she needed to stay out of the kitchen, because George was coming soon and we had to get a lot of work done.

She said calmly, "I'll clear out as soon as he gets here. Do you want some mushroom tea?"

"Words cannot express how much I don't."

"Don't be narrow minded. Why is it okay to drink brewed leaves and not brewed mushrooms? Think outside the box."

"I love when you use clichés to encourage me to be original. If I promise to defy convention in all other ways, will you please not make me drink mushroom tea?"

"Your loss," she said. "So George is coming back tonight?"

"What do you mean 'coming back'?"

"He was here earlier—working on your mom's office. He came yesterday, too. He wants to finish it before they get back."

"I didn't know he came by."

"Well, you were at school."

"He could have stuck around and said hi."

"He probably had plans."

Did he, though? Or was he just sick of me?

When he arrived, I opened the door for him but hung back a bit, feeling awkward now that he was there. I could still remember his disappointed expression when we parted the last time we'd talked, and it made it hard for me to look him in the eyes. Plus he'd since read my essay and that was embarrassing in its own way—I'd acknowledged some pretty ugly truths about myself. I felt exposed.

He probably thought it was stupid, anyway.

"Hey," I said, trying to sound normal and not succeeding.

"Hey," he said. "How's it going?"

"Fine. Come on in."

"Thank you."

This was going great.

We headed toward the kitchen.

"Heather coming?" he asked.

"Yeah, but I wanted to have time to talk about my essay first."

"Sounds good," he said without any real enthusiasm.

Grandma looked up as we entered the kitchen. She was sticking two slices of gluten-free bread into the toaster. "Oh, I'm sorry. I promised Ellie I'd clear out of here by the time you came, George, but I'm so slow. . . . Just let me finish making toast and I'll disappear, I promise."

I caught George's expression and realized how bad that sounded—like I was still determined to make my grandmother feel unwanted in my home. "It's fine," I said quickly. "I don't mind if you're here; I'm just stressed about how much work I need to get done."

"I completely understand," she said. "George, would you like a cup of mushroom tea before I do my disappearing act?"

"Mushroom tea?" he repeated uncertainly.

"Trust me, you don't want it," I said.

"I would love some," he said immediately.

"Excellent!" She beamed, delighted, then turned to me with sudden concern. "Don't get mad at me, Ellie. It will only take one more minute."

"I'm not mad at you. I don't know why you always think I am."

"I'm annoying," she said. "I know it."

I couldn't take it. She was going to make George think I was mean and uncaring. Not that he needed much encouragement in that direction. "Tell George about the movie we saw on Sunday," I blurted out suddenly, and felt my face turn hot as soon as I had—it was so obvious what I was doing. So pathetic.

"Oh," George said with a sudden sharp look at me. "You went to the movies together?"

"We did," Grandma said, bustling around, pouring steaming water from the teakettle into a mug she had filled with bits of something shriveled and ugly. "And we had so much fun. The movie itself was a little violent for my taste, but the popcorn was wonderful. And we all went out for frozen yogurt afterward."

"Yes, we did," I said, raising my chin defiantly and looking directly at George for the first time that day.

"Okay, here's your tea." Grandma handed him the mug. "Let it steep a few more minutes, then drink the top part. Don't worry about what's left in the mug. Just enjoy the liquid and throw the rest out."

"Thank you." He peered down at the mug's contents. "It looks interesting."

"Don't worry if you swallow something solid. Even the dirt is organic. Ah—my toast is done!" She put it on a plate, and carefully spread butter on each slice. George and I watched her in silence. "I'll take everything upstairs so I'm not a distraction. Work hard, you "two." She left, carefully clutching her mug in one hand and her plate in the other.

There was a pause. Then I said, "You don't actually have to drink that."

"Oh, thank God." He dumped his mug into the sink. He turned to me. "You invited her to go with you to the movies."

I nodded, still embarrassed that I had felt the need to blurt it out, but glad he knew. "Someone told me I should."

"I'd have thought that might have the opposite effect."

"I'm not that big a jerk."

"I never thought you were." There was another short silence and then he cleared his throat and said, "So let's talk about your essay."

"First tell me what you think of it. Do you hate it?"

"Hate it?" He sat down at the table. "I think it's great."

He liked it? My relief lasted about half a second before it turned into annoyance that he hadn't bothered to tell me before. "Your five-word email didn't give me a lot to go on."

"Sorry," he said. "I wasn't at my most communicative that night."

"Three or four more words would have gone a long way."

"I loved it. It was honest and unique and it made me want to know the girl who wrote it."

"You do know me."

He ignored that. "But, all that being said . . . it's definitely a riskier choice. The right admissions person will love you for being honest. The wrong one might wonder if you're incapable of accomplishing anything. You just don't know how it's going to be received."

"So I should use the other one?"

"It's totally your call."

"Don't do that to me!" I came over to the table and dropped into a chair next to him. "Personally, I like this one better."

"Me too."

I thought for another moment or two, then said slowly, "Maybe this is nuts, but I feel like I might not belong anyway at a school that would reject me for writing this. Does that make sense?"

"Totally," he said.

"I'd rather be appreciated for being honest than for being *glib*."

"I'm sorry I called you that. That wasn't fair."

"It's fine. Let's work on this one. I've decided."

We read through the essay together and he helped me find ways to strengthen it. "I'd add at least another sentence about the future and how you feel like you're figuring yourself out," he said. "I think schools care more about growth and potential than past achievement."

"Does this mean you think I have potential to grow?" I asked, half-joking, half-wistful.

"Yeah," he said. "You invited your grandmother to go to the movies with you, didn't you?"

"Because you told me to."

"Did I?" he said, and then shrugged and redirected me back to the essay. But when I glanced up, his eyes were on me, not the screen. He quickly looked away again.

twenty-five

Heather showed up too soon. George and I had worked steadily the whole time—I mean really steadily; no texting, even though I'd heard my phone buzz a few times—but I wanted more time alone with him.

I kind of wished I hadn't invited her at all—come to think of it, she'd pretty much invited herself—but when I let her in the house, she hugged me so warmly that I felt bad for having thought that.

"Let's do this thing!" she said. "Let's submit it and be done."

"Well, not really *done*," I said.

"We're both going to get in early, right? That's what you keep saying." Big blue eyes begged for reassurance.

"Right," I said. "Of course." For the first time, I felt

uneasy about my optimism. There would be no going back once we clicked send. She'd have used up her early decision shot.

It didn't matter—Luke would call, and they would let her in.

But would she even like it there? It had become my first choice after I'd visited and loved everything about it. But Heather had never actually toured the campus; she'd chosen it because I had. Because I told her to.

"George is in the kitchen," I said, forcing a smile.

But she was already ahead of me. "George!" she sang out, bounding through the foyer and running to greet him. She was wearing a flippy little black skirt and a tight pink sweater, and her hair had been plaited into a bunch of tiny braids and then twisted and pinned into a loose, low knot. In the brighter light of the kitchen, I could see that she was wearing more makeup than usual—lots of eyeliner and mascara.

"Hey there!" George said. "I hear you're just about ready to hit the send button."

"I'm terrified," she admitted, dropping into the seat next to him, which had been mine . . . but whatever. "Do you think my essay's good enough?"

"I do!" he said.

Her face lit up. "And do I really have a shot at going to Elton with Ellie?"

"Ellie might not get in," he said. "You might not

get in. Either or both of you could get deferred. But I'm sure you'll end up where you want to be when all of this is over."

I noticed he had managed to dodge her question.

"There's no way I'll get in if you don't," Heather said to me. "You're so much smarter than me."

"We can both get in," I said. "It's not either/or. And everyone says applying early raises your odds like a million percent. Which is what we're just about to do."

"Right," she said. "And then we should celebrate. Maybe we could all go out somewhere?"

I hid a smile. I knew what she meant when she said "we all." "I'll text Aaron and see if he's free."

"Great!" she said, and showed her dimple. "You should come, too," she said to George, which proved what I'd always known—that she was nicer than I was. It wouldn't have occurred to me to invite him along, but it was a good thought, given how much he'd helped us both.

"Thanks," George said. "I can't."

"Why not?" I asked, genuinely curious.

"Plans," he said curtly, and looked down at his phone, which had just lit up.

My phone buzzed, too: Aaron had texted me back, saying he was free after nine. "Let's pick him up at his place," I said to Heather. "You've never seen it, right? It's unbelievable. It's like my favorite house in the world."

"Your house is *my* favorite house in the world," she said.

"That's because you haven't seen Aaron's yet. Plus, you know . . . Aaron lives there." I grinned at her.

"Do you still need me here?" George asked, getting to his feet.

"Yes!" Heather said instantly. Then, "I mean, if you don't mind . . ."

He sat back down.

She said, "I want to go over my short essays with you. And my long essay. All my essays."

"You guys go ahead," I said. "I need to change my clothes if we're going out."

"You might want to read through that essay again," George said to me. "If you're really planning to send it in tonight."

"It's fine." I waved my hand airily. "Good enough."

He sighed. "At least you're consistent."

"If it's too perfect, they won't believe that I'm as bad about follow-through as I say I am. Form should follow function or something like that."

"In that case, you should end it in the middle of a sentence."

"Is that a dare?"

He held up his hands. "No! Just a joke. Please don't do anything that will make your mother angry at me."

"Fine. Then we'll leave it as is, shall we?" I tossed my

head and left them alone in the kitchen.

I figured since Heather was already dressed up, maybe we'd go out somewhere nice, so I put on a short black dress that had an empire waist and lacy bra-like shoulder straps and paired it with cherry-red Doc Martens so it wouldn't look too sweet. I took out my topknot and braided the hair at my temples back into a circlet around my head, with the rest of my curls set free to tumble in whatever direction they wanted. (Sometimes I thought of my hair as being alive. Like a pet I needed to groom a lot. That's not weird, is it?) I stopped by my grandmother's room to let her know we were running out—she was already ready for bed—then went back downstairs.

"Well?" I said when I reentered the kitchen. "What do we think?"

"Oh my God, you look so beautiful," Heather breathed.

I laughed. "I meant about your essays, not about me. But thanks." I gave a little twirl that ended in a curtsy. George had looked up when Heather did, but he didn't comment on my changed appearance, just turned back to her laptop. They were sitting right next to each other so they could both look at the screen—so close their shoulders were almost touching.

"What do you think?" Heather asked him.

"It all looks good to me. I don't think we'll accomplish much fiddling around with it more."

"I'm scared," she said, and kind of clutched at him, which was so Heather. I once watched a horror movie with her and I literally had bruises on my arm afterward.

"Come on," I said, and marched over to the table. "Let's do this thing. We'll read our apps quickly through one last time and then send them in. Agreed?"

"Let's do it," Heather said.

Fifteen minutes later, after we'd both read through our applications carefully, we counted down from ten together and hit submit at the exact same moment.

"Woo-hoo," I said, and we high-fived. "We did it!"

"We did it," she echoed.

There was a moment of silence.

I sat back in my chair. "This is really anticlimactic."

"That's why we're going out," Heather said. "To make it more climactic."

"I don't know what kind of evening *you* have planned," I said, and she blushed and protested that she didn't mean it that way.

"And on that note . . ." George stood up. "My work here is done. I mean, except for my other work here."

"I can't believe we're not going to see you anymore." Heather jumped to her feet, her little skirt swinging with the motion. "That's so sad!"

"You're done with your application," he said. "That's good, right?"

"Unless we don't get in and have to apply to more

schools. Which I probably will."

"No, you won't," I said automatically.

"If you do end up having to write more essays," George said to her, "I'll be happy to help you."

"What about me?" I said. "Will you help me if *I* need to write more essays?"

"You don't need my help. You always end up doing whatever you want, no matter what other people say."

"That's not true," I said, stung. "You totally helped me. I wouldn't have written that second essay if it hadn't been for you."

"What are you talking about?" he said. "You wrote that completely on your own. I didn't even know you were doing it."

But I wrote it for *you*. It was weird to me that he didn't realize that. That the essay was my side of a conversation I was having with him—but apparently he didn't even know we were having it.

"You wrote a new essay?" Heather said to me. "What's it about?"

"How I don't finish stuff I start."

"Really? You wrote about *that*?" She looked worried. "That seems a little weird. Do you think colleges will be okay with that?"

I shrugged, not interested in discussing it with her right then. "The point is," I said, addressing George, who was packing his laptop into its sleeve, "you helped me more than you realize, and I'll need you if I have to write more essays. Even if it's just to bounce ideas off of."

"Well, let's hope it doesn't come to that," he said lightly, and stood up, tucking the laptop under his arm. "I'll come back tomorrow to work on your mom's office, Ellie, but it'll probably be when you're in school. Take care, both of you. Congratulations on submitting your applications."

"You'll stay in touch, right?" Heather said.

He smiled at her. "Of course. Call me the second you hear from Elton. Good or bad news. We're in this together."

"I will," she said. "And if it's a yes, then we'll all go out and celebrate together, right?"

"Absolutely." He gave her a quick hug and then nodded at me. "Bye. Enjoy your night out." He walked out of the kitchen.

Heather and I just stood there for a moment, gazing at the doorway.

And I had thought hitting send felt anticlimactic. . . .

twenty-six

Heather called her parents and told them she'd sent in her application. I wanted to call mine but had to wait: it was five in the morning in London.

Heather was very quiet on the drive to Aaron's, so I asked her if she was okay.

"Yeah," she said, staring out the window. "It just felt so weird. I thought more would happen at the end. But we all just sort of sat there and then George left."

I glanced over at her. "Be happy. We're about to see Aaron."

"Fun." She didn't sound as enthusiastic as I'd expected, but I understood her dim mood; it was sobering sending off the application. It should have felt like the start of something, but instead it felt like something had ended. "Where do you think he was going?" she said after a moment. "George? Do you think he, like, had a date?"

"Nah," I said. Then: "I mean, maybe. I don't know. He did keep checking his phone, which isn't like him."

"Has he ever mentioned a girlfriend?"

"Never."

"Do you think he'd tell you if he was going on a date?"

"Probably not." We were both silent for a moment and then I said, "I bet it wasn't a date."

We reached the Marquands' front gate, and I punched the call button on the keypad. No one responded. "That's weird," I said after an entire minute had gone by and I'd pressed it a few more times. "He said he'd be here."

"Try texting him," she suggested, so I did.

No response to that either. Since the gate was tall and solid—designed to block prying eyes—I couldn't tell if there were any lights on in the house or any movement around it.

"Do you have their home number?" Heather asked.

"No. I'll try his cell but he's not answering my texts." I let it ring a few times, and then to my surprise and relief, he actually did pick up, but the first thing he said was "I can't talk."

"We're in front of your house," I said. "Can you come out?"

"Wait a sec," he said. "No, wait . . . Don't wait."

It sounded like a joke, so I laughed, but he didn't.

"Just . . . go home," he said in a strained voice. "I'll come over when I can. If I can."

"Are you okay?" I asked, but he had already hung up.

"What's wrong?" Heather asked.

I stared at my phone, bewildered. "I have no idea."

Heather and I decided to ditch our plans, since Aaron had said he'd meet us back at the house and I felt too worried now to just go out without him. Instead we picked up sandwiches and chips at Whole Foods and brought them back to my house, where we ate them in front of the TV—Grandma was watching *The Stoned Housewives of Dippity-Do* or whatever it was, and Heather wanted to watch it, too. Before it was over, her parents called to say they'd like her to come home soon, since it was a school night. "I'd argue with them if there was a reason to," she said as she packed up her laptop, "but since we're not really celebrating—"

"It's fine," I said. "Go."

"You have to let me know what's going on with Aaron as soon as you find out. And also whether George went on a date."

"I'll pass on any information I get."

Poor Heather. She looked pretty deflated as she dragged herself out to her car. No wonder: she had made herself look so pretty for Aaron and then he'd totally flaked on us. What was going on with him?

I called Mom around eleven—it was still early in London, but I figured Jacob would have woken her up by then. "Is everything okay?" she said.

"Stop worrying every time I call you. I just wanted you to know I submitted my application to Elton. The deed is done."

"Wow," she said. "Congratulations!"

"How's it going there?"

"Meh."

"What's wrong?"

"Remember how I told you Jacob liked Bob? The male babysitter we got through the hotel? He was amazing and was making my life so much easier—but then he had some kind of family emergency and now he can't come anymore. We've tried two other people since then. One of them was really young and she quit after the first day because Jacob wouldn't stop crying. She was in tears when I came back to the hotel. I mean, literally in tears. She and Jacob were both crying in different corners of the room. . . . It was ridiculous."

"What about the other one?"

"More competent, but I get this weird vibe from her. Like she hates Jacob."

"Seriously?" I pictured my wavy-haired little beauty of a brother. "How could anyone hate him?"

"I don't know. Maybe I'm wrong. It's possible I'm really as insane as Luke keeps telling me I am. It's just . . . she babysat twice and both times I felt like she couldn't even bring herself to smile at him. That he was just like this *difficulty* she had to deal with to get paid. I don't want Jacob to be with people who feel that way. So I don't want to use her anymore. But I also don't want to leave him with another stranger. So it's been me all day for the last couple of days, with no breaks. Luke's already left for the set today—it's going to be a long, lonely day here for me."

"I have a great idea: Grandma should fly out and help you. That would solve all our problems!"

She gave a weary laugh. "Nice try. She's all yours. Luke has tomorrow off, and he said he'll take Jacob and I should go get a massage."

"You should get ten massages."

"You deserve one, too," she said. "Sending in your college application . . . that's amazing."

"Save the praise for when I get *into* college," I said. "But I'll take the massage. Can I schedule one with Margo?"

"Sure," she said. "Enjoy yourself now because when we get home, you are going to be spending a lot of quality time with your little brother."

* * *

It was almost midnight. I had given up on hearing from Aaron and was getting ready for bed when I finally got a text.

I need a place to crash. Can I come there?

Like for the night? What's going on??

No response.

About fifteen minutes later, the monitor in the upstairs hallway buzzed, and I opened the front gate, then crept downstairs to let him in. I was glad Grandma was a sound sleeper and already in bed.

Aaron looked . . . weird. Disheveled and tense and not at all like his usual cheerful, polished self. Even while he bent down to kiss my cheek, his eyes were darting around nervously, and as he stood back up he kept thrusting his fingers through his hair and tugging hard at the ends. He was dressed in gray sweatpants, a T-shirt in a slightly different gray, and flip-flops. "Can I come in?" he asked, blinking rapidly. "And sleep here?"

"Yes and sure, but you're going to have to tell me what's going on."

Aaron sat down heavily at the table, hunching his shoulders with his head thrust forward.

"What is it?" I asked, sitting across from him. "What's going on?"

He looked at me. Then he looked away and ran his fingers through his hair again. "You guessed, right?" he said.

"Guessed what?"

"You know. What's been going on . . ." He shifted in his chair. "At the Halloween party, I could tell you had guessed. I was going to just tell you everything that night—it would have been a relief to have someone to talk to—but then I got the sense you didn't really want to hear about it and I got that. I mean, why would you?"

At the Halloween party? Wait—was this all about being in love with me? "I'm so confused," I said.

"Crystal," he said. "Me and Crystal."

"Did she kick you out? Was it because you're so messy?"

He stared at me like I was an idiot. "No," he said. "Jesus, Ellie, really? You didn't know? I thought . . . I mean, you saw us at that Starbucks. . . ."

"Oh, wait," I said slowly. "Oh, Aaron. Oh my God. You and Crystal? As in . . . *you and Crystal?*"

He dropped his head into his hands.

"Oh my God." I was stunned. "Oh my God." Then, "But you hate her."

"Yeah, no," he said, raising his head again with the ghost of his usual grin. "Not so much."

"You kept complaining," I said. "About how she was driving you crazy and how she and your dad—" I stopped. "Your dad," I said. Then, "Oh, Aaron."

"Shh," he said, even though I wasn't talking anymore.

"Don't. It's his fault. In a way." He rose suddenly to his feet and started pacing around the table, his hands twitching at his sides. "I mean, he was totally ignoring her. She's like the most amazing, beautiful woman in the entire world, and he was never home and even when he was, he barely talked to her. She came to me crying one night. I'd thought she was so . . ." He ran his fingers through his hair again, searching for the word. "You know. Cold. Cut off. Almost inhuman." He shook his head vehemently. "But she's not like that, I swear. She'd just been hurt. That's why she seemed like that. She was trying to defend herself against how mean he could be. And it's so hard with a baby. I felt so bad for her. I just wanted to help her not be lonely."

"Sounds like you succeeded."

His mouth twisted into something that wasn't a smile. "I guess." He sank back into his chair and held his hands up in supplication. "You just have to know that she's actually incredibly sensitive and caring and emotional. The way she seems—that's just a mask."

"Maybe." I was skeptical. "But no matter what, she's married to your father. That's . . . weird." It was a lot worse than weird, but I settled on the gentlest word I could think of.

"She's closer to my age than to his, you know."

"And that makes it okay?"

He said helplessly, "We were alone together so much.

It wasn't like we planned it. Things just happened."

I could picture it: the beautiful young woman, bored and lonely and feeling like motherhood is draining her of her sex appeal, stuck at home with nothing to do because her famous husband is always at work or out schmoozing . . . and then along comes this incredibly handsome, dynamic stepson and the place is alive again and he makes her laugh and he's *there*, and day after day they see each other and they eat dinner alone together and the baby's off with the babysitter and she starts to look forward to their evenings together, when it's just the two of them, and sometimes their hands touch when they're passing food . . .

So much made sense now. Like that time I ran into them at Starbucks—they had probably snuck out to be alone together. No wonder she had acted so weird and couldn't wait to get away: she was probably freaked out that I'd seen them, afraid I'd guess what was going on.

But all I'd seen was a kid being dragged out to a coffee shop by his stepmother. It hadn't occurred to me for a second to look at it any other way. Which maybe meant I was incredibly naive.

And the way she had acted so cold to me—almost rude . . . she probably felt like I was some kind of rival. Aaron had flirted shamelessly with me in public—so much so that even *I* thought he was in love with me. Crystal must have known that he was trying to mislead everyone, but maybe it still bugged her to see the two of us walking around together, openly teasing each other and holding hands, when she had to keep her distance and be all stepmotherly.

"I get it," I said. "Really. And I'm not judging you, but I still feel bad for your father."

"You should have seen him half an hour ago," Aaron said. "You wouldn't have felt bad for him. You would have been terrified of him. I know I was."

"Did he find out? Is that what was going on tonight?"

He nodded, sinking down low in his chair and staring at his own knees. "Crystal told him. It was crazy. I—you know how I had plans with you tonight? She was upset. She's sort of jealous of you—"

"I can't imagine why," I said. "It's not like you were all over me at the Halloween party or anything. It's not like you bent me over backward and gave me a steamy kiss in front of the entire guest list. Oh, wait, my bad, it was *exactly* like that."

"I'm sorry," he said. "I knew my dad wanted us to go out, and I thought that if he saw us together a lot, he'd assume we were and . . ." He trailed off.

"It's great," I said. "I can take being someone's beard off my bucket list."

"Are you mad at me?" He sat up so he could reach across the table and touch my arm. "I didn't think you'd mind. I honestly thought you knew what was going on."

"You're just lucky I didn't buy into all the flirting. I could have been really hurt right now."

"You're not, though, right?" he asked, studying my face anxiously. "You're not heartbroken or angry or anything, are you?" I rolled my eyes and he gave a short, mirthless laugh. "Right. No. Good."

"But I might have been." I didn't want to let him off the hook too easily. It was only luck that had kept him from hurting me—I had completely misread the situation.

"But you aren't."

"But I might have been." I let it drop. "So why did Crystal tell your dad tonight?"

"God knows. She'd been a wreck all week, kept saying she was sick of hiding things, that she couldn't stand to sneak around anymore."

"Did you feel the same way?"

"Not really. I mean, I didn't like sneaking around either, but it's not like we could run off together. I'm eighteen. She has a baby. Realistically . . ." He stopped.

Yeah, it was absurd.

"Anyway, she'd had a lot of wine tonight, and got mad at my dad about something and started going on about how he was never home and I was more of a husband to her than he was and then he was like, 'What are you talking about?' and then . . ." He flinched. "And then she told him exactly what she was talking about. While I just stood there like an idiot, not knowing what to say or do until he turned on me and scared the hell out of me."

"He threw you out?"

"Sort of—he told me to get out of his sight."

"What happens now?"

"Hold on. Text." He pulled his phone out of his pocket and looked at it. "Crystal," he said. "But my dad could be looking over her shoulder, for all I know. I'd better be careful." His thumbs started moving over the screen.

"A little late for careful," I said as I watched him. "Don't you feel bad for him? At all?"

He put down his phone. "If he had been a decent husband, this wouldn't have happened."

"Don't pretend this is all his fault and you're some kind of innocent bystander."

"I'm not saying that."

"Michael's Luke's best friend. He's like my uncle."

He held his hands out and said simply, "I do love him, you know. He's my dad. It kills me that I've hurt him this much. But I don't know what to do about it."

I relented. He was my friend and he was in pain. "You can stay here until you figure it out."

"Don't tell Luke or your mom, okay? You can say my

dad and I had a fight, but don't tell them about Crystal and me. Please?"

I wasn't crazy about hiding things from them, but I also wanted to respect Michael's privacy and let him decide whether or not he wanted to tell his friends, so I agreed.

twenty-seven

I put Aaron in Jacob's room for the night. (Grandma was in the guest room near me, and the other guest room was downstairs, which felt too far away.) "There are teddy bears," I pointed out. "Feel free to hold one if it will help get you through the night."

"I will." He soberly picked out a chubby little blue guy from the pile of stuffed animals and clutched it against his chest. "Thanks, Ellie. You're a good friend."

I said good night, but I couldn't fall asleep for a long time. I was too freaked out, not only by what Aaron had told me, but also by my own stupidity. I'd misread every signal he'd sent me over the past couple of months. All he had wanted to do was confide in me about this ridiculous affair he was having, but I'd assumed the big secret was that he was in love with *me*. God, I was an idiot. And a narcissist.

At least no one knew. That was the one thing that

made it endurable: I'd kept my assumptions to myself. It was an argument for never telling anyone anything ever.

If only that were a viable way to live one's life.

I was also relieved that Heather hadn't ever come on too strong with him. She didn't have anything to be publicly embarrassed about either. I felt bad though. I never should have encouraged her to like him. But at least he didn't know she did, and I'd tell her the truth about him and Crystal as soon as possible—I had promised not to tell Mom and Luke, but I hadn't promised not to tell *her*. She might be disappointed but it was no huge tragedy—they'd never even kissed.

I fell asleep eventually, and woke up early the next morning to the terrifying sight of Grandma's face near mine. "There's someone moving around in Jacob's room!" she hissed in my ear, and I sat up with my heart pounding before I remembered that I knew who was in there.

I explained the bare minimum—that Aaron had come over and we'd talked until it had gotten so late that he'd just stayed over.

"I don't know if your mother would approve of boys sleeping over on school nights," Grandma said.

"Which part is the problem?" I asked. "The boy part or the school-night part?"

"You tell me," she said with a broad wink.

"Aaron and I are just friends. Really." There were few

things I could say with as much sincerity and certainty.

"Well, at least you put him in a different room." She winked conspiratorially. "I don't think I have to tell your mother about this." Then she went downstairs to scramble some eggs before Aaron and I left for school.

I never ate much in the morning—I just wasn't all that hungry—but for her sake I forced down a couple of forkfuls before I pleaded lack of time and raced out the door. Aaron didn't even pretend to eat anything, just told Grandma he was sorry but he couldn't face any food right then. He looked pretty exhausted, and I doubted he had slept much, if at all. He promised to let me know what his plans were later that day, and then we took off in our separate cars to go to our separate schools.

I ran into Ben on the way to my car at the end of the day. We were talking about whether we should cap the amount people could spend on gifts for the holiday donations, when Arianna appeared and pounced on us.

"You look so cute!" she said to me, shaking my arm in a friendly way. "I love love that outfit! You have to take me shopping—I'm such a clothing loser."

"You always look good," I said.

"That was so much fun the other day," she said. "Going to your house. It's such a great house. Ben was just saying we should wrap the donated gifts there."

"It's a good location for everyone," Ben explained.

"Let's just meet here at school," I said. "Keep it easy."

"But then we can't do it on a weekend," Arianna said. "And weekdays are so busy. Oh, there's Lulu! She still has my bio notes—be right back." She darted off across the parking lot.

I turned to Ben and lowered my voice. "Look, I don't want to sound mean or anything, but Arianna kind of snooped around my house, taking photos and looking at stuff, and I'd rather she didn't come over again. It's fine for just the two of us to meet there, but not if she's coming. Okay?"

Ben's jaw tightened. He said icily, "Yeah, okay, whatever. We can just do everything at school from now on." He took a step away and turned his back on me.

Ugh. I was hoping he would agree that Arianna had been pushy and inappropriate, but I guess he felt some kind of loyalty to her since he'd brought her onto the committee in the first place. Now I wished I hadn't said anything. I tried to backpedal. "It's not a big deal or anything." I forced a smile even though he wasn't even looking at me. "I mean, maybe she just got lost in the house." *Yeah, so lost she confused upstairs and downstairs. Happens all the time.* "But actually it probably is easiest to just meet at school anyway."

"Whatever."

Arianna pranced back to us. "They're in her locker. She's going to get them. So . . . what did I miss?"

"Nothing." Ben bit off the word like he was going to chew it for a while. "Good-bye, Ellie."

I scurried to my car, relieved to get away and annoyed at myself for confiding in him. I glanced back at them as I got in my car. Their heads were together and they were both looking in my direction. This was Not Good.

I felt unnerved enough to call Riley from the car and tell her the whole story. I needed someone to reassure me that I hadn't done anything wrong. But as soon as I said, "So I said something to Ben about how she'd snooped around—" she cut me off and said, laughing, "Oh, shit, Ellie, why did you do that? You know they're going out, right?"

I almost crashed the car. "What? Are you serious? Of course I didn't know. Neither of them ever said. No one told me!"

"It's been all over her Instagram recently—tons of photos of the two of them together, kissing and stuff. It's only been official for like a week, but she'd been working on him for a while."

"Crap," I said. "No wonder he took her side."

"Don't worry. She's desperate to be friends with you. She'll probably let it go."

"Yeah," I said. "Someone who's desperate to be friends with me won't mind at all that I said I never wanted her in my house again."

Riley laughed like I'd said something funny.

twenty-eight

The second I got home from school, Grandma was on top of me, asking me to tell her all about my day, pushing some pockmarked quinoa cookies on me—"no eggs, no gluten, no sugar, just a bit of agave!"—and asking me what we should do for fun. I said I needed to get some homework done before I did anything else. She told me I was a good girl and let me escape to my room, where I had every intention of keeping my word and doing homework . . . as soon as I had talked to Heather and flushed the cookies down the toilet.

"I just found out that three other kids from my school applied early to Elton," Heather moaned the second we could see each other's faces on our laptop screens. "And they're all smarter than me."

"Don't let it worry you. It'll be fine. Plus I have something really important to tell you."

"Something good?"

"Not really. But it's intense. You have to promise not to tell anyone else."

"What is it?"

"Seriously. No one can know. This isn't one of those *Tell everyone you tell not to tell anyone else* kinds of situations. This is a *You will never be my friend again if you tell anyone* deal."

"I promise," she said. "Seriously. No one hears anything from me. Are you okay?"

"I'm fine. I'm more worried about you."

Her eyes grew big. "Why? What?"

I took a deep breath and ripped off the Band-Aid quickly. "Aaron Marquand is having an affair with his stepmother. His father found out last night."

Her mouth dropped open. She snapped it shut. "Are you serious? Oh my God!"

"Crazy, right? I had no idea. I mean, obviously or I would have told you."

"Wow," she said. "You hear about these things but you don't think they happen in real life."

"I guess they do." I studied her face, relieved to see that she looked more bemused than upset. "So you're okay? I was nervous about telling you."

"Why? Am I that big a prude?"

"No. I just meant . . . you know. Because you liked

him and I kind of encouraged you. I swear I had no idea about this."

She blinked. "What are you talking about? When did I ever say I liked Aaron? He's cute and nice and all but I've never thought about him all that much. He's a little manic for me."

"You don't have to feel embarrassed about it. You had no way of knowing."

"I'm not embarrassed," she said, almost irritably. "I just never said I liked him."

"Yes, you did! In my kitchen! We were talking about Aaron like a week ago and you asked me whether I liked him and when I said I didn't, you said you did but you were worried he was too sophisticated for you. Remember? And I said—" I stopped. "Why are you laughing?"

"Because you totally misunderstood me!" She was almost helpless with giggles. "That's so funny. We had that whole conversation and we were talking about completely different people. I meant *George*. Did you seriously think I meant Aaron?"

"You said something about how cute he was, and he'd just left the room—"

"So had George," she said. "That must have been why you got confused! That's so funny."

"You said he was cute," I repeated. "So I thought—"

"I happen to think George *is* cute, even if you don't. I like nerdy guys. I thought you knew that about me."

"I guess." I was too bewildered to argue. I was having trouble processing this.

"Why would I ever say that *Aaron* was too sophisticated for me?"

"I don't know." I tried to collect my thoughts. "I guess it does make more sense the other way. George probably *is* too sophisticated for you. He's definitely too old for you."

"He's only a couple of years older. My dad is six years older than my mom."

"It's different when you're middle-aged."

"But they were like eighteen and twenty-four when they met!"

"Oh. Right."

"A lot of girls date older guys," she added. "I feel the same way you do about high school boys. They're lame. George is like a real person—that sounds stupid, but you know what I mean. And he's so nice. We text sometimes, you know."

I shook my head slowly. "No, I didn't know that."

"You were the one who told me I should text him!" She put her hand to her mouth, laughing. "Oh, wait—I guess you meant I should text Aaron. Well, I thought you meant I should text George, so I did. Just a couple of times, telling him how worried I felt about college stuff and how my college counselor is totally burned-out and overwhelmed." She grinned and her dimple carved a comma into her right cheek. "So he said he'd help me figure out some new choices if Elton doesn't work out. I didn't even ask him to. It was totally his idea."

"Has he asked you out?" My body tensed up as I waited for the answer. Heather could easily end up hurt—George was way out of her league, even if they could surmount the age difference. He was smarter, funnier, and . . . I didn't even know what the word was, but he understood people in a way she didn't.

"Well . . . he did say we should get together once I hear from Elton, either to celebrate or to figure out my next step. I think he feels like he needs an excuse to see me, like he can't just show up at my house. Which I get." She tucked a lock of hair behind her ear. "There's my mom for one thing . . . but also it's probably weird for him that I'm still in high school. We're really alike, though."

Heather's cheerful obtuseness had never annoyed me so much before. "Really? I wouldn't have said that at all. You guys seem really different to me."

She opened her big blue eyes wide. "Are you kidding me? Haven't you noticed when we're all together how he and I agree about almost everything? *You're* the one who's always on the other side of arguments. And we work so well together—he never makes me feel stupid."

She shot me a sideways look. "Unlike other people I could name."

"Is that directed at me?"

She flung her hand out. "You're doing it right now—making me feel like I'm too stupid for someone like George to even notice."

"I didn't say you were too stupid. I said you were too young."

"And unsophisticated, which is just another way of saying stupid!"

"No, actually, it's another way of saying *young*."

"I don't see what your problem is. If he likes me and I like him—" She stopped. "Unless you like him, too? Is that what the problem is here?"

"George?" I dismissed that thought with a ripple of my fingers. "Of course not. He's my SAT tutor, Heather. And he's Jonathan's brother, and Jonathan's like *my* brother, which makes him like a brother to me—"

"It's the transitive property," she said brightly. "See how much math I remember, thanks to him?"

"Plus he's just not . . . I don't know. I don't want to be mean, but he's just such a *George*."

"That's what I like about him," she said with a little smile. "But you and I have always had different taste in guys. Anyway, that's how I thought you felt. I just wanted to make sure, since you were being so weird about it."

"I wasn't being weird. I just don't want you to get hurt."

"Why would I get hurt?" she said. "George is the nicest guy I've ever met."

"Yeah." A pause. "You really think he likes you?"

"I do," she said, her face turning pink. "I know that sounds conceited, but . . . he kept looking at me last time. Not in a gross way. In a nice way."

"You did look amazing." I remembered how much care she had put into her outfit and makeup that night. "Is that why you were so dressed up?"

"Maybe," she said, a little coyly. "But let's not talk about this anymore. I don't want to jinx it."

And she wondered why I questioned her sophistication.

I ended our chat as soon as I gracefully could and just sat there for a while, paralyzed. I couldn't believe I'd misread yet another situation. My ego had taken a lot of pounding over the last twenty-four hours, all of it deserved.

I tried to remember the original conversation with Heather. I could have sworn she'd said she liked Aaron. Plain as that. But clearly she *hadn't*. I should have felt relieved about that, since it meant her heart wasn't broken by the news he'd been in love with his stepmother all this time, but I didn't; I felt annoyed.

Heather could drive me crazy, I reminded myself. She

was sweet and loyal and trustworthy and dear in all sorts of ways, but she could also be a little misguided and clueless. Like saying that George was interested in her . . . That was ridiculous, wasn't it? I would have noticed if he liked her.

But *would* I have? Clearly, my radar sucked: I hadn't realized that Heather liked *him*. I'd thought all her little secret smiles were for Aaron. And I'd also thought that Aaron liked *me*—it never even occurred to me for a second that he might be in love with someone else. And why hadn't I picked up on the fact that Ben and Arianna were a couple, even though they'd driven over to my place together?

Apparently I wasn't the sensitive and intuitive Queen of Emotional Subtleties I'd always thought I was.

But still . . . Wouldn't George have flirted with Heather if he liked her?

Well, maybe not *flirted*. George wasn't the flirtatious type. The thought of him doling out little meaningful looks and touching her lightly on her arm . . . No. Definitely not.

But he would have signaled his interest in some way, right? Like . . . you know . . . finding excuses to work with her one-on-one. Being patient and encouraging, no matter how anxious she got. Softening his voice whenever he talked to her. Smiling at her more than at me. Much more than at me.

All of which he had done. Repeatedly.

I twined my finger around one of my curls so tightly that it hurt my scalp when I tried to extricate it. I swore out loud.

And what about the bunny? That stupid little stuffed bunny? He gave *her* one and not me. I had forgotten about that and Heather never even knew that I hadn't gotten one. But I bet if I told her now, she'd see it as one more sign that he liked her.

And maybe she'd be right.

Maybe the age difference didn't bother him. Maybe the intelligence difference—because there *was* one; he was a lot smarter than Heather, even if it was mean of me to think it—didn't bother him either. Maybe he just liked that she was upbeat and good-natured and easygoing and honest and sweet—all the things *I* liked about her.

Plus she wasn't a spoiled, conceited, narcissistic brat. Next to me—and he'd only ever seen her next to me— she had to look even better. Nicer, anyway.

And why shouldn't he like her? Why did it seem so wrong to me?

It was the age difference. He was just too old for her, even if neither of them saw it that way. Guys that much older only went out with girls that much younger because they wanted to take advantage of them in some way—

No, that was ridiculous. George wasn't about to take advantage of anyone. My mother trusted him. Heather trusted him. *I* trusted him. He was trustworthy.

But still . . . there was an awfully big age difference. Well, not *so* big—less than three years. But he was out of college; she was just going in. That was weird. Not unheard of. But weird.

I wished I had gotten Heather to see how awkward it would be for them to date. Would a guy his age really want to go to a high school prom? Of course not. And would she want to go to parties where everyone else was over twenty?

Yeah, she probably would. I would. I often *did*, with my parents.

Not that that was the point. The point was that it would be a mistake for the two of them to date. I couldn't even imagine it. Heather was so clearly wrong for George. I could see why she had a crush on him but not how he could crush back.

Wait a second—*could* I see how she could have a crush on him?

I fiddled with another curl as I thought about that for a moment, absently stretching it across my upper lip, mustache-like.

George was sort of cute, if you liked the hipster-nerd

type (minus the hipster). There was nothing actually *wrong* with him. He was no Aaron Marquand—no bronzed, blue-eyed young Adonis—but Aaron was a bit of a cliché. There were tons of guys like him on TV with their flat abs and white teeth—Generic Hollywood Dudes.

And George had a better smile than Aaron: Aaron's was mischievous and general, a grin that announced his good humor to the world, but George's was rarer and more personal—if you got a smile from George, it meant something.

I knew this better than anyone; I'd worked hard for some of those smiles.

I'd earned every one I'd gotten.

And that, I decided, was why I didn't want Heather to go out with George: He and his smiles belonged to *me*. He was *my* tutor. It was *my* mother who had hired him. We'd already spent a lot of days working together before I invited Heather to join us, and we had walked on a beach together in Hawaii.

He couldn't belong to Heather instead of to me. He was mine. My tutor. My friend. The brother of my step-father's production company president . . . or whatever the hell Jonathan's title was.

The point was, he belonged to me and to my family, and not to Heather.

But you can't go around telling people not to go out

with other people because they "belonged" to you in some weird way.

So I was just going to have to let whatever was going to happen between the two of them happen. No matter how wrong and unfair it felt to me.

twenty-nine

Aaron let me know by text that he wanted to stay over again at our house that night, but he came back pretty late. I ran out into the hallway when I heard him on the stairs—I'd given him a key and the gate code that morning—and he said, "Hey. Hope I didn't keep you up."

"It's fine." I raised my eyebrows. "I smell Crystal's perfume."

"Nose like a dog. The police should adopt you."

"Where did you see her?"

"My house. I had to pick up some clothes." He raised the duffel bag in his hand. "I tried to get in and out quickly but she was home and wanted to talk."

"What about your dad?"

"He was out. Trust me, I checked."

"What did she say?"

"A bunch of things." He dropped the bag of clothing

on the floor. "Mostly about what a mess their marriage is. Dad refuses to go to couple's therapy and she said she's starting to wonder if they even have anything worth saving."

"What about you and her?"

He stared at the floor for a moment, a muscle flickering in his cheek. Then he looked up and said, "Your father's your father, you know?"

I did know. Not because of my biological father, but because of Luke. "Do you think he'll forgive you?"

"I'm going to go see him this weekend so we can talk. We've texted a little, though, and I think it'll be okay. . . ." His shoulders sagged. "She kept crying tonight. She feels like she's losing everything."

"She had his baby. He'll take care of them."

"Yeah, financially. But it still seems unfair."

"It *is* unfair," I said. "The fallout's going to be much worse for her than for you."

"That's not true," he protested. "I've never felt this miserable before."

I didn't say anything. I believed he was unhappy now. He probably felt guilty and unsettled and anxious. But pretty soon he'd move back in with either Michael or his mom, and soon after that he'd go off to college, and soon after that all of this would feel far away, just some crazy thing that happened during his high school years.

Nothing would really have changed for him.

But Crystal and Mia's life would take a completely different path now.

I patted Aaron on the shoulder and told him to try to get some sleep—and felt grateful I had never actually fallen in love with him. He was a gorgeous mess.

When I got home on Friday, I was surprised to see George's car parked in the gravel circle in front of our house.

I found him in the kitchen, leaning against a counter and chatting with Grandma. He jumped to his feet when he saw me, almost like he'd been caught doing something he shouldn't. "You're home early, aren't you? I thought I'd be gone before you got back."

"My teacher got sick and canceled class. Are you trying to avoid me?"

He flushed. "Of course not," he said. "I just don't want to be the guy who's always underfoot around here."

It's funny: Now that Heather had told me she had a crush on him, I found myself looking at him differently. More closely. Scrutinizing his face to see what she found so attractive about it.

Like everyone else in the universe (except maybe their immediate family), I had always lumped him in

273

with Jonathan as just a Nussbaum-looking kind of guy, but now that I was trying to look at him with Heather's eyes, I could see a lot of differences. George was taller and thinner than his older brother, and his shoulders were broader; he stood up straighter; his hair was thicker; his nose was smaller.

In fact, Heather was right: he *was* kind of cute. Not drop-dead handsome—more the kind of cute that grew on you over time. And it was the unstrained kind of cute—he never seemed to care too much about how he looked, which I liked. There was no gel in his hair; his wardrobe was way more functional than stylish; he had a Timex watch that had probably come from a drugstore; his mother probably still bought his pajamas and boxers—because he was probably uncool enough to wear old-fashioned plaid boxers—

Not that *that* was any of my business.

"I told him he's always welcome to hang out here," Grandma said to me. She was at the table, eating something that looked like a heap of chewed-up and regurgitated raw grains—and knowing her, probably *was*. "He's doing such a good job on your mother's office! Everything is labeled and in its proper place." She swiveled in her chair to look at him. "I'm sad you're almost done—the house feels too big with just me and Lorena rattling around in it during the day. And Ellie and Aaron are really only here at night."

"Aaron's here at night?" George said with an unsettled glance in my direction.

"Oh, yes." Grandma raked her fork contentedly through the piles on her plate. "He's been our sleepover houseguest the last couple of nights." Then she said, "Oops, was I not supposed to tell anyone, Ellie?"

"It's not like it's a secret," I said, uncomfortable with the fact she was making it sound like it was.

"Your parents are okay with that?" George said to me. Then he shook his head. "Sorry. None of my business." He stepped toward the doorway. "I should take off. I'll be back on Monday to finish up the office."

"On Monday?" I said, following him out into the hall and then the foyer. "Why not tomorrow?"

"Your grandmother likes having people around when you're at school," he said. "Might as well wait and come then."

"Okay." He was reaching for the door and I was still a couple of steps behind him so I raised my voice a little to make sure he could hear me. "Heather said if she doesn't get into Elton College, you'll help her figure out where else to apply."

He nodded, his fingers moving on the door handle like they were eager to turn it and be gone. "Right."

"Will you do that for me, too?"

"Sure," he said. "If you want me to. And if I don't have a full-time job by then. But I'm not worried about you."

"That's the difference?" I said. "You *worry* about Heather and not about me? That's why you said you'd do that for her?"

"That's one of the reasons," he said, and slipped out the door.

thirty

Aaron stayed with us until Sunday, when he and his father got together to figure things out. From what Aaron told me later, there were tears and accusations and explanations and apologies and hugs and more tears and more hugs . . . and the end result was pretty much what Aaron had prophesied: blood proved thicker than the wedding band Crystal had worn for a year and a half, and Michael found forgiveness in his heart for his son but not his wife.

He and Aaron moved into a suite at a hotel and left Crystal, Megan, and the baby in the beautiful, big house.

They're working out the details, Aaron texted me, when I hadn't seen him for a few days and wanted to know how it was going. *She'll prob get the house. We'll find somewhere else to live. The Peninsula's nice for now tho.*

You and your dad good?

Good an overstatement but we're ok.

Ever see Crystal?

No. Wouldn't do that to Dad

Too bad he hadn't felt that way about it from the start.

I had kept my word about not telling anyone (other than Heather), but Grandma read a lot of celebrity gossip blogs, and she grabbed me when I walked in the door after school one day and stuck her phone screen in my face.

"Look at this!" she said. "Look at this!"

The headline on the article was:

Music and TV Producer Michael Marquand and Wife Separating

"Is this why Aaron was staying with us?" she said, then—to my relief—continued without waiting for a response. "I don't blame him for wanting to escape. There's nothing worse than being in a house with a fighting couple. Poor kid."

I was happy to have that be the explanation.

Luke and Mom heard about the separation around the same time. Mom mentioned that Michael had called them in London to let them know that he and Crystal were splitting up and that he would tell them more in person. I didn't offer to supply any additional details.

They came home the Saturday before Thanksgiving, and after we'd had dinner and they told me some stories about their trip, Luke left to go see Michael.

"What about Crystal?" I asked Mom after he'd gone. We were tucked up together under the covers in her bed. She was exhausted from the trip and time difference, but wanted to talk. Grandma was putting Jacob to bed. "You going to go see her?"

"Not right away," she said, rubbing her cheek sleepily against her pillow. "I want to enjoy being home for a little while. And also . . ." She sighed. "We really weren't that close. There's always been this wall with her that I couldn't get past. And I don't like the way she stares at Jacob when he's crying—she gives him this cold fish eye and then glares at me like I'm a bad mother."

"You may be projecting," I said.

"Maybe. God knows I can be hypersensitive."

"Besides, you're a much better mother. You know that, right? You actually take care of us. She always seems annoyed when someone hands Mia to her, like she shouldn't be her responsibility."

"At least they've got Megan. It's okay to be a bad mother if you have a good nanny."

"Can I quote you on that?" I asked. "The tabloids would have a field day with it."

"Let that be the worst quote they ever get out of me."

She shifted her legs under the covers. "So what do you think happened with Michael and Crystal? Did Aaron tell you anything about why they're splitting?"

I didn't want to lie to my mother. And I really wanted to talk to her about it. But I had promised to keep Aaron's secret. Of course, if she *guessed*, it wouldn't be my fault.

"I think she maybe had an affair," I said carefully.

Mom seemed suddenly more awake. She wiggled up to a sitting position. "Who with?"

"I think he was a younger guy."

"Younger than her or younger than Michael?"

"Both?" I said it like I wasn't sure; the word was honest, even if my tone wasn't. "But I didn't really want to ask Aaron a lot of questions about it." True enough, right?

"Right. We probably shouldn't pry." A pause. "I met her trainer at the Halloween party—I got a weird vibe from him, like he was a little too comfortable there."

"Interesting," I said. "Now tell me more about London. Did you go to Harrods?"

Luke stayed out late with Michael, and when he got back, he knocked on my door and asked if we could talk.

Michael had told him everything. "I'm confused," Luke said, pacing the floor of my bedroom, his hands thrust in his jeans pockets, deep shadows under his eyes that could have been cast by the dim light or printed there by his exhaustion and the time change. "We all thought the two of you were going out—I mean, at Halloween he couldn't keep his hands off you. That kiss—"

"I know," I said, cutting him off. "Halloween was weird—I guess he was trying to make everyone *think* he and I were going out, to cover up what was really going on—but there's never been anything between us other than friendship. That kiss was basically a joke."

"So I don't have to hate him?"

"Not for my sake. But maybe for Michael's?"

He shook his head. "Michael blames Crystal, not Aaron. Which I get—she was the married adult in the situation." An enormous yawn carved a hole in his face. "God, I'm tired. If you're fine, then I'm going to bed. To *my* bed. I'm so happy to be home."

"Hold on." I smiled my most beguiling smile. "Now that you're back, I have a favor to ask you."

"And fear enters his heart. . . ."

"This one's easy."

"I'll be the judge of that."

"I just need you to call Elton College on Monday and tell them they should accept both me and Heather. I mean, not in those words. You have to be diplomatic about it—just tell them that you're . . . you know . . . who you are . . . and that your stepdaughter and her friend are both applying and then say something like you just wanted to make sure they got our applications and they're complete—or whatever. It probably doesn't really matter *what* you say—just so long as they know that Luke Weston is on the phone. And maybe mention that you'd be willing to perform if I got in there. . . ."

"Ellie . . ." he said, and I could tell from his tone he didn't immediately love the idea. Which meant I'd have to talk him into it.

"It'll take you five minutes," I said. "Maybe less. They just need to hear your voice."

"Would you even want to go to a college that only let you in because someone famous called?"

"It's what happened with high school, right? Coral Tree let me in after they saw you—"

"You were a good candidate," he said. "Straight As at your middle school and you rocked those ISEEs. *That's* why they let you in. I didn't ask them for any special consideration."

"Yeah, but you went on the tour and they got excited."

"I went on the tour because I wanted to see the school. Not to impress them."

I clasped my hands together and shifted to my knees. I couldn't believe he was saying no. "Please, Luke. You have to. It could make the difference between getting in and not."

"Your scores are incredible and so's your GPA," he said. "You'll get in on your own—if not there, then somewhere else—and that's a lot better than getting in because you have a famous relative."

I let my hands drop. "It's not me I'm worried about," I said. "It's Heather."

"Why?"

"She's just . . ." I stopped. Then I said reluctantly, "Her scores and her grades aren't great."

"Then maybe she *shouldn't* get in," Luke said. "If there are stronger students, is it really fair for her to get in over them because she knows me? Wouldn't that be a lousy way for college admissions to work?"

"Oh, don't get all idealistic on me," I said, irritable because I did kind of agree with him. But not enough to back down. "People pull strings all the time. So why not us?"

"Because it's wrong," he said. "And because I have faith my brilliant girl will get in without my help. And her friend will, too—if she deserves to. Good night, Ellie." He left.

I dropped back onto my bed, now truly worried about Heather's chances of getting in early. I had banked so much on this one phone call, sure that Luke would make it for me. He always did what I wanted. I was in shock that he'd refused. And kind of embarrassed that I'd asked.

I was beginning to regret pushing Heather so hard to apply there with me. Now that I didn't have any way to actually help her, I was scared I might have steered her right into the path of a painful rejection.

The next morning Mom wouldn't stop talking about Aaron and Crystal (Luke had filled her in on the situation) until I finally lost patience and said, "You seem a little too obsessed with this whole younger-man thing. Luke getting too long in the tooth for you?"

"Stop it," she said. "I'm not obsessed with it. I'm horrified by it."

Grandma was in the kitchen with us, mixing some hot grain cereal at the stove and looking not unlike a witch stirring a cauldron in her long purple bathrobe. She said, "Every married woman fantasizes about sleeping with a single young man."

"No, they don't!" Mom said.

"They're just not honest about it." Grandma rapped her spoon on the side of the pot to clear it. "People aren't truthful about their emotions. That's what gets everyone in trouble. If we can recognize that even our worst thoughts are natural, we don't have to act on them. Repression causes bad behavior. Everyone knows that."

"I'm repressing something right now," Mom muttered.

thirty-one

I fell asleep trying to get some homework done that afternoon. When I came downstairs a little while later, still groggy, Mom was searching through a kitchen drawer. "Why can't I ever find a pen when I need one?" she said. "I buy them. And then they disappear."

I said, "Hey, George," with a yawn. "Didn't know you'd be here." He was standing near the kitchen table, where Grandma was sitting with Jacob on her lap, the two of them playing a game together on the iPad. "I thought the office was all done."

"He's running a couple of errands for me," Mom said. "As soon as I make a list. Which I would do if I had a pen."

"You could just text me the list," George said.

"Good idea. Why don't I ever think of that?" She glanced around. "And . . . I left my phone upstairs. Hold on." She ran out of the kitchen.

"Efficiency is not her middle name," I said.

He flashed a bland smile and turned to Grandma. "So when do you go back to Philadelphia?"

"Friday," she said. "I'll be happy to get back to my regular routine, but I'm going to miss my time with this little girl. We've had fun together, haven't we, Ellie?"

"Totally," I said, and plunked myself down in the chair next to her. I looked up at George. "We really did."

"I'm glad," he said, and this time his smile was more sincere.

Mom came back into the kitchen, waving a pen. "I found one on the whatchamacallit—credenza—and saved myself a flight of stairs. Okay, now first I want you to go to Barnes and Noble—" She scribbled the words *Overcoming Autism* on the back of an envelope. "Look for this book—it'll be in the special needs section for parents. If you see any other books with *autism* or *Asperger's* in the title that look good, grab those, too."

"Why are you buying those?" I asked.

"Because I want to read them. And then, George, I need you to go to the Apple Store—my car phone charger broke. I need a new one." She wrote that on the list and then told him to stop at a wine store and buy a good bottle of wine for them to take as a hostess gift to some party they were going to the following night. "You need anything, Ellie? Mom?"

"I need something fun to read," I said.

"You know what you want?" George asked.

"Not yet."

"Text me when you do and I'll look for it if I'm still there."

"Or you could get it on the iPad," Mom said.

"I like real books," I said. "And I'm in the mood to browse. I'll go with you to the bookstore, George."

"I've got to do all these other errands . . ."

"I'll do them with you." I wanted to spend some time with him, figure out whether he really did like Heather or not—maybe I could get him to say something about her while we were out together.

"Okay," he said. "If you really want to."

In the car, I kept glancing at him. He was being very quiet. Polite and not unfriendly. But quiet.

I said, "It's getting dark so early these days."

He agreed that it was.

Then we were silent again.

His voice, when he spoke again, was surprisingly gentle. "I don't know how to say this, but I feel like I need to say something. . . ."

"What?" Oh, God. Was he about to tell me how much he liked Heather? I'd thought I wanted to know, but now I had a sudden overwhelming desire to plug my ears and hum so I wouldn't have to hear it.

"It's just . . ." He glanced over at me and then back

at the road. "Jonathan filled me in on the Marquand situation. Luke told him, and he knows how close I am to your family and felt I should know, too. I hope it's okay."

"It's fine." I was relieved that he wasn't talking about Heather, but not exactly thrilled with this topic either. Why was life such a cringe-fest? "So . . . ?"

"I just wanted to make sure you were okay."

"Okay? Why wouldn't I be? I mean, it's sad that they're separating and all that but—"

"I know the *whole* story," he repeated. "Even the part about Aaron and Crystal. How they were—" He cut himself off and started again. "What he was doing to his father." Quick glance at me again. "And to you."

"He wasn't doing anything to *me*."

"Come on," he said. "I know you want to defend him, but sneaking around with Crystal when he was going out with you—"

I stared at him, torn between horror and amusement. "Aaron and I were never going out! Never. We were always just friends."

"That's a little hard to believe."

"Because he was all over me at Halloween?"

"And other times."

"It was all a mislead—so people wouldn't notice that he and Crystal were obsessed with each other."

His eyebrows drew together, in confusion, not anger.

"But you were always together. He was always over here. Spending nights when your parents were gone—"

"Because his father had thrown him out! For sleeping with his stepmother!" I bounced in my seat, frustrated, desperate for the world—or at least George—to understand the situation. I was tired of explaining it and tired of being seen as some sort of lovesick punching-bag. "I felt sorry for him. I barely even saw him when he was here—he slept in Jacob's room and didn't come back until late each night. I swear to you I'm not the slightest bit heartbroken or anything like that. I just feel bad for all of them. And relieved I'm not involved."

He didn't say anything for a moment. Just gazed through the windshield, his forehead creased. Like something hadn't computed right, and he was running new figures through his head. Then he said, "You two always seemed pretty cozy together."

"Yeah, well, that should have been a giveaway right there—no chemistry. Just coziness." I gave a short laugh. "Trust me, if we'd actually liked each other, there would have been a lot more awkwardness."

"Good point." He rubbed his forehead with the back of his wrist. "I was pretty far off base."

"It's okay. Luke went there, too. It's that stupid Halloween party—Aaron fooled everyone." I heaved an exaggerated sigh. "I just hope this doesn't happen to me *every* time a guy pretends to be in love with me to cover up the fact he's actually sleeping with his stepmother. It could get old."

He laughed, and things felt normal again. I was relieved that the weird tension between us had been dispelled. But also oddly let down. There had been something electric about that tension—something that made me feel like we were forging into some new territory together. But now we were back to being just plain old George and Ellie.

At least he seemed willing to talk to me again.

We split up at the bookstore. I went all the way up to the third floor to look at the fiction but I felt restless and couldn't focus. I stared at the spines, but I couldn't make sense out of any of the titles, so I wandered around the floor aimlessly for a little while, then rode the escalator back down.

I found George in the parenting section, searching through some shelves. "Oh, hi," he said, standing up. "That was fast. You find anything?"

"No. I'll get something later. Are you done?"

"I guess so." He picked up a small stack of books.

I wanted coffee, so after he checked out, we wandered over to the store's Starbucks.

"I'll get us a table," I said, taking the books from him. "Get me a vanilla Frappuccino. Extra whipped cream. And some kind of muffin."

"You sure you don't want to just mainline a bunch of

sugar packets?" But he got in line.

I was leafing through one of the books he'd just bought when he brought his coffee and my muffin to the table. "They're still making your Frappuccino," he said.

I looked up. "This is unreal."

"It always takes a few minutes."

"Not that. This." I held up the book. "Have you looked at this? At any of them?"

He sat down. "Just the titles and covers. Why does your mom want books on autism anyway?"

"Seriously?" I said. "You can't guess?"

"Because of Jacob?"

I nodded.

"I kind of figured, but no one's ever mentioned it before."

"Did you think that Jacob might be autistic?" I asked. "Before Mom asked you to get these books?"

He hesitated, then said, "My cousin's daughter has Asperger's. Jacob kind of reminds me of her sometimes. But what do I know? Has he been diagnosed?"

I shook my head. "The speech therapist raised it as a possibility, that's all. But I'm kind of freaking out here—I just picked this book up and started reading . . . and it's like they're describing him. Like right here, it says that some autistic kids stare at fans. I've seen Jacob do that a million times. Other stuff, too, like wiggling fingers in front of his eyes . . . or how he hates to make eye contact." I shut the book and dropped it on top of the others. "I think maybe Mom's right to be worried."

"Maybe. But don't panic or anything. My cousin's daughter is totally great. She's a little quirky, but in a good way."

"Does she do therapy?"

"Tons of it." He took a sip of coffee. "There's a clinic near them that they go to that my cousin says is great. I could get the name for your mom—it's in New York but they'd probably be willing to talk to her and they might know of a good place near here."

"Thanks. I think Mom wants to start looking into stuff like that, but Luke's really opposed to it."

"Why?"

"He thinks it's wrong to slap a label on Jacob. He says people on the Westside are way too quick to—" I stopped because George had suddenly jumped to his feet. "Um . . . did I offend you?"

"I think I heard them call your name. Hold on." He crossed the room and came back with my Frappuccino, which he put in front of me with a wrapped straw.

I thanked him and he sat back down and took another sip of his coffee. "What do you think I should do?" I flicked at the books. "Mom and Luke are in such different places about this."

"Maybe Luke would be willing to at least read one of the books? The more information he has, the more likely he is to see what she sees."

"He'll just get annoyed if Mom asks him to."

"Then *you* ask him."

"Why would that help?"

"Because no one can say no to you."

I thought about that a moment, as I sucked sweet vanilla goo up through my straw. I swallowed and said, "Do you mean that in a *you're too charming for anyone to say no to* sort of way or a *you're spoiled and they give you whatever you want* sort of way?"

"Does it matter?"

"My ego says yes."

"Then for the sake of your ego, let's go with the charm thing."

That wasn't a satisfying response. I picked at the muffin, but it had blueberries in it and I didn't like blueberries. I should have been more specific, but I'd kind of assumed George would know what I liked.

thirty-two

As we ran the other errands, we talked more about the Jacob situation. When we were in the car, I read bits out loud from the books we'd bought, and then in the stores, we discussed the things that reminded us of Jacob—like the delayed language—and the things that didn't, like how a lot of these kids avoided being touched, and Jacob loved being in our arms.

Nothing seemed obvious except, we agreed, that it couldn't hurt for Mom and Luke to bring Jakie to an expert who could evaluate him.

When we were finally heading home, I suddenly felt the full weight of what we were talking about. The books made it all seem very real. "I just want him to be okay," I said, rolling my head sideways to look at George as he drove.

"He will be," he said. "He *is*. He's smart and adorable and sweet. What's not okay about that? And your mom is willing to do whatever needs to be done to help him."

"I'll try to talk Luke into being more supportive."

"You'll succeed," he said. "You could talk anyone into anything."

"Not really. I—" My phone buzzed, interrupting me. I glanced at it. "Heather," I said, and put the phone away without texting back.

"How's she doing?"

"You don't know? She said you guys text sometimes."

He raised his eyebrows. "She did? I think we've exchanged one text since you took the SATs. Maybe two."

"That's weird. She said it was more."

He shrugged and I studied his face for some reaction to the mention of Heather. There wasn't any. I pushed harder, suddenly desperate to know for sure whether he was indifferent or interested in her. "It's just . . . I think she might kind of like you." She had told me not to say anything to him but that was when I thought she was talking about Aaron, so it didn't count, right? "And she seemed to think you might be interested back. Are you?"

"Are you being serious?" he asked warily. "Or just finding a new way to tease me?"

"I'm serious."

"I think she's a nice kid," he said slowly.

"You know what I mean."

"Yeah, then no. I want to help her with the college stuff but that's all. I'm sorry if I gave her any other impression." We were at my house. He punched in the code and we waited for the gate to swing open. "Do you think I need to do anything about it?"

"Nah, you're good," I said, suddenly feeling very cheerful. "It's nothing you did. She gets a lot of crushes on teachers and people like that. She gets over them." As we pulled into the driveway, I said, "We're not *that* much younger than you, you know. Just a few years."

"I know," he said. "It's not necessarily an age thing. It's more who she is. I just could never see her that way. It's not like . . ." He stopped talking as he put the car in park. He turned the engine off, avoiding my eagerly curious gaze.

"Not like what?"

"Nothing." He opened his car door and got out.

I jumped out my side and came around the car, meeting him by the trunk. I put my hand on his arm to keep him from opening it. "Wait. Not like what?"

"Nothing. Don't forget the books."

"You were going to say it's not like the way it is with me, weren't you?" My heart was thumping wildly in my chest. Leaping and thumping. I felt sick and excited. And suddenly enlightened.

Maybe I hadn't been jealous of Heather just because

George was my tutor. Maybe I had been jealous of Heather because she said he liked her, and I didn't want him to like anyone—except me.

George opened his mouth and closed it. His beautiful dark-green, dark-gray eyes—they *were* beautiful, even if I'd never admitted it to myself before—avoided mine as he said, "Ellie—"

My fingers pressed into his arm. "Just admit it. That's what you were going to say. You know I'm not going to leave you alone until you do."

"Man, you're pushy," he said.

"I know."

"And conceited."

"What else?"

He stared at my hand on his arm and said, "And if someone walks into a room that you're in, he's not going to notice Heather. Or anyone else, for that matter." He passed his free hand over his forehead like it ached, then said in one big rush, "Or what time it is or whether there was something he was supposed to be doing in there or where he is or what his name is."

A thrill of pleasure shot through me. "Someone?" I said. "Meaning anyone? Or someone specific?"

"We need to go inside." But he didn't move.

"Not yet."

"You think you can order people around," he said. "You're overbearing and dictatorial."

"Are you still listing things that are wrong with me?"

"The last act of a desperate man," he said. Then, so quietly I could barely hear him: "I thought you were in love with Aaron."

"Never. Not even for a second."

"It doesn't matter." He shook his head as he carefully slid his arm out from under my grasp. "I shouldn't have said anything. Your parents trust me. I'm supposed to be tutoring you."

"Oh, for God's sake," I said. "You're only a few years older than me. Aaron slept with his *stepmother*. This is nothing."

"Yeah, Aaron's not exactly a role model."

"You really hate him, don't you?"

"Not a big fan," he admitted.

"Because you've been jealous of him. Because of me." I grinned right up into his face—the thought delighted me so much I couldn't not grin right up into his face.

A very small, reluctant smile played on his lips. "That may have influenced me slightly. But he's still a selfish jerk."

"Admit you were jealous of him." I took his hand and threaded my fingers carefully through his. He let me do what I wanted, watching me silently, his fingers tense and taut in mine. It felt daring and almost wrong to touch him like that—but also thrilling. I wasn't about to stop. "It's too late to go back to just being my tutor," I said. "Now I know you like me. I didn't before, because you have a strange way of showing it. Always criticizing me—"

"You need to be criticized," he said. "You're spoiled. Your family lets you get away with everything. And Heather idolizes you and the world fawns over you and Aaron is even more spoiled than you are, which is saying a lot—"

"You adore me, don't you?"

"But you're not hopeless. Someone just needs to shove you in the right direction now and then."

"Yeah," I said dreamily. "You should shove me. Except not literally."

"I'll say this for you." He gazed at our entwined hands. "You take criticism better than anyone I know."

"Only when it comes from you."

"And why's that?" he asked in a suddenly unsteady voice.

I moved a step closer. So close I could feel the warmth coming off his body. "Are you trying to get me to say something nice to you? Don't you think you're being a little needy?"

"I've said nice things to *you*."

"One nice thing. In the middle of a lot of mean things. You just called me spoiled."

"You haven't answered my question." He tugged on my hand and I came even closer. Our bodies were almost touching. From this close, he seemed surprisingly tall. But then, I probably seemed surprisingly short.

I tilted my head back. "I forgot what it was," I said, feeling very distracted by the way his fingers were moving up my arm, pulling me against him.

He put his mouth near my ear and said softly, "Why don't you mind it when I criticize you?"

The breath of his words on my ear made me shiver. "Because you're the only person whose opinion matters to me?"

"That's got to be an exaggeration."

"Yes," I said, keeping my face angled up but closing my eyes because all this closeness was making me a little dizzy. "It probably is. But only a slight one."

His arms went around me and tightened. I gasped a little, not because they were too tight—just because they were there. "What now?" he whispered.

"I don't know. This is weird."

"Too weird?" His arms instantly dropped down.

I opened my eyes so I could look at him. So I could look at *George*—the guy whose approval and instruction had come to mean everything to me without my knowing how or when, and who definitely had more than approval and instruction in his eyes right now. "No," I said. "I like weird."

"It's not too late to stop this."

"Oh, yes, it is," I assured him, and I went up on

tiptoes so I could put my lips on his and end the uncertainty. I don't like uncertainty. Or waiting around for other people to do things I'm perfectly capable of doing myself.

I'd never kissed anyone before. I'd never wanted to. A couple of guys had tried to kiss *me* back in middle school, in the back rooms and corners of parties, but I always pushed them away. And in high school, I had avoided even flirting with anyone. Aaron had landed that one theatrical kiss at the party, but it didn't count. So pressing my mouth against someone else's—this was a new experience.

Which meant it was exciting and scary—and also lovely and ridiculous and forbidden and delicious—everything all at once, and also nothing all at once because I had closed my eyes again, which made everything disappear except the warmth of his mouth against mine and the gentle shock when our tongues touched and the feeling of wanting more and more and more and not wanting it ever to end and wanting more and feeling too much and the clutching of our fingers against each other's arms and backs and shoulders and the wanting more and more and more until my brain felt like it was going to explode with both having and wanting so much.

It was like being overfed and hungry at the same time. I'd never felt anything like it before.

I didn't hear the gate or the car motor—just the sudden loud spray of gravel close behind us. We jumped back, hastily releasing each other as Luke drove into the four-car garage.

But instead of going directly into the house, he came back out to the driveway and squinted at us.

"Hey, guys. What are you doing out here?" The casual tone would have been reassuring, except it was arguably a little *too* casual.

Which meant he'd seen us before we'd broken apart.

I said, "We were just on our way in. We have to get the bags."

"Yes," George said. "The bags." His eyes sought out mine, a little desperately. Luke was his brother's boss. And he was *Luke*. And he'd seen us kissing.

"All right," Luke said easily. "I'll see you two inside." But he kept glancing back at us as he went into the house.

George got the bags out of the trunk, while I retrieved the books from the front seat. "Do you think he's okay with this?" he asked as we went up to the front door.

"He'll have to be," I said. My hands were shaking, but it had nothing to do with fear.

We carried our purchases into the kitchen. Mom and Grandma and Luke were all in there. They fell silent the moment we entered.

"I think we got everything," George said.

"I'm sure you did," Luke said, and Grandma giggled.

"Thank you, George," Mom said with a reproving look at her own mother. "You too, Ellie."

"You're welcome," George said, and there was an awkward silence.

"We're going to go get frozen yogurt," I said suddenly.

"We are?" George said. Then, "Right. Yes. Let's go."

We said good-bye and crept out of the room. Luke murmured something we couldn't hear, and all three of them laughed from behind us.

"Your face is bright red," I told George as he held the front door open for me.

"I can't imagine why," he said.

thirty-three

Outside, I said, "We don't have to get frozen yogurt. That was just a panic plan. We could go . . . I don't know . . ." A sideways glance. "Maybe your place?"

"I like the frozen yogurt plan," he said, opening the passenger door and gesturing inside. "I need a little time to process all this. You work fast."

"You work slowly," I said, and climbed into the car.

We filled big cups with frozen yogurt and he paid for them, which may have been gallantry or may have been because I'd forgotten to bring my wallet. "You do this to all the guys, don't you?" he said, carrying the cups to the table.

"Only the ones I want to take advantage of."

But when we sat down at a table and I lifted a spoon-ful of yogurt to my mouth, I suddenly didn't want it. "I can't eat right now," I said, dropping my spoon.

"I know." He shoved his own dish away. "I can't either."

I leaned forward. "Tell me."

"What?"

"Everything."

"Everything?" He sat back in his seat and pushed his leg against mine. I pushed back, just as hard. "I was born at Saint Vincent Hospital. . . ."

"Everything that has to do with *me*."

"Yeah, I should have guessed that was what you meant."

I reached out across the table. His hand curved up to meet mine. I said, "Heather thought you liked her because you were always so much nicer to her than to me. And I thought maybe she was right. You need to explain that right now. Why were you so much nicer to her than to me? Why did she rate a stuffed bunny and I didn't?"

"Isn't it obvious?" he said. "I was terrified of showing how I felt about you. You were my boss's daughter and even if that was okay, you already had a boyfriend. A slimy, obnoxious snake of a boyfriend, I might add."

"None of that is true," I said. "He wasn't my boyfriend and he's not a slimy snake."

"You can't deny he's self-centered and selfish."

"Yeah, but so am I—you said so yourself."

He shook his head. "No, you're not. Not really. Not deep down. But I think that's why it bothered me so much when you were mean to your grandmother—I could see how Aaron was changing you, how he was teaching you to only think about yourself, to be just like him."

"In fairness to him, I was *never* all that nice to Grandma," I said. "I mean, until you told me I should be."

"Yeah, that conversation . . ." He smiled at me ruefully. "I thought that was it for our friendship—let alone anything else. I didn't think you'd ever talk to me again. You couldn't get away from me fast enough."

"I was *embarrassed*. You had seen what a jerk I could be."

"I didn't think you were a jerk. Just that you were letting Aaron influence you too much. I felt like I had one last chance to make a difference."

"And then you gave up. You barely talked to me after that."

"What was I supposed to do?"

"Yell at me more?"

"Yes," he said. "Because girls like it so much when guys criticize them."

"I *did*," I said.

He laughed. "No, you didn't. You were good-natured enough to tolerate it, that's all. Which is actually pretty impressive. Most people would have been resentful."

"I liked that you cared whether or not I was a decent human being."

"You *are* a decent human being," he said. "You just forget to be when you're around Aaron."

"Stop blaming him for my defects!"

"It's how I see it."

"Well, you're wrong. I'm defective all on my own. Anyway, if you were worried I'd hate you for criticizing me, you could have thrown in a compliment now and then. Why didn't you ever say anything nice to me?"

"Too dangerous. I didn't want you to guess how I felt. It wasn't safe to look at you too much. Or smile at you too much. Or praise you too much—"

"Let's be honest," I said. "You were never in danger of *that*."

"Probably not," he agreed, and I liked the mischief in his glance.

"So you were nicer to Heather so no one would notice how much you liked me?"

"More or less."

"Then you're just like Aaron," I said triumphantly. "He paid attention to me so no one would notice how much he liked Crystal."

He shifted away, withdrawing his hand from mine. "That was completely different."

"Don't get mad just because I'm right."

"You're not right and I'm not mad." He fingered the end of his spoon, then looked up again. "But I'll admit I don't like being compared to that asshole."

"That asshole is one of my best friends," I said. "You have to learn to like him."

"The sad thing is that I like him better now that I know he had an affair with his stepmother than I did when I thought he was having a perfectly appropriate relationship with you."

"Wow," I said. "You totally lack any moral compass. Which may not be a bad thing." I snuck my hand under the table and touched his leg. "If we're not going to eat our yogurt, can't we just go to your place?"

He rubbed his temple, like his head hurt. "God knows I want to."

"So?"

"I just want to be careful. Go slowly."

"You've already ravished my virgin lips," I said. "It's too late to think twice."

"Your lips weren't virginal. I saw Aaron kiss you, remember?"

"Doesn't count. Neither of us meant it."

"Are you going to say that about every kiss you've ever had?"

"There haven't been any others," I said. "Seriously."

"Oh, God," he said, and rubbed his temple harder.

"That doesn't make me any younger," I pointed out.

"Just more discriminating."

"I guess."

He was going to rub all the way through to his brain pretty soon. I leaned in, trailing my fingers along the top of his thigh, and said, "Come on. I want to be somewhere alone with you. Are you really going to refuse? Why would you do that?"

He studied me for a moment, his eyes narrowed in thought. Then he grabbed the hand that was on his leg and crushed it in his. He said in a low voice, "Half of me wants to take you home and do all sorts of indecent things to you. And the other half wants to beat myself up for even thinking about you like that."

"Let the first half win for now," I suggested. "The second half can come riding in on a white horse later. Or just mind his own damn business."

"I pick B."

"Hold on," I said. "Wait until you've eliminated some of the other answers. Narrow your choices down first and explain to me how you know the answer is B."

"Because it's *right*," he said.

I basically tackled him as soon as we walked through the door of his apartment. I knew if I hesitated even for a second, he'd get all doubty again. (That needs to be a real word, by the way. It's very useful.)

It was a good strategy, even if we almost tripped

trying to make it to the sofa without letting go of each other. Actually, that was kind of fun. We laughed, our lips shaking and sliding against each other, and then got serious again.

He never did get around to beating himself up, although he did occasionally stop kissing me long enough to say, "You sure this is okay?" until I told him *I'd* beat him up if he didn't shut up and stop worrying.

What was funny was how little had really changed between us, even though everything had changed. We were still teasing each other; I was still playing the cocky, overconfident girl; and he was still rolling his eyes at me with a mixture of frustration and barely tolerant affection. I used to see it as sort of a fraternal thing, but now . . .

"Not fraternal at all," I said out loud when we were curled up together on his sofa.

"Excuse me?" he said, pushing himself up on his elbow to look at me.

"Nothing. But I'm curious: How long have you been . . . you know . . . adoring me from afar?"

"Who said anything about adoration?"

"Just answer the question."

"Way too long." He collapsed back down at my side. "You don't want to know."

"In Hawaii?"

"Definitely in Hawaii. Maybe even before. Do you

have any idea how beautiful you are? Or how much fun it is just to be with you?"

"Tell me."

He pulled my head onto his shoulder and pressed it down there, almost roughly. "No. You're conceited enough."

"Never enough." I raised my head and studied his face, then gently traced the line of his nose with my fingertip. It felt almost wicked to do something that intimate. His skin was pale and smooth, with slight purple shadows just under his eyes. It seemed perfect to me.

He lay there with his eyes closed, letting me trail my finger lightly along the outlines of his face. Then he grabbed my hand and pressed it against the side of his cheek. Then he opened his eyes. "Hi," he said.

"Hi," I said, and settled back down next to him, pressed against his side, inside the circle of his arm. Where I belonged.

thirty-four

Eventually he took me home. It was late, so I crept quietly up to my room, assuming everyone was asleep. I was lying on my bed, staring up at the ceiling, too dazed and happy to start getting ready for bed or do anything really, other than gaze at the spinning fan and wonder if the last few hours had been some kind of a dream, when there was a knock on my door and Grandma walked in.

"Well," she said, crossing her arms over her chest.

Nothing—really, nothing—could make me as sure that I wasn't dreaming as the sight of my grandmother in her striped long johns (yellow and green) with her hennaed hair sticking up around her head like a spiky red halo.

"Hi," I said, sitting up. "I didn't know you were still awake."

She came over and settled down next to me.

"Someone's in love! And I know who with."

"It's not exactly a secret."

"He's a good one. I approve."

I bit down on the sarcastic rejoinder I wanted to make—*oh, thank you, because of course I wouldn't dream of dating someone without your approval*—and just said I agreed: he was a good one.

"And now," she said, "we need to talk about condoms."

"Oh, God, no," I said fervently. "Please not now."

She waggled her finger at me. "If you're going to act like an adult, you need to be responsible like an adult."

"Can't I just enjoy kissing a boy for the first time without having to talk about all that? That's all we've done, I swear."

"You'd be surprised how quickly one thing leads to another."

"We both want to take things slowly." George did, anyway. I wasn't so sure and had done my best to break down his defenses that night. I'd almost succeeded. But not quite.

It had been fun trying.

My being impulsive and his being cautious—it was who we were. It felt right even when everything else between us had changed.

"Don't be afraid of sex," Grandma said. "It's good for the body—it revs up your circulation and improves brain function. But you do have to be *careful*. So . . . condoms."

"Got it," I said, deciding it was easiest just to agree with everything she said: arguing would lead to a longer discussion, and I really just wanted to be alone. Almost as much as I didn't want to have a Sex Talk with my grandmother.

"It's good to be practical, but never forget that sex can be spiritual, too," she went on. "There's the tantric approach, of course. And the many positions of the Kama Sutra. And yoga can open you up to better orgasms—but I had to stop doing yoga because of my hip problems. You're lucky you're young."

I nodded, my face blank. *I don't have to listen. I have to sit here, but I don't have to hear what she's saying.*

She nudged my shoulder with hers. "Experiment. I wish I'd experimented more when I was young and my body was like yours."

"Uh-huh," I said.

She put her face close to mine. "Your mother isn't as open-minded as I am," she whispered. "No one was wilder than she was as a teenager, but now she likes to pretend that none of that happened. So don't go to her if you have questions. Come to me." She shifted back. "My mother didn't talk to me openly about sex and it took me decades to learn everything I'm telling you

314

tonight. I want you to be an expert right away. So ask me anything."

"I will," I said. "Only not tonight. I'm really tired."

"Sex gives you energy," she said. "Did you know that? It doesn't work with men—they lose energy with sex. But women gain energy from it. Remember that."

"Yeah, okay," I said, and she smiled and, to my huge relief and with one more pat on my leg, finally left.

I couldn't fall asleep. I just couldn't. Most of it was happy, excited energy, but there was a tiny part of me that felt uneasy—the part that didn't know how I was going to tell Heather that I was totally in love with the guy she had admitted to having a crush on.

Eventually I gave up on sleeping, picked up my phone, and texted George. He was awake, too. We texted for a while. It was ridiculous—we had been together all evening but still had so much to say to each other. Neither of us was the sentimental type, so it wasn't gooey and silly, but we talked about what we should do together tomorrow and the next day and the next and about his frustrations with not having a real job yet and about my anxiety about leaving for college when I felt like Mom and Jacob still needed me—stuff like that. One thought led to another, which led to another. It could have gone on all night, but sometime after two a.m. I heard a wail from down the hall.

Jacob's crying. Going to get him

I dropped my phone and went to Jacob's room. He was sitting up in his bed, rubbing his eyes, and softly weeping.

"Hey, there, baby dude," I whispered, and picked him up. "What's wrong?" I carried him over to the rocker in his room and sat down. "Why so sad?"

He said something. It was definitely a word—I just didn't know *what* word. It sounded a little like "uggy" so I repeated it. "Uggy?"

He shook his head and said it again.

"Oggy? Uppy?"

He moaned in frustration and hit me—lightly—with his fist. He wasn't trying to hurt me, just letting me know I wasn't getting it.

"I'm sorry," I said. "I wish you could talk."

"Me too."

I looked up over his head and saw Luke in the doorway.

"He wake you up?" he asked as he came over to us.

"I was awake anyway."

He put his hand on my shoulder and squeezed it gently. "I can take him if you want to go back to sleep."

"I'm okay. I just wish I knew what he was trying to tell me. I think he had a bad dream or something and he's trying to tell me what it was about."

"Uggy," Jacob said again.

"Uggy?" I repeated, and his body became rigid with fury.

"No!" He collapsed against me, sobbing.

"See?" I said to Luke. I stroked Jakie's back. "You know what he means?"

"No idea." Luke sat down on the corner of the bed nearest us. "Poor little guy. He's so frustrated."

"You'd be frustrated, too, if you couldn't speak the language."

There was a pause.

"Luke?" I said.

"Mm?" His hair was sticking up funny and he was wearing retainers—his teeth were shifting but of course he couldn't have braces put on, what with his TV appearances and music performances, so the orthodontist made him retainers to wear at home whenever he could. Sometimes I wished all the women who adored him could see him like this. He just looked so *normal*.

I touched the top of Jacob's head and said quietly, "I really don't think Mom's being crazy when she says there may be something going on with him."

His face tightened. "I never said she was crazy. I'm just trying to protect him from being boxed into a corner at the age of two."

"He's almost three. You should look at those books Mom bought today. A lot fits."

"Your mother just starts jumping to conclusions—"

"It's not jumping to a conclusion if you've really thought about it—it's *reaching* one, and that's different." I hugged Jacob hard. "This guy is amazing. He's smart and cute and wonderful and nothing changes that. But I want him to learn to talk to us. Don't you?"

"He's in speech therapy."

"I know but maybe there's more we could be doing."

"I want what's best for him, Ellie. You know that. I'm just not sure that what he needs at this stage of his life is a bunch of doctors and a label."

"Mom's not sure either." I rocked Jacob slowly. "But can't you guys try to figure it out together? You could read those books and talk to the therapists and if the two of you just keep talking to each other about it all—"

"Ellie—"

"You've told me a million times that you love me and would do anything for me. Well, this is what I want you to do more than anything else in the world: I want you to listen to what Mom's saying. Really, really listen. Please, Luke?"

He sat there for a moment, staring at Jacob, who was calm now against my chest. "I promise," Luke said finally, with a sigh. "You always win, don't you, little girl?" He held out his arms. "I'll take him now. You go back to sleep."

"Okay." I got up and let Jacob slide into his arms,

where he settled down contentedly against Luke's broad chest. "Good night."

"Hold on," Luke said. "We haven't talked about *you* yet."

"What about me?"

"You know how I feel about those Nussbaum boys. I trust them more than anyone else in the world. But George is a lot older than you and in a different place in life and—"

I stopped him with a raised finger. "You don't need to worry," I said with my most disarming smile. "He doesn't have an attractive young stepmother. So I think this could really work out."

Luke laughed, just like I'd hoped. "There are other potential issues, you know."

"He's a good guy," I said more seriously. "He would never take advantage of me in any way. But I will probably take advantage of him in every possible way I can."

"Good," Luke said. "That's exactly how I want it to go."

thirty-five

had to tell Heather. We always shared the important stuff. And keeping this a secret from her would only make my betrayal worse when she eventually found out.

I called her from the car on my way back from school on Monday. After we'd said hi, I took a deep breath and told her that her friendship was one of the most important things in the world to me and that it was hard for me to tell her what I had to tell her.

"What's going on?" she said. "You're scaring me. Did you hear about college? You did, didn't you?"

"No. This is about George."

"He told you he doesn't like me. Oh, God. Did you bring it up? Why would you bring it up?" The hysteria in her voice was mounting.

"It's not that!" Deep breath. "It's just . . . he and I are sort of going out now."

"What?" she said. Then again. "*What?*"

"I didn't know," I said. "When we talked about him and you said you were interested, I swear I wasn't—or at least didn't know I was—or I would have told you. But then we were running some errands together and somehow I just realized that I liked him and he realized that he liked me and things kind of went from there."

"Let me get this straight," she said, her voice trembling and tight at the same time. "You waited until I said *I* liked him to decide that *you* liked him? Is that what you're saying?"

"The last thing I wanted to do was go behind your back or hurt you."

"Oh, well, thanks," she said. "Thanks for not wanting to hurt me." Then, "What about everything you said? How he was too old for me? How it was weird for a guy his age to date a high school student? About how you didn't want to date until you were in college?"

"I know, I know," I said. "I was stupid and wrong about everything, especially about myself."

There was a long pause. Then: "Well," she said in a very cold, very distant voice, "I guess this proves what I've always known, which is that the great and powerful Ellie Withers gets everything she wants and I don't get anything I want *ever*."

"Heather—"

"I have to go," she said, and hung up.

Once I was home, I tried texting and calling her but

she wouldn't respond, and later that night her mother answered her cell phone and told me to leave her alone, then hung up on me.

It hurt a lot. Especially since I blamed myself for her unhappiness: I'd thought she liked Aaron when she liked George, and I'd thought I didn't like anyone when I basically worshipped George. If I'd just been more aware, less dense . . . But the damage was done.

The one thing that cheered me up a little was that Luke and Mom went out to dinner alone that night, and Mom told me after they got back that Luke had—for the first time—let her talk freely about her concerns about Jacob and told her he'd read whatever she wanted him to with an open mind. "I've never loved him more," she said, and even though she said it lightly, I don't think she was actually joking.

Tuesday was the last day of school before Thanksgiving. That afternoon the members of the Holiday-Giving Program assembled food baskets for the shelter residents. Students and their families had been donating nonperishables for the previous few weeks, and then that morning everyone brought fresh bread and frozen turkeys. Most of them were donated by school families, but Skyler's uncle had a friend whose family owned a supermarket chain, and they had donated a few dozen turkeys, so we were in good shape.

We gathered in the student lounge to pack the baskets, which were really just cardboard boxes, also donated by the supermarket. We had the core group of me, Ben, Skyler, Riley, and Arianna, and then a bunch of volunteers to help us. It was pretty hectic, but even with all the running around and heavy lifting, I couldn't miss the bolts of hatred Arianna was launching at me.

Yes, my self-proclaimed "best friend" (at least on Instagram) was now apparently my worst enemy. She sighed loudly when I gave directions, glowered when I thanked everyone for coming, turned her back on me whenever our paths crossed, and told everyone who would listen that I was a snob who thought that because my stepfather was famous, everyone was supposed to worship me. I knew exactly what she was saying, thanks to Riley, who spent the afternoon listening eagerly and reporting every word to me, despite my attempts to convince her that I actually didn't *want* to know every single horrible thing being said about me that afternoon.

"She's so awful," Riley said with horrified delight. She liked drama. "She's just tearing you apart out there. Do you want me to tell her to stop? I will if you want me to."

"I honestly don't care what she says about me," I said. "I just want to get these baskets packed."

I really *didn't* care about Arianna, but I was disappointed in Ben. He had always been friendly in a businesslike kind of way. We had been good teammates. But now he was cold and standoffish, abrupt to the point of rudeness. Maybe I should have admired his loyalty to his girlfriend, but mostly I just felt disgusted with them both. Was I supposed to have tolerated her inappropriate snooping just *because* my stepfather was famous? I wished I hadn't said anything about it to Ben—and I wouldn't have if I'd known he was her boyfriend—but she was the one who had behaved badly, not me, and it bummed me out that Ben couldn't see that at all.

We finished packing up the boxes and loaded them into Skyler's mother's minivan, then Skyler, Ben, and I drove them to the shelter, where people there helped us unload them. The warmth and gratitude of both the staff and the residents made me feel a lot better. This was what mattered. Even Ben seemed touched enough by it to say an almost civil "Happy Thanksgiving" to me when we parted back at school.

A little while later, I walked into my house with that incredible feeling of lightness that comes from knowing you have five days of vacation ahead of you—and will be seeing your new boyfriend as often as possible during those five days—and found Lorena and Grandma sitting and chatting in the kitchen.

Lorena was a good listener and Grandma loved talking, so they had always gotten along well, but I think the last couple of weeks, when they'd spent a lot of time alone together in the house, had turned them into real friends.

"Where is everyone?" I asked, joining them at the table.

Grandma said, "Your mom and Luke took Jacob to an appointment with that doctor she wanted him to see."

"The developmental pediatrician? I thought they couldn't get an appointment for like two more months."

"The office called this morning—there was a sudden cancellation."

I raised my eyebrows. "And Luke Weston's kid just happened to jump to the top of the waiting list?"

"We don't know that," Grandma said primly.

"I'm just glad for Mom's sake."

They walked in a little while later. Luke was carrying Jacob, and Mom was close behind them. Lorena was instantly on her feet; she held her arms out for Jacob and whisked him off.

Mom said, "Who wants to make me a cup of tea?" as she sank down on a chair.

"I will," said Grandma, getting up. "You relax and tell us what happened at the appointment."

Luke said, "I should go work out. I had to cancel with my trainer today."

"Not yet," Mom said, and patted the chair next to

her. "Let's all talk about this for a second."

He sat down and reached for her hand. I breathed a sigh of relief at the sight of their clasped fingers—whatever they'd heard hadn't driven them further apart. "What did the doctor say?"

They looked at each other and then Mom said slowly, "She does think Jacob falls somewhere on the autism spectrum. But she also thinks he's incredibly bright and that he can learn pretty much anything we want him to, with just a little bit of work."

"Okay," I said. I felt like I should have a bigger reaction to the news, but we'd been inching toward that possibility for so long that I guess deep down I'd already kind of accepted it. "It makes sense, right? What do you think, Luke?"

"You'll be happy to know I listened quietly to the doctor."

"Because you promised me?"

He nodded. "But also because you were right. It was time for me to shut up and listen. Plus I really liked her."

I beamed at him. I felt like a proud parent. "And?"

"I told her I still don't like the idea of labeling a two-year-old, and she said she completely understood and that the label didn't matter anyway—the important thing was just to recognize that Jacob's a little behind other kids his age and we need to help him catch up. Which I'm fine with."

"Me too," Mom said.

"Whatever it takes." He brought Mom's hand to his mouth for a swift kiss. "Can I go now?"

"You may go," she said. "And thank you," she whispered to me as he left the kitchen. "I don't know what you said to him, but it made all the difference."

"I have awesome powers of persuasion."

"Yes, you do."

"Speaking of which . . . can I persuade you to let me stay out past one tonight? I'll just be at George's. You know you can trust us."

"Curfew's midnight," she said. "Same as always." Grandma put a cup of tea in front of her and Mom nodded her thanks while Grandma sat down with her own cup.

"I know," I said. "But I'm on vacation. And you should be proud of me for not sneaking home later than curfew without permission even though you're usually asleep and don't even notice what time I get home. I'm always honest with you. Which is why you can trust me. And it's not like I want to go drinking or anything. I just want to hang out in George's apartment and watch movies with him, and it's so much nicer not to have to rush home early."

"That's all?" she said. "You're just going to watch movies?"

"Yeah," I said.

"I used to tell my mother that, too," she said, and the two of them looked at each other and laughed a little too loudly.

"Don't worry," Grandma said to her. "I already had the condom talk with her."

"And I endured it without complaining," I said. "For that alone I should get one night without a curfew."

Mom laughed some more and gave in.

thirty-six

Crystal took the baby (and Megan, who never seemed to get any holiday off) back to her parents' house in Boston for Thanksgiving, so Mom invited Michael and Aaron to have dinner with us.

We ate in the dining room, which we saved for big formal dinners—which meant we almost never used it. I don't know about the adults' end of the table, but Aaron, Jacob, and I had fun at ours. We piled mounds of mashed potatoes on our plates and sent cranberries crashing through them on skateboards made of turkey, while Aaron told me stories about life in the hotel—it sounded like he was basically an older, male version of Eloise, wheedling everyone who worked there to give him free food and drinks, making friends with the other guests, and driving the staff crazy. He was having fun, he said.

"I'm over all the drama," he told me right after he

had stuck green beans in the corners of his mouth and pretended to be a walrus to amuse Jacob, who just stared at him, then looked away again, unimpressed. Aaron tossed the beans back onto his plate. "I'm avoiding it in the future."

"Make it your New Year's resolution," I suggested.

"That'll be one of them," he said. "Sticking close to good friends I can trust—that's another."

I fluttered my hands to my chest in an exaggerated *You mean me?* kind of way and he grinned and raised his wineglass to me. We were both drinking wine, but I was still on my first glass and he was on his second. Or third.

The plates had all been cleared when George and Jonathan arrived—they'd had dinner with the Nussbaum clan first, but had been invited to join us for dessert.

I watched from a distance as Luke got up to shake George's hand and Mom reached up to give him a hug and a kiss, and I felt as lucky as people were always telling me I was.

Jonathan circled around the table and reached me first. He leaned over to give me a kiss and whispered in my ear, "I want you to know I don't approve of this at all. You're way too good for him." He cuffed me on the shoulder and nodded in Aaron's direction. "Hello," he said coldly. Apparently (and probably not coincidentally) he shared his brother's dislike of Aaron.

Jacob stretched up his arms and Jonathan scooped

him up. "All right then," he said, and carried Jacob over to the adults' end of the table, where he sat down next to Luke, arranging Jacob comfortably on his lap.

George said hello to all the adults before coming to our end of the table, so he reached us a minute after his brother.

"Happy Thanksgiving," he said, and rested his hand on the back of Jacob's former seat. "Mind if I sit here?"

"Do you really want to know or are you just being polite?" Aaron asked.

"I'll take that as a yes," George said, and sat. I nodded a greeting at him but didn't indicate in any other way that for the previous couple of days we'd basically spent every hour we could alone in his room, twisted around each other. I got home at four in the morning on Tuesday night—or, rather, Wednesday morning—but last night I had to be back at midnight. Mom wanted me up at a normal hour to help her get the house ready for guests.

I hadn't told Aaron about me and George yet. This was the first time I'd seen Aaron since things had changed, and it seemed awkward to just bring it up out of context. And why should I rush to tell him about my private romantic life when he'd kept his a secret from me? It felt good to turn the tables, to have information he didn't. I mean, if he'd asked me specifically about either George or my love life, I might have said

331

something, but Aaron didn't ask people questions about themselves. He liked the conversation to be about him.

The three of us chatted for a while about nothing important. Aaron kept trying to make George feel like an outsider: he'd whisper funny little observations into my ear that George couldn't hear and catch my eye whenever George was talking, making faces and mouthing words to distract me from listening.

At one point, when George was still in the middle of telling us a story about his sister's boyfriend, who had come to their Thanksgiving dinner and been terrified at the number of brothers all sizing him up, Aaron cut him off by turning to me and abruptly saying, "I feel like we've been sitting here forever. My butt hurts."

"We could all move to the living room."

"How about we sneak out to a movie?"

I glanced over at George.

"You could come too if you wanted," Aaron said to him begrudgingly.

"Thanks," George said. "I don't want to strand my brother—we came in one car."

"So how about it, Ellie?"

"I'm fine staying," I said.

Aaron leaned forward and lowered his voice. "I'm going to scream if we sit here any longer. Can't we just run out and do something? Anything? Just us two?"

"I'm really happy here," I said, and shifted sideways

in my chair so I could lean back against George. His arms went around me just like I knew they would—not in a proprietary way, just settling me against his chest. "You see?" I said to Aaron. "Happy."

He stared at us. "Excuse me?" he said.

I put my hands over George's and pressed them hard against my arms. "He's a really good tutor," I explained.

It took him another moment. "You two?" he said. "Seriously?"

"Define 'seriously,'" I said. "I mean, I make a lot of jokes about it. . . ."

"I can see why." He forced a laugh. "This is . . . unexpected. You could have said something."

"Yeah, I really should have," I agreed. "I hate when people sneak around and don't tell you the truth about their love lives, don't you?"

"Ah, I see what you did there. Clever." He stood up. "Excuse me. I'm going to need a lot more wine to process this." He picked up his glass and stalked down to the far end of the table, where another bottle had just been opened.

We sat quietly for a while. I watched Jacob—now on Grandma's lap—methodically stab his pumpkin pie with a fork until it was completely dead. Apparently he wasn't a fan.

"When you move your head, your hair tickles my nose," George said sleepily.

"Your nose tickles my hair."

He slid his fingers up my neck and tugged at my curls from underneath. "There's so much of it. Maybe you should cut it all off."

"Never!"

"It's just dead cells, you know."

"Yes, but my dead cells are so much more beautiful than anyone else's."

"Vain, aren't we?"

I tilted my head back to look up at him. "Have you *seen* my hair? It's extraordinary."

"It is," he said.

My phone buzzed and I moved back into my own seat to glance at it.

Meet me in the kitchen.

"I'll be right back," I said, and got up. I went into the kitchen, which was amazingly clean. The servers Carlos had arranged for us had left already, but they had washed all the dishes and counters and put all the leftovers in the refrigerator. You wouldn't even have known that an entire Thanksgiving meal had been cooked and eaten there that day—except for the good turkey and pie smells that lingered in the air.

Aaron was leaning back against the counter, his arms tightly folded across his chest, his wineglass next to him.

"We need to talk about this," he said.

"Why?"

"Because it's so clearly a mistake."

"And again I say, why?"

"Because you're—" He waved his hands in the air. "You're fireworks and symphonies. He's moldy books and everything that's boring. And he's way too old for you."

I regarded him amiably. "Aaron, my love, are you really going to go there? Living in that glass house of yours and all?"

"That's *why*!" he said, flailing his arms around. I was beginning to think maybe he'd had too much to drink. "I've been down that road. Learn from me. There are healthy relationships and sick ones. There are right people and wrong people. I can teach you, little Ellie grasshopper. I can lead you in the right direction, but you have to trust me."

I put my hand on his arm. "Here's the thing: I like George a lot, and if you can't be nice to him and about him, *he's* not going to be the one I cut out of my life. Got it?"

"Really?" he said like he couldn't believe it.

"So really. Just be a good friend and be happy for me."

"Bleargh," he said miserably. "Happiness."

I squeezed his wrist. "I know things have been bad. They're going to get better."

He pushed my hand away. "Traitor," he said. "You

were supposed to belong to me. What about *my* needs? What if I'm sad and lonely and you're the only person I can stand to be with, but you're off with *him*?"

"Then I guess you'll have to wait for me to come back."

"If I have to, I will," he said. "But I'd rather have you all to myself. I'm supposed to be the most important guy in your life."

"Yeah, no," I explained.

thirty-seven

was alone in my room when I found out online that
I'd been accepted to Elton College. I screamed and
Mom and Lorena came running in, concerned. Once I
explained, we all jumped around for a while and they
hugged me, and then I said, "I want to tell George in
person. Don't call or text him, Mom."

"Why would I?"

"You told him my SAT scores without my permission."

"That was when he was your tutor, not your boyfriend," she pointed out. "And I was paying him for the
time he spent with you. I've stopped doing that, in case
you hadn't noticed."

"I should tell him to submit a bill," I said. "He's been
putting in some long hours with me over the last couple
of weeks. Lots of late nights . . ."

"I don't want to hear about it!" she said, putting her
hands over her ears. She was in a much better mood

these days, willing to laugh and be silly. Jacob had a whole weekly regimen with various therapists and had added about fifteen more words to his vocabulary in just a few weeks, and Mom had said to me a few days earlier that knowing he was getting help and seeing him respond to all the interventions made her feel better about everything. And I could see that in her face every day—that little line between her eyes had virtually disappeared.

She dropped her hands and said more seriously, "But can you still apply somewhere else? You got in so easily—maybe you didn't reach high enough. The Ivies—"

I cut her off. "Too late. I'm committed now—early decision, remember?—and it's good news, so don't harsh my buzz." I slipped my feet into flip-flops, twisted my hair into a knot, threw on a sweatshirt, and was out the door before she could say anything else.

It was late afternoon on a weekday, and traffic was predictably hellish going over the hill into the Valley. I listened to music and tailgated every car in front of me. Not that it helped.

About halfway there, I got a call. Heather. My stomach tightened. It was the first time she'd called me since I'd told her about George. I'd texted her a bunch of times, asking her if we could please just talk, but she never responded. I kept trying; she had a right to be mad at me, and I had a right not to give up on our friendship.

But now she was breaking the silence. She must have heard from Elton.

I hoped she was calling to say, "Hey, since we're going to be going to school together, let's make up!"

Please let it be that.

I hit the car's Bluetooth speaker and said hello. I heard weeping on the other end, then finally some broken words. "You got in, didn't you? Didn't you?"

Crap. "Yeah. You?" But I already knew the answer.

"I listened to you!" she sobbed. "I listened to you and you told me I'd get in and I could have applied somewhere better for me. I didn't even want to go to Elton—I let you talk me into it—"

"Then maybe it's not so bad," I said, torn between irritation and remorse. "You'll get in somewhere you like better."

"You've been a bad friend to me." She hung up.

I reached George's apartment about fifteen minutes later. When he opened his door in response to my knock, I said, "I got in," and burst into tears.

He pulled me inside, shut the door, then sat down with me on the sofa while I told him about Heather. "She's so unhappy. And it's all my fault. I've ruined her life in every possible way. What do I do now?"

He gently brushed his knuckles against the tears on my cheeks. "Don't panic. She'll be okay."

"You were right. You said she wouldn't get in just

because I wanted her to, that I should stop pushing her to apply there."

He didn't say anything. He wasn't the *I told you so* type but we both knew it was true.

"I've lost my best friend. I had already hurt her and now she hates me even more."

"You didn't lose her. She loves you and she knows you love her. Just give her some time to recover."

We sat like that for a while, my legs across his lap, my head on his chest. Just being with him made me feel better. I inhaled the salty-sweet scent of his neck (no cologne, just him, thankfully) and felt better. I wished I hadn't had to hurt Heather to end up here, inside George's neck, but I didn't regret the outcome.

But then . . . I sat up suddenly and moved away from him. "You don't seem all that happy for me," I said accusingly. "About Elton, I mean."

"I am," he protested. "It's great news. I'm not surprised but I'm happy for you."

"Then why don't you *sound* happy?"

He looked down at his hands. "Connecticut just seems very far away, that's all."

"Oh," I breathed, suddenly understanding. I threw myself on him and pinned him against the sofa. "That's a very good reason for you not to seem happy." I straddled him, then leaned forward and dropped my head until my lips met his.

* * *

A day or two later, George showed me a list he'd made of schools that he thought Heather would like and could get into. "She said her college counselor wasn't very good and had hundreds of kids to oversee, and her mother didn't strike me as a clear thinker, so I went ahead and did some research. I could email her this. Do you think she'd be okay with that?"

"Print it up," I said. "I'll take it to her."

"Really? You think it'll be okay if you just show up?"

"I'm hoping that if we're face-to-face, I'll be able to convince her to forgive me."

When I got there, her mother answered the door and said stiffly, "Oh, Ellie. What are you doing here?" Our last exchange had been when she asked me to stop calling Heather's cell, so it was pretty awkward.

I asked to see Heather, and Mrs. Smith called out, "Heather? Come to the door, please."

Heather came down the stairs and stopped short at the sight of me.

Her mother said, "You didn't tell me you were expecting Ellie," and Heather said in a faint voice, "I wasn't."

I slipped past Mrs. Smith—who hadn't invited me in—and went right to Heather. I said, "Can I talk to you for just like five minutes? Please?" and she hesitated but then said a reluctant okay—she was incapable of being cruel—and led me up to her room.

Once the door was closed, I said in one breath, "I misled you and I also hurt you. I'm sorry in every possible way. I love you and I need you in my life. Can you ever forgive me?"

It was *Heather*. That's the thing. Maybe someone else would have made me suffer a lot longer. But that wasn't who she was. She was made to like people and I was her best friend. So she burst into tears and we threw our arms around each other and hugged for a while and I apologized about fifty more times, and pretty soon she was telling me it wasn't my fault, that she understood, that she had made her own decision about applying and she knew it, and pretty soon after that, she was chattering away again, confiding in me about school and friends and her parents, just like always. Or almost like always—neither of us mentioned George, which meant things weren't entirely normal between us. He was such a big part of my life now that I had to keep editing things I wanted to tell her. But the important thing was that we were friends again.

Later—after we'd left the house and gone out for cupcakes and more tears and hugs—we came back and looked up the colleges on George's list. One was less than two hours from where I'd be in Connecticut, and we both got stoked for that, but I was careful this time not to push her or act like I knew what I was talking about. I'd learned my lesson.

"I'm over Elton anyway," Heather said, leaning back against her headboard—we had curled up on her bed with the laptop. "If all the kids are like you, they'd be smarter than me and I'd just feel stupid for four more years. Anyway . . . it was always more your choice than mine."

I couldn't argue with any of that. And didn't.

thirty-eight

Over the next few weeks, Aaron and Michael moved out of the hotel and into a huge and beautiful penthouse apartment in Santa Monica with a view of the ocean. Crystal kept the house. She and Michael were working out some kind of joint custody agreement, which for now mostly involved Megan's carting the baby back and forth and having to take care of her in two different places. Crystal was going back to acting, Aaron said. He never saw her alone: one of the conditions of his getting to stay with his dad in LA was that he wouldn't. He admitted to me that it was sort of a relief. He was over her.

Whatever Crystal felt about the whole thing remained a mystery: she was completely out of our lives. Mom and I did spend time with Mia when she was at Michael's, though. She was still the world's cutest baby, as far as I was concerned.

Arianna continued to tell everyone at school that I was stuck-up, and Riley continued to come rushing to report it to me no matter how much I made it clear I didn't want her to, but none of this affected my life much. The kids who fawned over me because I was Luke's stepdaughter still did; the ones who I'd always hung out with stayed loyal; the ones I didn't know well may have believed Arianna but it didn't matter: we had only one more semester together and I could survive a few dark looks and mutters for that long.

Right before Christmas, we finished collecting donations for the Holiday-Giving Program and handed out the presents at the annual party at the shelter. To my relief, Ben was civil—almost pleasant—to me when we were working together. I didn't know whether he had softened because he knew he had been unfair to me or because Arianna was losing a little of her luster as a girlfriend, but I was glad either way. It made the whole thing more pleasant.

Luke wasn't able to come to the party, but even if some people came hoping to see him (thanks to Arianna), they didn't leave too disappointed. Once they got busy entertaining the little kids and handing out presents, most of the students had fun, and I knew a lot of them would sign up again next year—with or without a celebrity tease.

As we were cleaning up at the end, Ben told me, a

little uncomfortably, that he thought we should make Arianna the president of the program for the following year, since she was the only junior who had run any part of it. I instantly agreed. He looked surprised, but I figured she *had* worked hard and earned her place at the top.

And I'd be at college. She couldn't bug me there.

Aaron got accepted early to the USC film school, which was his first choice, so he was as relaxed as I was as second semester got under way. We got together a lot in the evenings when neither of us had any other plans, going out for frozen yogurt, drinking boba tea, trying new restaurants (Aaron got his father's assistant to book us some of the hardest-to-get reservations in town, using Michael's name), and being generally hedonistic and sugared-up.

George was never thrilled to hear I had plans with Aaron, but he wasn't the kind of boyfriend who was going to tell me what I could or couldn't do. (Not that I would have gone out with anyone who *was*.)

"It would be easier if he were just a little less cool and handsome," he said once when I came over to his apartment after having dinner with Aaron. "Or if I were a little *more* cool and handsome."

"Cool and handsome is overrated," I said.

His smile was pained. "So you agree I'm neither?"

"You're everything good and smart and funny and kind and wonderful and exciting and wonderful," I said.

"But not cool or handsome."

"*And* cool and handsome. And wonderful."

"You said *wonderful* three times," he pointed out, and then caught me against his chest and covered my mouth so I couldn't say anything else for a while.

Spring came. Heather got into five of the seven colleges she'd applied to and freaked out over having so many choices. I pointed out that that was a good thing, but she still spent days agonizing and calling me constantly to discuss their different merits.

In the end, she *didn't* pick the one in Connecticut, near where I'd be. She kept apologizing to me, explaining over and over again that her dad really wanted her to go to Steventon and it actually looked perfect and she felt less guilty making him pay for a college he was enthusiastic about, and repeatedly assuring me that it had been a tough decision, because she wanted to be near me. I told her it was totally fine. At this point I was just relieved and happy that she seemed excited about going off to school in the fall.

I had already met a bunch of my future classmates online and had found a few I really liked, including two who wanted to room together. They only knew me as Ellie Withers and had no idea Luke Weston was my stepfather, so their enthusiasm and interest seemed genuine, and I was feeling pretty optimistic about having a more normal social life in college than I'd had in high school.

Mom kept tweaking Jacob's therapies, increasing his time with the ones she liked and pulling away from the ones she didn't, and he was doing great, saying a ton more words and getting frustrated much less.

We were hanging out in the family room one day when he called out, "Mom. Look!" and we both jumped to our feet—it was the first time he'd ever said her name just to get her attention.

He pointed to the floor, where he'd been busily arranging some plastic letters. Most of them were in a long row.

"What's a jacobellie?" Mom said, studying it. Then, with a delighted laugh: "Oh, it's his name and yours put together!"

"Did you know he could spell?" I asked, dumbfounded.

"I had no idea."

"He's a total genius!"

"There's definitely a lot more going on in that little head than we realize." She called Luke to tell him and I could hear him shouting with excitement at the other end of the line.

Thanks to Luke and Michael, in May, George finally

landed a job—as the assistant to the vice president of development at a TV studio. It wasn't the writing job he'd hoped for, but he had reached a point where he was just happy to have full-time work. His hours were long, and he always had scripts to read on the weekends. I complained that he wasn't paying me enough attention, and he came up with a solution: that I stop complaining.

We'll Make You a Star had gone on hiatus in April, so Luke was desperately trying to write and record a new batch of songs for the album he wanted to release the following fall. It kept him busy, but the Luke who was being creative was always happier than the one who was the TV star. He didn't love that job, but it paid the bills and—he would have been the first to admit—gave him the leverage and power to put out the kind of music he wanted to.

My grandmother started dating some senior citizen and informed me soon after that their relationship had become "physically intimate." I jokingly reminded her to use condoms, and she said seriously, "Well, of course pregnancy isn't an issue for me, but STDs are. You know what those are, right? STDs?" I told her I did and got off the phone quickly, before she could give me more information about that than I wanted, which was really any information at all.

* * *

I didn't want George to go with me to my prom. "You're too old," I explained. "It would be incredibly awkward for you to be around all those high school kids, and I'd feel guilty dragging you around, making you meet people who just want to see who Luke Weston's step-daughter is dating. You'd hate it. Aaron's up for it and he's used to all the fame-whore weirdness."

"I'm all in favor of not going," he said, "but couldn't you not go, too? Especially not with him?"

"It's the only high school prom I'll ever have. And who would you rather I went with? You know you don't have to worry about Aaron."

"Can't you go with a gay friend?"

"The gay guys in my grade all have dates," I said. "All the girls who don't have boyfriends were fighting over them. Anyway, I've already asked Aaron and he's already said yes."

"Fine," he said. "Just come over to my place after. No flying around all night on Aladdin's magic carpet."

I promised. Mom knew I was planning to be out all night anyway—everyone stayed up on prom night.

She and Luke took a ridiculous number of photos of us when Aaron came to pick me up for prom. As we posed, his arm around my shoulder, he reminded me that he was going to put me through all of this again in a week, at *his* school's prom.

He clutched me a little too tightly during the last dance of the night, so I pulled away and said, "Let's sit this one out."

The limousine dropped us off at my house and I walked him to his car. He leaned against it and said, "Sometimes I think I made a mistake, missing my chance with you."

And I said cheerfully, "You never had one."

I don't think he believed me, but I didn't care. I quickly pecked him on the cheek and ran inside to get my stuff.

It was past midnight by the time I got to George's apartment.

"Wow," he said when he opened the door to me. I was still wearing my ivory-colored prom dress, which was very tight in the bodice with a long, flowing skirt. It had, as Mom pointed out, cost more than a month's rent at our old apartment. I'd brought a change of clothes in a bag, but wanted George to see me all done up. "Your mother sent me a photo but it didn't do you justice."

"Do you like my hair?" Mom had hired Roger to style me, and he'd straightened my hair with a flat iron, then pinned half of it up, and let the rest of it fall to my waist, which it did when it was completely straight.

"It's pretty," George said, and touched it lightly with

his fingertips. "But I wouldn't want you to straighten it all the time. I'd miss your curls."

"Don't worry," I said. "It took three hours to get it like this. I may never do it again."

We went inside and he said, "Will you hate me if I do a tiny bit of work? I just finished reading a script and I need to write down a few notes before I forget."

I pouted. "If you'd rather work than be with me . . ."

"Not fair," he said. "I'd rather work *and* be with you. Come sit next to me." He led me over to the tiny table where he worked and ate. And did everything else that could be done on a table. His apartment was small, narrow, and dark. It was my favorite place in the world.

I sat down with him. "How was it? The script?"

"I kind of loved it," he said. "I mean, it's a mess and needs a ton of work, but it's got this incredible idea and these moments of pure genius."

"So you'll help the writer make it much better."

"That's the goal."

"It's what you do," I said. "Take something that's a little rough and messy and make it much better."

"Is that what I do?" he said, amused.

"It's what you did with me, wasn't it?"

"The raw material was very good," he said. "Moments of pure genius."

"I was always a great idea," I agreed. "You know what else is a great idea?"

"What?"

I knocked the script off the table. It fell on the floor.

George didn't get around to picking it up until the morning.

Read the first chapter of

Claire LaZebnik's

epic
fail

The front office wasn't as crazy as you'd expect on the first day of school, which seemed to confirm Coral Tree Prep's reputation as "a well-oiled machine."

That was a direct quote from the Private School Confidential website I had stumbled across when I first Googled Coral Tree—right after my parents told me and my three sisters we'd be transferring there in the fall. Since it was on the other side of the country from where we'd been living—from where I'd lived my entire life—I couldn't exactly check it myself, and I was desperate for more information.

True to the school's reputation, the administrator in the office was brisk and efficient and had quickly printed up and handed me and Juliana each a class list and a map of the school.

"You okay?" I asked Juliana, as she stared at the map

like it was written in some foreign language. She started and looked up at me, slightly panicked. Juliana's a year older than me, but she sometimes seems younger— mostly because she's the opposite of cynical and I'm the opposite of the opposite of cynical.

Because we're so close in age, people frequently ask if the two of us are twins. It's lucky for me we're not, because if we *were*, Juliana would be The Pretty One. She and I do look a lot alike, but there are infinitesimal differences—her eyes are just a touch wider apart, her hair a bit silkier, her lips fuller—and all these little changes add up to her being truly beautiful and my being reasonably cute. On a good day. When the light hits me right.

"It'll all be fine," Juliana said faintly.

"Yeah," I said, with no more conviction. "Anyway, I'd better run. My first class is on the other side of the building." I squinted at the map. "I think."

She squeezed my arm. "Good luck."

"Find me at lunch, okay? I'll be the one sitting by herself."

"You'll make friends, Elise," she said. "I know you will."

"Just *find* me." I took a deep breath and plunged out of the office and into the hallway—and instantly hit someone with the door. "Sorry!" I said, cringing.

The girl I'd hit turned, rubbing her hip. She wore an incredibly short miniskirt, tight black boots that came up almost to her knees, and a spaghetti-strap tank top. It was an outfit more suited for a nightclub than a day of classes, but I had to admit she had the right body for it. Her blond hair was beautifully cut, highlighted, and styled, and the makeup she wore really played up her pretty blue eyes and perfect little nose. Which was scrunched up now in disdain as she surveyed me and bleated out a loud and annoyed "FAIL!"

The girl standing with her said, "Oh my God, are you okay?" in pretty much the tone you'd use if someone you cared about had just been hit by a speeding pickup truck right in front of you.

It hadn't been *that* hard a bump, but I held my hands up apologetically. "Epic fail. I know. Sorry."

The girl I'd hit raised an eyebrow. "At least you're honest."

"At least," I agreed. "Hey, do you happen to know where room twenty-three is? I have English there in, like, two minutes and I don't know my way around. I'm new here."

The other girl said, "I'm in that class, too." Her hair was brown instead of blond and her eyes hazel instead of blue, but the two girls' long, choppy manes and skinny bodies had been cast from the same basic mold. "You can follow me. See you later, Chels."

"Yeah—wait, hold on a sec." Chels—or whatever her name was—pulled her friend toward her and whispered something in her ear. Her friend's eyes darted toward me briefly, but long enough to make me glance down at my old straight-leg jeans and my THIS IS WHAT A FEMINIST LOOKS LIKE T-shirt and feel like I shouldn't have worn either.

The two girls giggled and broke apart.

"I know, right?" the friend said. "See you," she said to Chels and immediately headed down the hallway, calling brusquely over her shoulder, "Hurry up. It's on the other side of the building and you *don't* want to be late for Ms. Phillips's class."

"She scary?" I asked, scuttling to keep up.

"She just gets off on handing out EMDs."

"EMDs?" I repeated.

"Early morning detentions. You have to come in at, like, seven in the morning and help clean up and stuff like that. Sucks."

"What's your name?" I asked, dodging a group of girls in cheerleader outfits.

"Gifford." *Really? Gifford?* "And that was Chelsea you hit with the door. You really should be more careful."

"I'm Elise," I said, even though she hadn't asked. "You guys in eleventh grade, too?"

"Yeah. So you're new, huh? Where're you from?"

"Amherst, Mass."

She actually showed some interest. "That near Harvard?"

4

"No. But Amherst College is there. And UMass."

She dismissed that with an uninterested wave. "You get snow there?"

"It's Massachusetts," I said. "Of course we do. Did."

"So do you ski?"

"Not much." My parents didn't, and the one time they tried to take us it was so expensive that they never repeated the experiment.

"We go to Park City every Christmas break," Gifford said. "But this year my mother thought maybe we should try Vail. Or maybe Austria. Just for a change, you know?"

I didn't know. But I nodded like I did.

"You see the same people at Park City every year," she said. "I get sick of it. It's like Maui at Christmas, you know?"

I wished she'd stop saying "You know?"

Fortunately, we had reached room 23. "In here," said Gifford. She opened the door and went in, successfully communicating that her mentoring ended at the room's threshold.

Over the course of the next four hours, I discovered that:

1. Classes at Coral Tree Prep were really small.
   When we got to English, I was worried that half
   the class would get EMDs or whatever they were
   called because there were fewer than a dozen kids

in the room. But when Ms. Phillips came in, she said, "Good—everyone's here, let's get started," and I realized that *was* the class.

2. The campus grounds were unbelievably green and seemed to stretch on for acres. I kept gazing out the window, wishing I could escape and go rolling down the grassy hills that lined the fields.

3. Teachers at Coral Tree Prep didn't like you to stare out the window and would tell you so in front of the entire class who would then all turn and stare at The New Girl Who Wasn't Paying Attention.

4. Everyone at Coral Tree Prep was good-looking. Really. Everyone. I didn't see a single fat or ugly kid all morning. Maybe they just locked them up at registration and didn't let them out again until graduation.

5. Girls here wore every kind of footwear imaginable, from flip-flops to spike-heeled mules to UGG boots (despite the sunny, 80-degree weather), EXCEPT for sneakers. I guess those marked you as fashion-impaired.

6. I was wearing sneakers.